Zero Tolerance

50

FARRAR
STRAUS
GIROUX

Thomas Richards

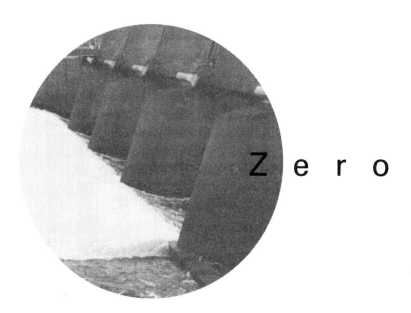

Zero

Tolerance

Farrar, Straus and Giroux
New York

LIBRARY OF CONGRESS CATALOGING-IN-PUBLICATION DATA
Richards, Thomas.
    Zero tolerance / Thomas Richards.
        p.   cm.
    ISBN 0-374-29662-6 (alk. paper)
    1. Vietnamese Conflict, 1961–1975—Fiction.   2. United States.
Bureau of Reclamation—Fiction.   I. Title.
PS3568.I3168Z47   1997
813'.54—dc20   96-15656
                                                                      CIP

For my mother and father

5854

Zero Tolerance

1

My brother cut the throttle. What he'd heard a second before was very faint, but they were voices, he was sure they were voices. He wanted to hear more. The gunboat pushed on upriver, silently drifting past rows of orchards and terraced fields of rice, toward the place where the Mekong River was going to jump its banks and cut to the sea. Slow there it was again, that voice. It was weak because my brother thought this river was weak and about to die. He knew from the Monongahela that no river was undying. This river clocked along finite as any, and he marked time on it, not seeing it change even though all it did was change, endless depositions since that first day, early January 1968, five years ago, but now it seemed more like five thousand, when he'd taken two Bureau of Reclamation engineers out on the Mekong to site some kind of dam. The survey boat had just rounded a bend toward Da Trinh Sanh, the same place he was heading now. The two engineers stood next to him, talking but not to him in their lingo about a strange kind of dam cut low in the earth. To my brother this Da Trinh Sanh was just another place on the river, a place like any other far as he was concerned, so he was only half listening, mostly wishing he was back on the Allegheny reach of the Mon where the river was dull and the sun shineless, when the talk stopped and the two Reclam men froze in awe before the drift of the river. The depth finder showed thirty-eight feet.

Did they know then? Did they know that a day was coming when tomorrow would not course for this river, a 29th of November diverted from its 30th? One of the engineers was midlands British and the other was a U.S. Indian. My brother had kept his distance from Navier-Stokes but felt drawn to Petard Davidson, something about him reminded him of a cracked compass, maybe it was the lines in his forehead, but he trusted him. Petard had reached across him and throttled down, taken off the wool ski cap he always wore pulled down over his ears no matter how hot it got. He remembered now what he'd told him that day five years ago on this bend in the river, the village just coming into view. He'd told him they were looking for the blind part of the river, a dark part black even at noon, a hole in the river where there was no shape or substance to anything. He said the surface of a river was paper with writing on it but if you listened close you could hear the old lays being sung from below, said the Vietnamese knew this, said their word for river was *song* and once you got that you got it all. You didn't have to be literate to read a river. All rivers had their writing but some, big old rivers like the Mekong and the Mississippi and the Nile, were singing rivers with wide mouths and deltas. These were rivers washed and sieved by the hands of slaves, didn't matter what they were slaves to, rice or cotton or maize, the swaying lines of reapers with aching ocher hands were the same. Sometimes they sang when they worked, and when they did, they sang the river's song. These old songs were all alike and when Petard spoke about them, my brother knew he knew them. They were inside him the way the Mon was. Now, five years later, my brother cleated his lips and started to hum, groaning back a song to the blind singing bottom of the lower Mekong, but his humming dribbled off wordless when for the first time he heard the clear running voice of the river coming at him, telling him, *You, too, are a river.*

That was all he heard. An L-19 spotter flew low overhead, engines grinding over the voice, drowning it out, then banking off toward where he knew the river must go. The Mekong was going to be diverted before it split into two rivers not twelve miles into Vietnam. If he were up there he'd be able to see the levees, two raised lines of earth with nothing between them, nothing yet, running in a dipping line from Diversion Point Da Trinh Sanh all the way east to Saigon. The levees were mostly dirt and trees, traditional stuff, just high enough to keep the river from spilling over. Some channels had been dug deep to give the river a nice gradient slide. Air-portable bulldozers from the 65th Engineers were dredging canals. Pylons and revetments went in at possible breakout points. Dam and locks were fitted into the levees along with pumping stations. Four tailing stations were ready to pump out the necessary power to push the river over a few uphill stretches, they weren't high, not more than a few feet above sea level, but they were long. The force of the diversion would dig the channels deeper if they held just for a few days. The distance across the delta plain to Saigon was a hundred and thirty miles, same length as the Monongahela River from Tygart Dam to Pittsburgh. The Bureau was doing everything it could to get it to roll right into downtown Saigon. My brother didn't know the details, didn't know how the Bureau could get a river to *want* to change its course, but he knew the changing meant the virtual destruction of Vietnam. The Delta was going to be a silt bar: how the Vietnamese could ever go along with this was beyond him. The ARVN had been reorganized into an Army of the Delta. NVA regulars were working on weirs. China'd sent a unit too, they were experts in *shui li*, benefit of water, the classical Chinese term for hydraulic engineering, and they reported directly to Petard Davidson, now Chief of the Department of Design, Reclam R&A. You name it and it was being done, silt and scour, dredging and dikes, gambions, stanches and sluices. This was more than a dam across a valley. This was inundation.

"Harper?"

"Yeah?"

"What's that up ahead, Harper?"

The men on the boat weren't Bureau and they were nervous. They didn't get why a slight white line of concrete should rise a few feet above the river like Long Dam was the lip of a bowl, didn't get why the line ran off east far as they could see, didn't get why a river wide as a lake was being routed round the site through diversion tunnels they couldn't even see. Most of all they didn't get this not shooting at the river. River fighting was the worst. The VC used swimmers, drifting mines, and the only way to clear the river was to spray fire at anything floating, fire till the guns were too hot to fire, and he was glad it was over. The Travers plan seemed to be working. The 20-mm. and 40-mm. cannons were zipped up but each of them'd slipped a few clips into his pocket. Every time my brother edged the boat near the bank he heard the clicking of safety catches on carbines. The men watched him when he throttled down, breathing down on the river like he was reading a wet newspaper floating by. They hated being close to the shore, scraping the edges of old rubber plantations, but they also hated being out in the murky middle of the river. What they knew about the operation wouldn't fill an index card. Their orders were to secure the river once it'd been diverted. From where to where they didn't know, east, they weren't sure how far east but they'd heard rumors, dams being built where there was no river, how could that be, six dams built to classical proportions on the outskirts of Saigon even though the burbs were VC turf.

These guys weren't from rivers, they were from cities, Gary and Detroit and Baltimore, places where there were no dams, and they wore sunglasses with starched fatigues. Why a bunch of engineers had taken over the war in the Delta they didn't know, but early in 1973 the Army and the Navy had pulled out under cover of Vietnamization and now the Bureau of Reclamation was running the war. Brought over as part of the Mobile Riverine Force, they didn't even know they were part of the Bureau of Reclamation, not at first. They didn't get the way my brother steered a gunboat without a thought in his head, leaning over the wheel like that, his eyes skipping over the river ahead, looking for smudges on the river, little ash smudges on the river's forehead like the river was the put-out fire of heaven. There was haze on the river but the haze wasn't haze but engine exhaust. Behind him, the river was a rumble of boat engines. With all the racket, it was getting hard to hear the river and harder to see. My brother did his best, taking out a pair of binoculars and scanning the sweeping crescent ahead. Finally he cut the power and the gunboat drifted like a jar. Voices from below, fuck, that thing down again, what's this full-stop shit, you dotting your I's again, Harper, what the fuck are you up to?

"Listening," said my brother.

Listening for the turning of the river. A signal hadn't been arranged and yet my brother thought he'd know it when it came no matter where he was on the river. Some rivers pushed, Yangtze and Colorado and Klamath, but others had to be pulled, Nile and Mississippi and Mekong dragged by peasants through dike and ditch. When this river went from pull to push, that was it. Not a shot'd be fired but there'd be shooting, he was sure of it, a great planar dropping of the river from Da Trinh Sanh all the way to Saigon. It was going to be a natural disaster of epic proportions. That's because big rivers carry an epic volume of crud, till one day the crud builds up into a wall, sending the river spilling off in a new direction. Three thousand years ago the main branch of the Nile was the Rosetta River, till one day the water upped and left the loam of the land a silt bar next to a tidal creek. The Yellow River shifted four hundred miles once and there was mega-famine. If there'd been a war the river would have won it. Best disasters in history, Petard'd told him, all natural disasters. They had its route mapped out, they were going to take it on a joyride and junk it in the South China Sea. It had all been worked out. Every last pressure drop was set down in advance by the Bureau at the Cavitation Center at Long Binh. He hadn't seen the exact numbers, the Bureau Chief, Navier-Stokes, was the only one who had, but he'd seen the model created from them fill up. The final welling, they called it, and it was fearful even in miniature. The model was the size of a small graveyard and it made the Delta into one big potter's field. The surface tension was high but it looked like it was going to work. For years they'd been building dams upstream, real reason for the Cambodia invasion back in '70 was to secure the Tonle Sap, the detention reservoir moderating the flood flow in the Delta, and now all they had to do was say the word, what word he didn't know, but he knew a diversion was more than music.

My brother remembered this much, and not much more. He remembered watching the land slide by, some parachutes hanging in trees by the river's edge, not like there'd been a jump but like the chutes were shrouds. He remembered throttling down to a final slow troll, feeling his way along the river beside the banks matted with bamboo, fingering with his free hand the prayer beads Jenna's friend Defosse had given him, and he remembered looking back and seeing the junks. Thousands and thousands of junks, all dipping with the same low bow you saw all over southeast Asia. Junks were boats with high overhanging sterns, flat bottoms, and near zero draft. They weren't like canoes. They were really more like rafts, Huck Finn rafts just floating along downriver with nothing to do but escape from slavery by drifting right into it. Looking behind him, what my brother saw was the largest armada of American boats anytime anywhere and he saw they were all riverboats, not a one with triple decks or tall narrow funnels or iron railings or belching smoke, but they were our riverboats all the same, no tugs or coal barges there either, but they were gambling boats and they were all about to turn inland. He spun the wheel and the gunboat plowed into the Kanh Xing Canal. That was the signal. He had reached the diversion point. He remembered the river of boats tailing him following his lead, fanning now into the deepened canals behind as far as Cao Lanh.

2

"That's all," my brother told me. "I see us turning up the canal. Cao Lanh was behind us. Then it goes black."

"You mean blank?" I asked him.

"No, black. If there was light I'd remember. But it's like everything happened in the dark."

My brother ran his fingers through the lightly oiled roots of his hair, now just turning gray. He had been talking for over an hour.

"Wait here," he said. He went off to the bar and came back with a shot glass of whiskey in each hand. He didn't offer me any. He downed each of them in a single gulp.

"Don't the others remember?"

"That's the point," he said. "None of us remembers enough. I know my part. Petard knows his. Travers knows a little less and Jenna a little more. But the pieces don't all fit together."

"Why don't they?"

"I don't know. They just don't."

My brother stopped talking. "Maybe they never will," he said. "Maybe we're getting too fucking old." He had been working in a mill in Eureka and true, he was getting old, old the way you age in a mill, hands yellowed and cracked at forty, but unshrunken overall, his eyes steamed over with exhaustion. I thought I saw tears forming in them but he shuddered and shook his head hard like he was trying to shake something out of it. Then he was up on his feet and out of there. There was a single pool table in another room in the bar and he led me to it. He racked up the balls under the light of a long fluorescent bulb hanging by wires over the table. My brother bent low, closed an eye, and took aim. The balls cracked across the tattered green felt and a couple dropped into side pockets. He kept shooting. Every few shots he twisted his cue stick into a piece of chalk, keeping an eye on the position of the balls on the table. Looking hard at me and not at the balls, he'd smack a few more into the pockets.

"I remember the canal," he told me between shots at the scattered balls. "What it looked like. The straightness of it. Nothing curved in the Delta. The canals were perfect. At the right time of day, from the right angle, they were like strips of aluminum foil, the way they caught the sun. They were beautiful. You wanted to go out and walk on them. I'd never seen a body of water with so much sun on it. I couldn't take my eyes off it. It was like a spell cast over us, the line of the water, your eyes following it falling away into green fields of rice. It took one of my side gunners, Stosser from Chicago, tugging at my flak jacket to jolt me out of it. *Lieutenant Harper? Sir? The sun's gone down. Sir, the sun's gone down.* That's what he said. You get it? The light on the canal wasn't coming from the sun. It was coming from the water. Even when the sun went down, the canal was still bright silver. I wanted to turn back but there was no turning room. I could only push the gunboat ahead into the light. My men were scared, they were clutching their weapons and asking me, Lieutenant, how can a river be light as day in the dark of night? What kind of river is this? Is this what these gook rivers are like? Or—"

His voice stopped there. A full stop, not trailing off the way it sometimes did. His eyes blinked. My brother tried to smile over the silence. He pinched his shirt and raised it off his stomach. He was sweating through it. He didn't like being hot, he never did, but these days, carrying those extra pounds over his belt, even pumping a pool cue made him uncomfortably hot.

"Or?" I asked.

"Or did we do this? They were more scared of this than anything. Of us doing this to a river."

He wasn't looking at me now, he was looking out the window of the bar, out past the buzzing neon and the drooping power lines to the long sad row of storefronts that reminded him so much of home. Lights were on in some of the buildings. My brother narrowed his eyes, not seeing the mountains in the dull pink distance—those were real enough—but the dispersed shadows of a ghost town. That's memory for you. Here he was in East L.A., watching the heat waver over sand and asphalt, and all he saw was our old house on the river. I know, I saw it too.

There were two bedrooms on the third floor, one facing the river and one the town. My brother's bedroom was the one facing the river. That was twenty years ago, before a chain of narrow lakes backed up the river from Brownsville all the way to Point Marion. Guttenberg, Pennsylvania, was dead. The name was there on the map but that was about it. From up in the hills you saw two roads dropping into town, dropping then meeting the water, a grid of a town beginning at the waterline, then going all cloudy and vague.

My brother lowered his voice. "You been back?"

"Once," I said.

"Did you see anything?"

"The outline. You have to be high up."

He continued to look down the street, away from me. At the corner was an empty motel with cracks in the walls.

"Any sign of the house?"

"I saved a couple of bricks. I have them in a box somewhere."

"How long did it take?"

"A year to flood the valley."

"Petard said it took five on the Klamath," he said, shifting his weight from one leg to the other, looking at the ground and then at me. He wasn't thinking about the Klamath River. He didn't want to ask, but he wanted to know, so he blurted it out. "How did she take it?"

"You know Lydia. She said she let them do it."

"You still call her that?"

"It's what she wants."

Lydia was our mother. She always made us call her Lydia and not Mother because she said the river, not her, was our mother. Sometimes, though, the two were so mixed up in my head I couldn't tell if the Monongahela River was our mother or if our mother was the Monongahela River. The Mon was a river born to a dam in the blue hills above Fairmont, West Virginia. The Mon didn't begin or end. Beginnings and endings were for free open rivers and the Mon had more dams and locks than any river in America. A dam every ten miles slackened the river into one long lull, a great sectional stillness extending a hundred miles north to Pittsburgh. The Mon was a slave in states where water was cotton and rivers were middle passage for coal. My brother and I grew up around the coal barges, feeling the black sting of coal lashed over the river and the patience of the waters beneath, barges moving over them like they didn't know every cusec, every cubic foot of flow, had a past. Our family was the last in the Mon Valley who remembered what the river used to be. We were born into the river, born to love its brown lentil flow, lensing out thick at the middle and thinning out at the edges, a river strong and firm at its center but weak and unfocused at its banks. Guttenberg was a lump on a bend in the river five miles north of the state line. The river ate away at the town like a famine and maybe two hundred houses held on, starving for land. The land was low and the soil was rocky and we all grew up waiting for the old lock gate at Mile 87.6 to wear out, for the river to push through and take the town in its arms, smooth its damp hair back and lay its face down to sleep. We didn't fear flood. Our mother taught us that flood was day, that only drought was night, said when she was a little girl, back around her tenth birthday, she'd said something to the river she hadn't meant and couldn't take back, just a few words, but the waters had receded and the Monongahela nearly gone dry. That one far spring when it rained all April and the river kept on rising higher every day, Lydia took her blue plastic shovel and built an earthwork round the garden back of the big old house, and when the waters came running in, she took towels and stuffed them under the jambs of all the doors at ground level, and when the waters came running, she took all the labeled cans in the kitchen, Sugar, Coffee, Salt, Tea, and emptied them onto the wet floor to feed the river's hunger, and when the waters kept on running, she ran upstairs into her attic bedroom and said a few words in a bitter language she didn't even know she knew. She didn't say much but she meant what she said and that was enough. The waters slowed through the town, it rained and rained but the river dropped, dropped back into the channel and didn't come back for a year. Years later, after the town was flooded for good and she'd moved west to live with me in California, her thin mouth still tightened talking about it. She hadn't said river go back, she'd said river go dry and the river'd heard her, heard her and cut her off. Lydia really believed she had a voice in the running of the river; she thought the river listened to her. She didn't know why. Guttenberg was a nothing town two miles from the state highway, seven from Belchertown, twenty-seven from Waynesburg, ninety from Pittsburgh, and half a continent away from the great anointed dams of the west. But the next time a flood came she was careful what she said, and her parents, my gramps Darian and grandma Flo, had to tear her away from the river she held onto like a sleeve, her dress wet in front like she'd been washing dishes.

That was in 1930. The old house on the river had been a hotel back in the days when there'd been regular ferry service across the Mon. The hotel had four stories and then some. Being brick, it stood out from the sagging staggered rows of wood-frame houses, wood in name only because up close they looked like they were made of cardboard and linoleum with crushed tin cans for roofs. The bricks were rubbed slick with grime, the trees around them black in fall and mostly bare even in spring. The only road into town ended at the hotel and split around it, not going anywhere really, not anymore, because the old dock'd gone under when the first locks jacked up the river level eighty years back. The back side of the hotel was the front because the back dropped down to the river, and our mother's bedroom, the one she later gave my brother, faced the river. Nights in that bedroom she slept with the river cursive around her. Under her blanket down on her back Lydia watched the shadows of the barges flickering across the ceiling. It was then she felt the river, the river all over her, coming to her from places where there was not even a river. The people in town were wrong. The Mon wasn't a river in decline. She'd seen the resignation in all the faces, so beaten it was pious, the sad withdrawn acceptance that the river was over and done with, the town trapped in the clutch of engineers able to bend the river to their will easy as her wrapping a straw around her little finger. She tried to tell them what she felt but they all thought she was nuts. They gave her that squinting WPA stare people in Guttenberg gave outsiders. Lydia didn't know what to do; these people'd lost the Mon; their faces were worn down to tar paper like the houses they lived in. Most of their houses were empty now, sold to the Army Corps, their furniture piled outside and left to rot, most going west like I did later, leaving behind dinettes with speckled white tops, chairs with polestar cushions, beds with rusted mesh springs. Up by the state highway, two miles or so, was an empty lot full of nothing but the rotted unsprung sofas of generations.

Lydia had faith in the river. She felt it for a certainty that the river would run as long as there was beveled ground. There it was on the map, 128 miles long, incompressible no matter how hard the U.S. Army Corps of Engineers held it down. The town was another matter. The water tower in Guttenberg leaked even on days when there wasn't any water in it, and when there was, the water juiced out of the tap like pulp squeezed out of an orange. The acid drainage from the old mines'd gotten into the water way under town, and that was why the rocks along the river were two colors, gray above water and orange under. Some creeks flared pure orange from all the sulfur, draining into lakes that were crystalline blue-green, a neon blue glow with none of the sky in it because it was blue from within. There weren't any mines in town and hadn't been since Lydia was little, and by the late fifties, when my first memories kick in, all that was left of them was a rusted coal tippet, a dinosaur's broken neck halfway up Lectern Hill, and those hills across the river, the black lung hills rising gray above the graveyard. Lydia said the first time she ever saw clear water was in a shale barren down in eastern West Virginia, and when she poured some of it into a glass it didn't sizzle but made a running sound like the sloosh of trains she used to hear running three miles east of town, freights headed west, always headed west, full of everything but coal because there was no coal left anymore, freights pulled by a big black GP-9 diesel over rails warm to the touch. She did her best to make the yard halfway decent, planting a garden that was the best place in town. A little garden with carrots and potatoes growing in gley soil, a rice paddy almost because the water had nowhere to drain to. The soil was ironless because all the iron was in the river, in the refractory glide of those big black barges pushed by tugs. There were hills on the other side of the river with nice runoff but they were a river away, not quite a hundred yards, but you had your choice, row across or walk around. Rowing was slow because the river always had other ideas and they never went in straight lines. The other way was down and up a long winding dead road, ten miles down counting telephone poles all the way to the creaking iron bridge at Point Marion, then ten miles back, following a road back on the wrong side of the river, least it always seemed wrong to Lydia because it took her farther and farther away from home, past an old abandoned glassworks and past Potter's Beach, not much there either, just broken misfired old pots glazed down to sand, looping back all the way to the wild overgrown graveyard where people from Guttenberg had always buried their dead, over there on the other side of the river it took so long to cross.

My father was buried in that graveyard. He was lockman to the river at Lock and Dam 7 at Mile 87.6 counted south from Pittsburgh in river miles, long blocked coagulant miles he spent fifteen years running rectum to. He was a dropout engineer and that's the way he saw it, a life spent at the colon end of a canal. He gave up a lot to marry Lydia but expected to get a lot back, too much probably. I think he thought there was some magic the river'd teach him if only he sat next to it waiting for a vision so abundant there'd be no closing the shutters on it. But the river rolled along on its way to some far strange place, keeping its secrets under a dark scum of snow and leaving him alone in his hut for nineteen years to watch the icicles freezing around him. He called it a hut, but the lock building was really more the size of a small town bank. The windows were very narrow, barred and covered with a wire mesh bolted into the rough stone walls. A few of them had fans in them but they were never on and the blades spun in the wind with a creak. Early on, so early I don't remember much before it, I went in with my brother, who'd been there before, but all I remember doing is reaching up to open a locker where he stored his wide rubber hip boots and plastic helmet, yellow with no scuffs on it. Much later I noticed there were some small turbines in there to power the lock. I flicked the rim of one with the nail of my pinkie and it gave off a dim pitch. I kept pinging at the rotor casings to see if the sounds they made sounded good together but they didn't. They all sounded off, not all the way off but a century out of tune like the old baby grand in our parlor. I knew that whatever these things were, they didn't work and hadn't for a long time. I didn't know if something had jammed or blocked or what. All I felt was the sadness of my father sitting here in his heavy plaid shirt and rumpled khakis, hands rusting from arthritis and disuse, filling his iron stove with twigs and garbage and broken crates, civil servant to a river that wasn't listening to him and wasn't about to. He wrapped tape around his hands to make them a little stronger when he turned the head of the valve to adjust the gates, but the valve never turned and the gates never budged. Everything in the room was frozen, even his dreams in it, but he kept the brass polished on them. He'd spread out maps on a big oak table, different maps at different times, but the one that was always out was a Phillips 66 map of California, worn to chamois with fingering. My father's face was pelleted on one side with old acne but it seemed the face of a man much younger when he'd trace the path of rivers with his thumb and tell us, "See that blue line? It's the Klamath River. Those black crosses are for dams. Two big dams and the river runs right through them. Right through them both like they're not even there."

But this was a riddle from somewhere else. We had our own running riddle and he was lockmaster to it. In the lock at the dam a mile south of Guttenberg, the gates were open and the water didn't flow through them. Sure a little coughed through but not near as much as the laws of fluids said ought to. The floodgates were wide open and had been since 1934. By anyone's slide rule the river should've risen three hundred feet thirty years back. The town wasn't supposed to be there. I wondered why he wasn't doing anything but looking at maps but shouldn't have. There wasn't anything for him to do but sit there twisting his wedding ring like a movable valve. A couple times a week nineteen years running he'd walk half a block from the hut to the grocer's, where two aisles of cans and cake mix and TV dinners, Crisco and meat stiffened in aluminum trays and tins of SpaghettiOs, lay separated by a warped abraded floor. The grocer was a vat of a man, sitting on his stool behind the soda-fountain counter crushing peanut shells in his mouth, wearing shorts even in winter, when the blue veins streaking his legs flared indigo from the cold and bunched into leaves at his ankles. Dad paid him cash, not food stamps, and watched Wilbur snap his bills one by one, testing for stress, he always thought, for the giving way he'd once learned to measure in pounds per square inch. The bills passed but he could feel the strain in the look on Wilbur's face, a fat round face, the folds of his neck pinched into the dirty collar of a white rayon shirt, rigid with fat except for the eyes, gummy elastic eyes that said, I know you, you're the one married that Handy girl, you ain't from here but you sure act like you are. Dad knew better. He wasn't from here because here was the river.

"He knew it wasn't his river," I told my brother. "And I knew it wasn't mine. It was yours and Lydia's. Mornings I'd walk down to the hut and he'd make me breakfast. He'd fry eggs in an iron skillet without a hot pad in his hand. There was a hot pad on the wall but he never used it. When he died they came and took his things out of the hut. That's the only thing I saved. The hot pad."

My brother gave me an adhesive smile, all lips and no teeth: Lydia's smile.

I told him how up to the very end she'd tried to interest people in town in their own fate, serving up what everyone called Lydia lunches, meals laid out on TV trays, deviled-ham sandwiches, pickles, hot coffee, shortcake with frozen strawberries. But there was apathy over the town like they'd sprayed it with indifference. Most of the town was for sale but, except for the Corps, there were no buyers. Half the buildings were empty hulks with stickers on them, that same shield, tricolor with a caption dripping from the bottom saying the U.S. Government didn't tolerate vandals.

"She didn't give up," I told him. "She never gave up. Not even when the big boys came."

"The big boys?"

"That's what Lydia called the Bureau of Reclamation. They never seemed that big to me."

"Why's that?"

"There were only four of them. Four in a car."

It was March, I told him, late March '67. Dad wasn't three months in his grave. You were already in the Delta. Lydia was at home and I was minding the hut. A car came at night, driving without headlights up the frontage road, a Chevy sedan a bubbling black color like it'd burned and been painted over a couple of coats. There'd been more than usual of the river's freaks that month. Above L/D 7 the water was flooding the fields way into the woods. Below the dam the water was level and low. When they got out of the car I knew their faces. I'd seen them in town that morning, four grim men sitting bolt upright eating ham and eggs in a booth upholstered in blue-and-white plastic. No introductions this time, though, just a card put in the palm of my hand, Fresco Crew, Resection Division, U.S.B.R. The head one wore blue jeans, a cattleman's leather jacket, and soft stirrup boots. He didn't say much, save to ask me where he could get some local charcoal, the burning kind, not the drawing kind, and when I'd shoveled some out of a bin, he'd crumbled off a piece in his hands and done a quick sketch of me on the wall, just a couple of turning lines, but in a quick sweep he caught the spirit of my face, six seconds and there I was, complete, in charcoal, and all the fresco foreman'd said was, Fine, this'll do. He didn't dink around asking me for permission to enter. Bucket swinging in hand, he just went right for the dam, took out a pair of bolt cutters, and snapped the lock off the chain-link fence. I leaned against the sedan while they set up in the dark. In the back seat I saw a couple of knapsacks. I loosened the string on one, expecting to see their tools, clawhammers, wrenches with oil caked on the teeth, screwdrivers with clear plastic handles. But no, there was a blunt brush, an egg carton full of fresh brown eggs, a box of charcoal, a pad of tracing paper, a bolt of muslin, two or three pasteboard folios, several lengths of fine cutting wire, some clay pellets the size of BBs, a few plastic jugs full of distilled water, plus a few cans of orange paint, different oranges. When they'd popped open the trunk to get more supplies, I'd looked inside there, too. Mounted under the hood was a little boxwood panel, hinged in two places like an altarpiece and painted in a shallow style, all surface and relief, the images pale like chalk and faded like cloth. So they were here to do just what the card said they were going to do. They'd come to paint the dam in fresco.

"No big crew. No trucks. No heavy equipment," I told my brother. "Just this stuff."

I didn't get it. Lydia told me there were frescoes on the big dams out west but they went in after the dams were done. Lydia didn't think of frescoes as repairs or even as being part of a dam. To her they were surface stuff, art deco that went in last and mattered least. The black Chevy had California plates and so she guessed this must be one of those fresco crews who'd worked the California dams, the ones who wet down the walls, trued and plastered them, outlined figures in charcoal, the cinabrese faces of Indians mostly, faces noble the way gases are, proud and unreacting, marking them out with a fine pointed brush, tinting them the color of redwood, fattening the cheeks with lime, adding a drapery of folds under the eyes plus a little pink on the lips to wash out the sadness and give some relief. She'd thought they came to work the walls only after the concrete dried, to make a tribute to the people they'd flooded out, but here they were, rubbing it over with powdered pumice, then applying a sticky paste, gum and honey swirled in a bucket of river water. They were getting ready to paint it, brought in not after the dam was done to finish it, but before.

"It took them about a week. They did a kind of mural of the town. They left and we thought that was it. But a year later the water level was up three hundred feet and the town was gone."

My brother put out a cigarette in a can of beer and turned to me. Suddenly I felt his stare.

He said, "Have you been on the dam?"

"A couple of times."

"A dam has two entrances, north and south. There's a round brass plate on a block of marble by the north entrance. Do you remember seeing a plate like that?"

"I think so. A picture of a dam with the sky above and the fields below."

"That's it. Were there words on it?"

"There was a slogan running round the edge of the circle."

"Do you remember what it said?"

"Something in Latin."

"Anything under that?"

"It didn't say Bureau of Reclamation. It said something else. Something shorter." I paused and dredged it up. "Reclam R&A."

"I knew it," he said.

"They were really engineers, right?"

"I wouldn't call them that."

R&A, he went on to say, was his unit in the Delta. He didn't know what the initials stood for, but then everything in the Bureau was abbreviated. The United States Bureau of Reclamation: nobody ever said the name whole. They called it the Bureau, called it Reclam, or called it by a sub name like R&A, but the king-size name was something formal, a title reserved for ceremony like the full name of a king. The Bureau was old, old as a monarchy, older than America, with that weird flipping coin of an escutcheon and that Latin motto, *Vox Reclamantis in Deserto*, like they were desert fathers crouching in dry caves praying to some terrible parched god for rain. My brother said the Corps would put a dam almost anywhere, shit, they didn't care where they put them so long as they could think of names for them. Half the time they didn't even bother doing that, naming not being easy as you think, them just slapping a few numbers on the Mon, Lock and Dam 6, 7, 8, nameless numbered locks supposed to hold the river staggered in nine segments between here and Pittsburgh but never holding, not for long. The names were off and the numbers just crumbled away. That's why the Bureau never did anything without a name. If there wasn't a clear name for what they were doing, they stopped work and waited for one to well out of the ground. The transpiring names were often collective, dams and lakes named after mute dispersed peoples, river peoples like Petard's, the Diggers on the upper Klamath in northern California. And even then, a name in place, the Bureau'd lay a dam only if there were signs pointing to the right place on the river. The Bureau didn't try to correct runny old surveys, fact all they did was hunt for them, the threads of old lines traced along invisible bounds, stone walls buried two or three feet deep, tops of stakes rotted off, lengths of iron pipe sunk in sand. The lines were where they were and nobody in the Bureau had the power to shift them because every mark on the ground was a meridian you couldn't erase even if you wanted to. He'd seen them pace out a dam by walking back and forth over the site in a trance. He'd never seen any of them measure anything. Sometimes they drew pictures and the pictures had power, specific power; fresco was one of their arts. They weren't just surveyors, he said, they were sentinels, and they could make lines wake out of death.

"But why get rid of the Corps?" I asked.

"You never believed Lydia, did you?"

"In my own way, maybe."

"Say what you want to, but that's not believing." He reached for a saucer of limes on the bar. He took a section, squeezed it over his whiskey and soda, and stirred the ice cubes with his finger. "They're like you in the Corps. They don't believe either."

My brother had nothing but scorn for the Army Corps of Engineers. He said the Corps thought a river was a highway for barges but the Bureau of Reclamation knew better. A river was a necropolis and its hacking flow was the cough of the past. With their yellow machines the Corps dug canals like canals were something new, like nobody'd ever dug them before. The Bureau didn't dig. The Bureau disinterred. This was an agency prepped for all your lost cities wherever they turned up, surrounded by scar tissue of silted-up canals. Because reclamation wasn't about necessity. Reclaiming was the calling back of the land to what it had once been, for land could not be what it had not once been. When the Bureau built dams their dams were monuments, because, unlike the Corps, they built dams nobody needed. If a dam was needed someplace, they put it somewhere else. If one turned out to be useful, they took it down. If one irrigated a field, they poisoned the water and razed the field. Dams were for them pure exercises of power, auroras brought to earth to shoot pale volts across the land. Around every dam they strung bows of high cable and lit the desert with the sequent light of noble gases. Leave civil engineering to the Army. These were uncivil engineers with mysteries to stage. They'd managed to build most of their big dams during the Depression, when there was no money to build them. During the war the Bureau's black budget was bigger than the Pentagon's and not even the Pentagon knew it and wouldn't, least not till the very end of the war on the Mekong Delta, the war that turned the waters crashing inward and calmed American Reclam once and for all.

"Yokut Dam on the Klamath River is bigger than all the locks and dams on the Mon put together," my brother told me. "Next to the Bureau we're ants and our dams are stinking little anthills."

"Why bother about the Mon, then?"

"The Mon was free and the Bureau knew it. You don't build a dam without the water backing up on one side. The river had nine dams on it and didn't touch the town in thirty-five years."

"Aren't dams supposed to protect us?"

He let out his breath. "You know the answer to that. Lock and Dam 7 was opened in 1934. The river just wouldn't flood Guttenberg."

"Because of Lydia?" I asked.

I thought again of our place on the Mon, the porch lights on, Lydia sitting on the back steps watching the river. It was completely dark on the other side of the river, so I never knew what it was she was watching. Back then she had a pale face with jet-black hair pulled straight back from a center part and fastened with a rubber band. When she blinked and turned her head away from the river, you thought for a second she was slow and maybe she was because it took her a while to disengage, retreating with retarded motion from the river. Dad used to say she was a wild child all grown up. When it came to the river she wasn't just back in the first grade, she was back before grades in a river's childhood where there were no gradients, no dams, no towns, no anything, just a river running through an empty valley.

"I thought I had it too," said my brother.

"Had what?"

"What she had. A voice with the river."

"I don't know about voices," I said. "But I know she tried everything. Letters, calls, meetings, trips to D.C. Nothing worked, nobody listened, so we waited. I figured it'd be some sort of deluge, but when the end came, it was slow. It took five months for the river to rise high enough to flood the first floor of the house. You were gone then. She knew you were in Riverine and she thought that meant you hadn't given up the fight. She didn't know you were with the Bureau of Reclamation. She thought you were fighting a war on a river. She didn't know."

"Know what?"

"Know you were fighting a war *against* a river."

3

My brother put his elbows on the bar and held a glass in his hands, turning it in the light. The light in the bar caught the glass like a prism, and I found myself remembering May 1975, the month he came back from Vietnam. It wasn't long after my wife and I split up. I'd taken her to California with me, moving west to leave the Mon Valley once and for all, only to find myself in another valley full of Pennsylvania transplants. Linda Lee hated mill towns and it didn't take her long to figure out that a mill town was a mill town no matter where it was. Fontana air was full of taconite dust from the Kaiser Mills and a few stinging lungfuls were enough for her. She left me telling me she wasn't leaving me, she was leaving Southern California, but I couldn't go back any more than my brother could.

He stayed with me six weeks under certain unspoken conditions. No talk about money, no talk about plans, no talk about our mother, Lydia, who was then already in the west, staying with her sister in Santa Barbara, no talk about our father, who he always said was more my father than his, and no talk about Vietnam. It wasn't hard for him to keep to his end. I still pictured him wearing an oily blue shirt with his name in an oval, *Jim*, jumping at the sound of cars pulling into the gas station up at the state highway, the chair springing back up and him out the door, rag in hand and ready, but he'd changed. He had no energy. Dad had never liked to climb stairs, and now I often heard that familiar heavy reluctant footfall, slight pause, and outdraft of breath coming between creaks like each step was too much, except it was my brother. I never heard him laugh. He'd smile slightly but the smile would go quick as it came. He breathed fairly easily so long as he wasn't smoking. He didn't do much. Sometimes he'd go out for walks in Cypress Park and feed the birds. He was getting so big then I often wondered why he didn't crush them instead. He had a frame made for crushing and somehow it didn't make sense to see him quietly feeding the small twittering birds jumping for bits of bread around his boots. But mostly he slept, if you can call it sleep. The moment he opened his eyes he was wide awake and fumbling for a cigarette.

"Can't sleep?" I'd ask, coming in.

He'd lift his head and I'd see how red his eyes were.

"I get all the sleep I need."

"You've been up all night."

"I've been up sleeping," he'd say.

Up sleeping. I didn't know then how right that was. For a while he tried to sleep in the bedroom next to mine but he banged around so much after midnight I moved him to a converted garage in the backyard. He seemed to like it better that way. The bed in his room was pushed against the garage door. He emptied the drawers into cartons, stripped the mattress, and ran an extension cord out there so he could watch television at night. Days he'd open the garage door and sit in the driveway. For six weeks all he did was sit. Sometimes he'd talk about repairing things in the house, sometimes he'd call me and complain about all the junk in the backyard, hillbilly junk he called it, a bathtub filled with dirt and a stack of old rattan chairs, but he never lifted a finger, not even when the picture went out on his television and all he had was volume. After a while he stopped putting on his clothes and just sat in the driveway in a dirty white robe, watching the cars go by on Baseline Road. People slowed down to look at him, but when he looked back, they sped right up again. At night he'd sit in his garage and warm his hands on a portable heater, complaining how cold L.A. was in May. He had no curiosity, none.

"That house across the street," I remember telling him. "The pink and yellow one. It's the Landis place. Not the same Landises. These are Belchertown Landises, but they're related."

"Why'd they all come here?"

"Same reason I did. They came for work."

"Work where?"

"In the steel mills."

"Bullshit," he said. "The mills are all shut down here

same as in Pennsylvania. You know why they came here? They came here because it's a desert. Just like you. They came here to forget."

My brother was in his twenties then. I saw him maybe six times after that first long stay, always looking worse each time, slumped in a booth in some bar, drinking whiskey with lime, balling up napkins, his face gray and sullen. Cigarette after cigarette burned down to stubs in his hands. His life was over, he kept saying, over. He had all of three friends, Bureau friends from Vietnam, but they had their own lives now. Petard took care of Travers, and Jenna was off on her own in Turlock, working for the irrigation district. He had enough to live on because the Bureau took severance seriously, but he only wanted to make a real living somewhere, any living'd do because this wasn't living. He was sick of running from the past, not his past, that was easy enough, but from the Bureau's past; that was different.

He had a succession of shit jobs, one working in a Coke-bottling factory in Vacaville, another driving a forklift in a furniture warehouse in Richmond, another packing fish in flat rectangular cans, ten at a time, as they rattled by on a belt in a cannery north of Vallejo. He was at loose ends and he'd take almost any kind of job save the kind you had to wear a uniform for. After he bummed around for a couple of years, Petard brought him north to Eureka to work in the mill he worked in now. He had a hard time of it. Sometimes the memories hit him so hard and fast he had no idea what he was remembering. Why couldn't he remember what he couldn't forget? Trying, not trying to remember or forget but trying to talk to me in some bar somewhere, same as now, he saw himself trapped in a batting cage with baseballs thrown at him according to some hypercomplex laws of calculus way over his head. Curves shot over the shoulder, memory curves shot at him in a coinciding rush of flashes that seemed to come out of nowhere and go flying right back into darkness. He knew he couldn't write it all down. The flashes wiped him out; they still did. Drinking helped but not much.

"I didn't try to stop it," he was saying now, not turning his head to me, barely moving his lips. "I wanted to but I didn't know how. I'd be on the river—the Mekong was a big wide river and I'd feel it—the river moving under me just like the Mon. They didn't take river people, not for Riverine. The rest of the men on the boat were from cities. Water for them came from a fucking tap. They didn't know, couldn't tell. It was November and hot. The river was a mile wide and there was no shade anywhere. My guys'd crouch under the guns for shade. That was about the most protection they could get from those 144s."

"Why was that?"

"They were empty."

"Empty?"

"Those were the orders, empty. Reclam didn't want to take any chances with the truce. I told them we'd be shot out of the water if anything went wrong. The fuckers. They knew what the Viet Cong would do to us once they found out what we'd done to their river. But they just let us go upriver unarmed. They knew and they just let us turn off the Mekong and plow right up the Kanh Xing Canal. You know how narrow a canal is. We had three feet on either side and only a truce to protect us."

"Truce? Whose truce?"

"Ours and theirs."

"Who was us?"

"Reclamation was us. That was what the war was about in the end, reclamation. VC, ARVN, they all sent units to the dam."

"What about the peace talks?"

"They were a diversion. And besides, this wasn't peace."

"Did they have the authority to do that?"

"Authority?" My brother snorted out the word. "You're talking like a fucking journalist. Like Jenna before she saw what was what. Look, I don't know how many times I have to tell you this, but the Bureau doesn't answer to the U.S. government."

"Then how did they negotiate a truce with the Viet Cong?"

"Nobody negotiated anything. The truce sort of sprang up. I can't explain it. It took a long time for it to happen, but once they saw what we were doing they didn't fire on us."

"Why didn't they?"

"We were doing something they wanted us to do."

"Building them a dam?"

"Not just any dam. A dam they understood. A kind of dam they wanted so badly they helped us build it."

"But they turned on you," I said.

"On me?" he said, staring at me. His eyes were yellow and I couldn't see what was in them. "No, not on me. I made it through okay. Petard saw to that." Then, abstracted, running his fingers through his hair, long and slicked back and just turning gray, "Not on me, no. On everyone but me."

He wasn't drinking now but, elbows on the bar, he was looking at a row of old license plates nailed to the wall next to the mirror. Black-and-yellow California plates, dull and rusted, 1947, 1948, 1950, 1951. 1949 was missing. The sequence was random to me but it made some kind of sense to him. 1949 was Petard's year, the year Yokut Dam went operational. He said he knew why there were all those Indians in the Bureau, they were the ones closest to the Klamath, the Colorado, the Columbia, Dartmouths of them trained to go back to the rivers they loved and betray them. But not Petard.

"Petard's too smart for them," he told me. "He's got that tribe of his behind him. Nobody can kill off that tribe, and believe me, everyone's tried. Digger Indians, who ever heard of Digger Indians? They don't even have land anymore. He has absolutely nothing, but you know what? Navier-Stokes, head of all Reclam, is afraid of him. Afraid of Petard. Petard used to be Chief Engineer, Division of Design, Reclam R&A. He was the best they had. I told you a little about R&A. They're the elite unit. They move the earth."

"They what?" I asked.

"They move the earth."

"Of course they move the earth," I said. "They're engineers."

"No, I really mean it, *they move the earth.*"

"But that's what engineers do."

"They're not real engineers," my brother said.

"I thought you said Petard was an engineer."

"He was. But not your kind of engineer. Reclam has engineers who design and build dams but they're strictly low-grade. Dad was one of these and he didn't even make that grade. There are other engineers, higher engineers. It's an old art, it goes way back. Some engineers build dams but others design them. They call them chief engineers. You can't be trained as one. You have to be born into it. It's not something you can choose. They have to find you, or you have to find them. Usually it's both. These engineers can't stay away from dams. Petard couldn't. It's in the blood."

He went on to tell me that this highest grade of engineer was rare; maybe a few came along per generation. They were dangerous, too, because they could do a lot more than build dams. They could feel dams from the inside. He'd seen them build dams that couldn't possibly hold together, dams with not much more than a few inches of wall holding back a river, dams laid in place like the tensions that occur in bodies simply didn't apply to them. Given the right conditions, they could split a dam in two.

"Just by willing it?" I asked.

"I'm telling you, it's not a matter of will. No chief engineer wants to be one. Think about it: God *made* the heavens and the earth: it's that kind of power. They run from it but it catches up with them. It's just a matter of time for most. Look at me. I ran off to Vietnam thinking I'd never see another dam long as I lived."

"Are you one?"

"Reclam used to think so. It runs in our family. Lydia was. She kept that dam at bay for thirty-eight years."

"You're not, then?"

"They used to think so but not anymore, not after what happened at Long Dam. I could feel the waters running under me even when the river was a foreign river like the Mekong. But I couldn't move them. I was just a spectator. The river never came clear to me. It ran right under me and there was nothing I could do to move it."

"Maybe it skips generations," I said.

"It doesn't work that way," he said. "The line has to be continuous. It runs in families. If one doesn't get it, another does."

"That means?"

"Process of elimination."

"That means it's me?"

"*They* think it's you. I don't know what your power consists of. You're a writer. Maybe that's it. The engineers always have a way with words. But whatever the fuck it is, they think you've got the gift. Petard saw it in one of his sweathouse visions. He's always having visions. It's an Indian thing, visions. He saw you receiving the stories. That's how he put it, the stories. He says the stories have been waiting for you. He wants to meet you. He told me to take you up to Eureka and says he'll take care of the rest. I didn't want to. Half the time when I'm with him I don't know what's going on, but I can feel something's going on. They want to see you because they think you'll understand."

"Who's they?"

"All of them. Petard, Travers, Jenna."

"I thought you said Travers was crazy."

"Sort of, but he's still doing biology. He named one of his pet toads after you. Gailly Harper, a big green Cane toad."

"So what?"

"He didn't know I had a brother. He's been certified crazy since '73."

"Why isn't he locked up?"

"He's from an old family," said my brother. "Maybe they pulled some strings."

He drained the can of beer he held in his hand, mashed it, and stood for a time turning the can in his hand. He didn't want to ask me to come north then and there even though that's what he'd come to do. For the occasion of asking me for something, he had on a short-sleeved Hawaiian shirt that hung outside his jeans. He was clearly irritated at having to ask me for anything. He didn't know what more to say, so he looked down at his bar stool, rocked back and forth on it a little till he decided it wouldn't do. I watched him line up a row of stools near the window and check them one by one for wobble. He chose one that wasn't too rigid, the frame moved a little but not too much, he said it had good give and mumbled something about the Euler equation for a pin-connected column. I had to smile. He was a born engineer even when he was drunk.

4

The next morning my brother was gone again. He left beer cans strewn all over the living room, most with cigarettes stuffed in them. There was a sofa in the room, a couple of folding chairs, and a glass coffee table. A bus ticket to Eureka, California, was on the coffee table. When Lydia came out of her room she glanced at the ticket and told me he'd left for Humboldt County. The covers on his bed were neat, the clean sheets stretched across just the way she'd left them. He'd slept on the couch again. She went to the refrigerator, drank some tomato juice, and set out a chicken covered in plastic wrap. She looked at me and I looked away.

I avoided her till later in the day, when I took a jar of iced tea to her out in the front yard. We sat in the late afternoon, the hot part of the day in L.A., she on a lawn chair in the front yard, staring off up the valley, and me a few feet away on the top step of the stoop. Lydia was composed and matter-of-fact. She never talked much about my brother, not to me; I know she felt he'd left her and she was sick of leavings. But she accepted his leaving with an Appalachian fatalism she'd fought off for years but which now, having lost her battle with the Army Corps and living in exile with me in a California desert, she gave into it like she'd finally come into her birthright.

"You're still angry with him," she began.

"In a way."

"He wasn't a good brother to you. He didn't take you along anywhere. He didn't show you the river. He was always alone. Jimbo liked being alone."

I didn't know what to say but she didn't seem to expect

any answer and continued stitching, pausing sometimes to search for new strands of yarn in a bag by her side. The needlepoint was a pattern of red and green Christmas trees.

"He left before you were old enough to know why. He was afraid of your father. Not that there was anything to be afraid of. It's just that he didn't want to be like him. Walter felt it and so did I."

"He never liked Dad," I said.

"No he didn't," she said. "He thought he was weak. But he followed in his footsteps, followed him right into engineering school. He says he was drafted but I never saw a notice. You remember the postcards he sent. Two in six years. In '67 there was one from Muscle Shoals, Louisiana, saying he was in basic training there. But the cancellation mark said Denver. He is like your father. When there's something he can't understand he doesn't try to understand it. He tries to live with it, to put himself inside it. He wants to touch it, to turn it in his hands. He wants to become part of it."

"But he hates dams."

"I hate them too. Hate doesn't stop them from building them."

"You mean he joined the Bureau to stop them?"

"He wasn't the first. He might not tell you. He might not admit it to himself. He hates the Bureau. He hates them too much. If he'd hated them less he might have been a better engineer. That was Walter's story too. Hating himself for becoming an engineer then hating himself more for *not* becoming one. Why do you think your brother wound up on a gunboat?"

"He was in Riverine," I said.

"Riverine was guard duty. Can you picture your brother taking orders from anyone? He had something, an engineer's gift, a partial gift maybe, but he didn't want to use it. He stayed because he trusted the man who was building the dam in Vietnam. I haven't met Petard Davidson. I saw him only once, but I feel like I know him well. He lost his land to the Bureau and he's taking care of your brother now. He's fifteen years older than Jimbo, and not like him at all. Your brother could push a car up a hill but Petard has a different kind of strength. He lost a river, too, but he didn't run away from it. I don't know the whole story, but there's a river in California with two abandoned dams on it. Jimbo looks up to him for what he did. I think he's teaching Jimbo to be a brother to you."

"Jimbo drinks too much," I said.

"But he calls you."

"Sometimes," I told her. "He calls sometimes."

Lydia shifted her weight on the lawn chair so she could look straight at me. "He wants to take you up north."

"I don't want to go to Redding again just to look at the furniture. That storage locker is like a grave."

"I think he wants to take you on some kind of river trip."

"Did he put you up to this?"

"He asked me to talk to you."

"I knew it."

"He wants you to help him."

"What does he want? More money?"

"It's not what you think."

"He drinks a fifth a day."

"It's not that. He needs your words."

"My words? That's strange. He talks fine when he feels like it."

"He does and he doesn't. He can talk but he doesn't have the right words for what he saw. He says you have them. I think he's right. I've seen the drawers full of those stories you're writing. You never leave your room."

Then, fainter and more distant, not looking at me but far away into the past, "I gave you the room in back. I think I was wrong. You should have had the one facing the river."

Facing the river. Together and apart we sat there in my front yard in Fontana, California, remembering what had been, our high brick home on the river, the Monongahela River in Pennsylvania. Early on, Lydia gave my brother her old bedroom in back and me the one in front facing the hill and the tower. Our bedrooms were on the third floor. A curved staircase led from the hallway near the front door to the second floor. Lydia and Walter slept on the second floor. The way up to the third was by a narrow staircase cut off at floor level by a trapdoor. The door was hinged to the floor, and you opened it by pulling a rope threaded through a pulley screwed into the ceiling. You didn't have to yank hard. The pulling end of the rope had flat weights on it, so even if you just touched it the door popped open with a creak and a slam. The bedrooms had one rounded window each and they both had locks on them. The house was so old and thick he heard only barges and I heard only trains. So in a way I was raised with my back to the river. I was a Harper more than a Handy and there was something between Lydia and my brother that defied the generations. She had a way of nodding her head at him even when she was saying no and not taking her eyes off him. Sometimes they'd sit for hours on the back porch, watching the river. When I asked him what he thought when they were watching the river he told me he often wondered if the river knew where it was going. Did it know about the locks and dams ahead, did it pass the word back, was there warning, time to prepare, or did it flow blindfolded to the white barren tower at Waynesburg? Sometimes, walking evenings along the riverbank, he thought he heard a warning carried back, a cry pitched waterborne, a low audible wail, but when he followed it, wading into the river, no time to strip, jeans black in the water and boots sinking in the mud, crystal of his watch clouding with steam, all he heard was waves. If the Mon wanted to turn away from its severance, it didn't let on. It swerved unbending around him, moved with low stoic flow toward its fate, loosened the tunic on its shoulders and laid its head on the dam like a king.

"How do you know this?" I'd ask.

"You don't know anything, do you?" was what he'd say.

He was eighteen and I was eleven and I remember trying to think the way he thought, listening to him listen to the river, and not getting it, just watching the foam push by in the wake of barged coal. Why didn't I hear what he heard? When the river spoke to my brother all I saw was a voiceless moving jaw. The washup along the banks was junk to me but a shrine to him, a place to pray full of glass in green and amber and pink and blue, pieces of redware made of the same clay the bricks were, shallow fired jars, a ladle, some .22 caliber shells, porcelain doorknobs Dad used to collect. The back porch had a wet-dog smell, specially on days when the river was high, and I'd often give up and go inside to sit with Lydia in the kitchen. The kitchen was an addition to the hotel which made it the room nearest the river, and on cold days, when she couldn't get closer to the Mon, that was where she was, cooking but not really. The rows of fat blue glasses and chipped white dishes were unused, the drawer underneath full of dull knives, tarnished spoons, forks with bent tines. Along the river wall there were long shelves with jars on them, mason jars full of wild berries for jam, and a big pot of berries steaming on the burner. The way out to the river was by the kitchen door with yellow and red corncobs nailed to it. I got to the doorway quick enough but just stood there, not going in and not knowing how to say what I wanted to say, instead picking up a box of stove matches and scratching a match against the counter, watching the tip flare blue then red then white.

"The river doesn't talk to me," I said at last.

"I know," she said. "It talks to your brother."

"But can I make it talk to me?"

"It doesn't have to," she said, sealing a mason jar. "It talks through you."

Back in Fontana, Lydia set down her sewing and took a sip from the plastic bottle of iced tea. She slipped her feet out of her slippers and peered around the front yard. She was finished remembering, but not me. Suddenly I was back on my river again, my river the way it used to be, my father alive and next to me, my brother down by the river, playing river as he put it. My father'd rowed me across the river so we could look back at our town. There wasn't a dock over there. Knee-deep in mud he pulled us in and tied us down. Ten yards in and up were the P&M&B tracks, I never knew what they stood for, I always thought Pittsburgh and Monongahela and Beyond, because just beyond the tracks was the old hillside graveyard. The place was full of old dead stumps that'd never quite rotted away and April wildflowers pushing up blue and purple. The grass wasn't soft, it was hard and prickly to sit on. The trees around the clearing quivered in the wind. You could see our property all the way from one edge at the service road to the other where the garden ended. Lydia wasn't there because she was at another meeting trying to save the town. She was already a river fighter, not like my brother later in Vietnam, but there wasn't an inch of town she hadn't fought to keep above water. Dad, too, would have walked through walls to save that town if he'd have thought that walking through walls would have done any good. While Lydia begged and pleaded in front of a bored, bought-off magistrate, my father took my hand and smiled his tipped smile, the lines of it fixed on his mouth by his second-to-last stroke. In my memory he is always smiling like that, wiping his nose on the sleeve of his brown wool sweater and closing his eyes while he talked, saying the things he said to me, me and not my brother because I was the one who needed to hear them said, saying, Gailly the river takes back what the river gives, everything is a return to the river, Gailly someday the river will give you something, I don't know what, a woman, the river gave me a woman but maybe for you it'll be a voice or a journey or a song, but remember whatever you get you've got to give it back. The river gave me your mother and I know one day I'll have to give her back. It's good we live in a hotel on the river. The place you stay on the river is just a place you stay for a little while on your way back, and along the river there are many empty hotel rooms like ours where people live till they get called back to the river. When you're working, pumping gas like your brother or salting steel in one of the mills, look down at your hands and see the river lines in them. The lines in your hands are the rivers running through you. The lines'll always take you back to the river. Remember, the river's where you can begin again when you thought you were out of beginnings. Remember that when you can't remember anything else. The river is where you always begin . . .

And end. I told Lydia to tell my brother I'd take his river trip with him. She put down her sewing and looked, not to me, but down the street. The heat of the day was over and families were out in front of their bungalows, all sitting in wicker chairs. A boy with a baseball cap pushed back on his head mowed the lawn. A girl in a waitress uniform unlocked the door of a car. They all had narrow pinched faces, mark of the Mon Valley, and now they all lived in Los Angeles. She knew why. Nine dams between Fairmont and Pittsburgh meant a string of nine lakes where nine small towns had been. Mile 0.0 was at the mouth of the Monongahela River at Pittsburgh. L/D 7 was right in the middle at Mile 89.6 counting south. In California, too, we were right in the middle of the block, a long block where the houses had five-digit numbers painted on the curb. Over Fontana the sun was down, the sky was brown, and the sprinklers were on.

"The weather doesn't turn here," said Lydia in her lawn chair, more to herself than to me. "I keep waiting for it to turn."

Two ●

1

Eureka, California. I'd waited a long time at the bus station, sitting on the old curbing of US 1, blowing breath into my hands and waiting for the sun to come up. Eureka was like Pittsburgh, full of mills and barges and bars. This early in the morning no bars were open but the town hummed with neon signs. An hour passed and not one car. When a dim pair of headlights broke the dull ocean gray, I picked up my duffel and walked into the middle of the road. My brother had told me to come to Eureka, a mill town where the mills were still working, paper not coal foaming out of the plants where pulp poured into the ocean and glue into the air, because he'd said Petard was ready to talk, ready to remember, said they all were. But he looked away from me soon as he saw me, away, not down, and I knew I was on my own. He got out of the passenger side of the pickup and stood holding the door while I put my bag in the back, my arms shivering in the morning fog. The three of us in it, the pickup then turned around, turning back inland toward what was left of the great Klamath dams.

Petard Davidson was driving. My brother wasn't big on intros but I knew he'd been higher up than him in the

Bureau, way higher up. In the first light of day rolling toward the jagged horizon of the Klamaths northeast of Eureka, breaking open into the bottomlands of north coastal California, the old green Dodge pickup not taking the wet wind too well, I got my first good look at Petard since the bus let me off that morning. His face was wind-burned and divided into two by the stain of a tattoo. Cut into his chin was a flat black line about two inches long. Petard didn't like to show it off. It was there under his beard, a birthmark of sorts, but not there for anyone to see. He said there were two kinds of tattoos. Story tattoos that didn't mean shit and memory tattoos that pinched your nerves and made you cry for the past. This sure as fuck wasn't a story tattoo. It was there because it had to be there, because Petard was a Digger Indian and all Diggers bore the memory mark of the flood line.

The 1946 Dodge Petard drove was a truck conversion. The pickup was a beater but when he bought it he'd done it up good and the engine was better than a new one. New engines have new parts, the tolerances are close but never close enough, but he said if you rebuild it yourself you can grind them even closer. He'd taken apart the B-2-B, stripped it down to a bare ruined cab, down to flathead and block and pan, boiled out the block, checked for cracks, tapped off the corners of the cylinder heads and sealed them up again nice and tight. Mostly it ran fine now, taking in air through the grille, two bars laid across the radiator like braces on teeth, the bullnose with the dented boxy cab and the two-piece windshield running creeping and coasting up and down the Trinity Highway from Arcata on our way to Junction City, a place of converging roads near where Petard's first dam was. It was high rough country, and for most purposes the soggy old gas-station map Petard carried in his glove compartment, Skelly 1949, was about as good as any USGS product.

The road was a corkscrew. We were getting out of the Coastal Ranges with their wave-planed slopes of red iron soil, getting into the granite Klamaths, but there was no way to see the difference by looking out the window, because the granite was underground. The old black sea floor of the Pacific, pure ocean bedrock, had got thrown up onto land and crumpled into this Klamath outcrop a hell of a long time ago. Now the Klamaths were scrap of sediment jammed into a high trench at the edge of the continent. No even township corners here. The heavy black rock was a surveying nightmare.

"The USGS must hate these mountains," I said.

"The Bureau hates them more," said Petard.

"Because you can't reclaim them?"

"Because they're already claimed."

Petard had the wheel. I sat next to him, legs splayed between the three-speed column shift, and my brother sat next to me on the wide bench seat, pressing his face sullenly against the door glass on the other side. Along the western base of the range the land flattened out bald and featureless toward the ocean. Petard drove with the seat shoved way back and his legs stretched out, ankles thick and swollen into big high grommeted boots he never took off. He squinted when he talked but he wasn't really squinting, just focusing on what he was about to say like the words were coming up on the road just ahead of him. He was built like bedrock, thick wrists, big forearms, fat, but the fat was strong fat. He wasn't wearing a shirt, just an open vest, the crusty diamond-quilted liner from his army jacket, plus that pointy lama's hat flopping down around his ears, some souvenir from his alpine days in Vietnam back before Vietnam was our war, when he was an advisor to Thieu's wet dream to dam every river in the Annamite Cordillera. Like the truck, Petard gave off a faint leaking brake-fluid reek. For this trip he'd pulled the old black California plates off it. "Where we're going they got their own plates." He started telling me about where his tribe's name came from. Digger was the only word in the Digger language that was not native to it. The word came from somewhere else, no one knew where exactly, and it meant digger. Weird shit, the one word naming them being an English word what with the rest of the words in the language being regulation Algonquin, a very pure strain and nobody knew why, because Algonquin dialects, Cree and Fox and Sauk and Shawnee, were an eastern thing, but right here in Siskiyou County was this Digger-speaking tribe and, double weird shit here, the next tribe up, the Coos Bay Salish, spoke Spokan, a language with not one word in common with theirs, a language with no past tense while the Digger lingo made everything sound like it had already happened and was being remembered. The Diggers had not dug in low valleys for seventy years or so, they'd been pushed out of the low Sierra where they once lived, whites lived there now, up Placer County way, and the settlers'd gotten their digs in good, pushing them out then naming the whole fucking county after running water flushing heavy metal out of placer deposits, then naming them too, because, like Petard said, the name came later.

"Our enemies gave it to us," he said.

"You let them do that?"

"It always works that way. The people who hate you tell you who you are."

Out of a deeply tanned leather sack he handed me an oily hunk of acorn bread. I broke it in two, it was Digger food and Petard was very particular about what he put in his mouth. This bread was full of big brown acorns with no worm holes inside and I gave some to my brother, who ate it without looking to see what it was. Petard had taken charge back in Eureka, he'd pulled me into the pickup with me rubbing the green of sleep out of my eyes, saying we were here for a reason, the Bureau was leaving America and fuck if he wasn't gonna be in on it, he'd been waiting for this for a long time, too long. He said we were going to Witusa'a, that he'd take us that far then we'd be on our own recog, the Dodge was ours, Travers didn't live far from here and Jenna wasn't more than a day away in the Central Valley. Driving north from Eureka along Highway 96 above Arcata Junction along the Klamath River, watching the dippers breaking the brittle shell of the water, diving and feeding in waterfalls, my brother and I wanted to go have a look at Digger Lake, definitely the biggest ditch left in the area after the failure of Ah Pah and Tehama dams, but Petard said he hadn't been back in a long time and wasn't about to go back now. 96 passed a 16,000-kW power plant a few miles upstream along the western embankment of a small holding reservoir. Petard winced when he saw it. He said it brought back a memory, a bad memory from a long time ago but not too far away from here. He was from a little village on the bank of a small arroyo right under a place a lot like the place where that U-shaped generator is now. The place used to be called Yokut, it still had the same name but it was Yokut Dam now, and it had stood on stoneless alluvial soil.

"They always give dams Indian names," he began. "I went to school to learn about the mounds they were using to bury us."

2

Petard said he was still a kid in 1944 when the Division of Design, Bureau of Reclamation R&A, San Francisco, sent a fat man in a pin-striped suit to tell them they were going to build a dam to irrigate crops. He said he was a farmer, see, and that he came in peace. But what kind of farmer carried with him compass and chain, wye level and level tube, target rod and telescope? Think back, Petard said, the Diggers didn't have agriculture, they didn't till soil or dig ditches, they dug for acorns with a stick, they didn't live on squash or corn or cereal, they lived on hampers and granaries filled with acorns and their word for plenty was *anauchemineash*, acorn. Sure, they'd staked weirs to take salmon. But how could they possibly have known that what the man in the pin-striped suit was talking about was an earthfill built 405 feet above the valley floor, a three-gated gallery a mile long with intake towers the size of skyscrapers, diversion tunnels the depth of mines, spillway troughs the width of canals? The feds wanted to trade them benchlands for bottomlands. They might as well have offered them beads or abalone shells. The new land was dry, poor, strange, a place called Witusa'a but the pin man pronounced it like Warsaw, a ghetto of the remaining nations of the north of California, Karok, Shasta, Wintun, Miwok, all pressed into a dirty open camp ninety miles north of Willow Creek on 96. The man in the suit kept saying, see, it'd go easier for the Diggers if they just said yes to the feds, the others had and, see, look at them, but the Diggers just said no in about a thousand ways.

The meeting went on for a long time. There were lots of questions, lots of objections, but everyone knew what a few Indians said wouldn't count for much. The plan was going to be slow liquid death for the valley. To ward off the coming flood the shaman, Petard's father, Lew, stood and sang the song of the dead. This was the song of how the Diggers had once let their dead rot in the open air but gave that up because the wind was cold, how they then had laid them in the ground but gave that up because the ground was damp, how they then had released them into the waters but gave that up because the waters were roiled, how they at last had burned them in fire because fire was pure and returned their spirits to fresh bones. The women thumped their pestles in their mortar baskets, crushing acorns, approving. But the man in the pin-striped suit, some Cagney clone folded in fat, kept saying See? See? after every few words, talking broken English to them because he saw they were Indians and he thought Indians only understood signs and grunts. A lot of the Diggers didn't know English too well but they knew all too well that a shroud of water was falling over them, tight and dark and wet, and they knew what a fearful death a premature burial was, your body stiff but alive, knees under chin, hands against cheeks, wrapped in blankets and skins against the chill of *wesquaubenan*, the winding up in the deep cold ground. A few Diggers that had a smatter of Spanish from way back swore he was saying "Sí, Sí," that he was listening to them, but some knew better and said that it was all over even before the meeting began. They were sighted at the intersection of the cross hairs in a level tube. The Bureau's line of sight was fixed on them and it was too late to turn the scope away from them. The meeting was as open and closed as a pricking ceremony in a Digger sweathouse.

They were right. There was nothing they could do. The bus station at Weed was crowded to the doors with Indians, waiting for buses, standing around, sleeping curled up on long, high-backed mission benches. In the coffee shop Digger families, eight to a booth, ate stacks of buckwheat pancakes like it was their last meal. These were the ones who had taken the Bureau's money. Their buses were leaving for the roadhouse tents of Bakersfield, the watermelon fields of Fresno, the four-room shacks of Sacramento. The waitress was Nina, Petard's cousin but within marrying range, a Digger of twenty with an open face, clear brown eyes, long black hair, and a clean poppy smell about her. He'd known Nina since childhood when their fathers had built a sweathouse together. Nina had a clarity about her. Petard felt sure that Nina would stay and do the right thing; maybe she would help him with what he had a mind to do; but what he told her was that he wanted her to come out and see the night with him.

"I'd love to, but I have a ticket."

"For tonight?"

"For tonight."

"Why go," said Petard, "when you've got a good job?"

"I'm going to Berkeley."

"What's there for you?"

"You used to talk about going there. To the university."

He wanted to say, That was then, this is now, but what he said was, "Didn't know you could read."

He did not want to sting her but he stung her bad and right away he regretted it. Nina's face fell, the light went from it, she peeled his check off her pad and slapped it upside down on the linoleum counter. He turned the check and saw numbers, she'd written them in a row but she couldn't add, he knew that for a fact. There were no words there. Everything was falling apart. That night Petard took a crowbar and bolt cutters, cut a hole the size of a boulder in a chain-link fence, and forced open the door on the weatherboard contractor's shack built into the hillside just below the dam. The door popped open easily, it had been drawn shut by a leather strap over a nail, but Petard didn't know what to do once he was inside. He had not made any plans. Toward one end he saw a wooden shelf, waist-high, a bucket, a dipper, a basin, a bar of soap, a towel. Toward the other he saw a standing table slanted like the back of a grasshopper. He knocked it over and the maps slid across the floor. Forgetting for a moment why he was there, he knelt on the floor to pick them up. 19 USC Driggs 405 60/70°. *United Western Investigation, Interim Report on Reconnaissance, Report to the Chief.* T 1 3 N R 2 2 E S 3 6 B T. These were magic symbols to him but, look, follow the yellow and brown contours and, look, there was the dam: a huge plunging apparition, it was already there. The map said one, nine, four, one, three years ago. It was not a blueprint but a regular gas-station map of Northern California, Shasta Region, a glove-compartment map of the sort packed in his father's Ford pickup wedged between tire gauges, spark plugs, oily chamois cloths. Three years ago, full two years before the pin man handed out brochures and put the project to a vote, his village was already underwater!

Out of reflex he lit a cigarette and began to pace, and out of rage he pressed the hot orange burning tip to the map and watched it burst into flames. Seconds later the flames zipped across the trailer, the flames a very cold and fine sudden white that fired the two-by-fours like fuses set up in the bare walls. Petard had to double back across collapsing walls of flame. The fire burned the hair off his arms and singed his cheeks. He ran hard and as it grew dark outside he heard the roar of water coming from everywhere around him like a thousand voices echoing in a low natural stadium among the brown ratcheted mountains of northernmost California. He ran up into free unmarked Klamaths, above the road cuts, the weathered rock above him flaking off ungovernable underfoot. But then he saw the first of many hub and tacks, the fat stakes pounded flush into the ground, nailed with a strip of orange flagging tied around the head and a second flag hung on a branch above the stake. He wanted to pull them up but there were too many of them. The first station was the zero station, 00+00, the second fifty feet away, 00+50, at intervals to 62+00, a mile up. The stakes marked a road but the road began, not at the bottom of the mountain, but up near the top. Petard was confused till with a fainting stab of recognition he saw that the roads began where the water would end. Everything below the stakes was going to be underwater. The old black sea floor was going to go under again. There were copper-capped bench marks everywhere around him, some with a few inches of concrete poured around the metal cap, even here so far up, *my God how did they get here.* That night he made a bed for himself, climbing the Siskiyou higher and higher, the ground cold, the air colder, till it was two in the morning, bunching up some hard pine needles under an immense spread of trees, firs and ponderosas, sleeping facing the free open unfloodable inverted valley of the stars.

The day came. It was slow in coming but it came, four years nine months eighteen days later. He counted every single day. For more than two years the ancestral Klamath had been barely alive, hooked up to diversion tunnels that conveyed it around the dam site through four huge concrete-lined passages, two on each side of the riverbed running three-quarters of a mile through the cliffs. The feds waited for a day in low-water season when the pressure was low and the table was high. It came. As the sun rose, a steel bulkhead gate weighing more than a thousand tons was lowered, closing the portal of tunnel No. 4 and forcing the river into No. 1 and into the valley. The river was pronounced dead at 6:23 a.m. at a final elevation of 726.4 feet. Water impoundment, they called it water impoundment, but Petard knew it was murder. The last of the Diggers, a small band of fifty or so, stayed to watch as a spongy new lake rose over an area of 210 square miles. Lines of water hemorrhaged across the valley floor. For just a moment the water stopped rising. There was an announcement over a loudspeaker; a block had developed in one of the dam's valves. Petard and the Diggers knew the flow had stopped for them. The heart of the river beat still even if its lungs were full of water. They knew it stopped because he'd tried to make it stop, they knew because when it stopped it had come up as far as a man's chin, steady at the point where you could lean back your head and still take in air. As many as could, carrying deep conical baskets full of hazelnuts and manzanita nuts and purple whortleberries, waded in the reservoir, not many fit, the slope of the bank fell away fast, they crushed the nuts and berries with their bare hands and cast them over the rising water. The people of the valley were cast out, burning with the fire that was water. A strange calm fell on the dying valley. That such a day should have come and gone. The Diggers called the underwater village *tak-ekum quttuck*, well rising up to chin. The Bureau called the dam the Enterprise–East Yokut Feeder Pipeline and Canal Outlet Works Control Structure, Yokut Dam for short. The lake was called Digger Lake.

July 27, 1949. The south Klamath's last day of freedom. That was one reason the line was on his chin. There were others, Petard said, but this was the one that mattered most to him. The line marked the point of stoppage, the high mark of the water before the water wasted the Diggers and took them higher. As the water rose again the tribe fanned out in a broad circle above the valley. The men wore white feathered headdresses made from the long feathers of the yellowhammer, the sacred ornamental bird of California. The feathers were evenly laid together, making up a headband about four inches wide passing across the forehead and tied behind the head, leaving the loose strings to flop back and forth over the ears. The rim of the valley looked like lips wetted by milk. When the water rose above them a cry went up. The last fifty voices of the Digger nation joined for the last time as they lost the Klamath River. Petard did not hear the cry because he was crying, not loud, but his whole being was a cry. He picked up a crowbar and hit the dam but the dam was reinforced concrete and the tool dashed against it. There were legends about the ground moving at the end of the world, a lava flow, an unearthing of the underground, but nobody had said anything about the water rising and here was the end with all that water incising the uplands, filling the cavities like a diastole pulse. On one side of the dam the water was on. Coming were 200,000 acre-feet of active capacity, 87,780 acre-feet inactive, 470 acre-feet dead storage. On the other the water was off. The Klamath rapids were pipes now. The valley was a plugged sink. Petard wanted to find and burn that map he'd slashed and burned, Klamath Bench and Shasta Canyon, USGS 44° NW 1/4 Driggs 1° by 2° quadrangle, northwestern California, find this knowledge of water and burn it with fire, find all of them and burn them all, but through his grief he heard his father standing behind him, speechless, helpless, drunk, alone, so shitfaced he could barely stand but a true holy man anyway, sponging the ground with the flour sack he used as a robe, unwrapping herbs out of a brown foul newspaper from last year and laying on the little dry bare ground left an offering of angelica, balsam root, yerba santa, willow bark, brushing them around, moving his hands fast sharp sideways like the edge of a sickle reaping, and now pouring out the libation of a prayer, a prayer passed in such a light clear drowsy voice Petard strained to hear it, but his father could hardly get it out, saying, take me, then losing it, delirium trembling with capacity grief, sloshed now with water and not booze, trying again, saying, take me, and still not getting it out, but Petard sensing clarity coming and getting ready to draw it in, and then his father coming to the end of it all, coming clear, saying, take me, this time take me, take me and let my valley go.

"He knew nobody'd take him," Petard said. "But he meant what he said. He was willing to give his life. The tattoo was his idea. It marks the flood line, right along the chin, right under the mouth."

Petard said he knew what he had to do but he did not yet know how to do it. He had to get his valley back. They were not Indians; not anymore; after the flooding the Bureau of Indian Affairs had stripped away their federal credentials. Once the feds let his people go Petard swore he'd never let go of his people. Most let go of him. Nina did. Before the onrush of water there had been money, that payoff, the feds called it a dividend, and yes it had been a dividing, and after, when the dam held (the old promised a miracle, a break in the dam, but the old were old), there had been even more hands to reach out and take it. This land that was theirs was no longer land at all and so they left for the land of others. Long and laminar they dispersed, these last not for valleys and flood plains, San Joaquin and the shallow Salton Sea, but drawn one by one to the grounded starlight of the cities, first into one hole, the tenderloin of San Francisco, then into others, the log-skid rows of Seattle, the Portland longshore, gliding with slow and noiseless tread into ferral exile, digging the dry root of extinction, savoring its bitter taste. To be last is to be lost, Petard said, to carry the memory of your land within you like fog scattered by the fire of the California sun. Petard didn't take the water money. He took a job as a dungpicker for a circus, the Circus of the Siskiyous that summered in the Redding–Eureka–Yreka triangle and wintered in Weed, walking in circles behind a lone elephant in a small ring, holding tin pails under his hanging pizzle to catch the water pissing directionless on the treadmill. He felt at home with that miserable transplanted beast with his sad familiar focusless stare. During shows the bulk of big Mingo came between him and the gaze of the pink faces that whites called white. On cold days he pressed his hands into the wrinkled folds of skin to keep them warm. For the year and a half that he drew rutted circles in sludge he remembered Nina. Finally it came to him to leave. He had a trucker's wallet chained to his belt he'd filled with his savings, ones and fives mostly. The day he bought his first car, a '46 Pontiac, he tanked up full and loaded it up, not much to load, his spare plaid work shirts fit inside a knotted-up blue bandanna, 99, then it was US Highway 99 not Interstate 5, two lanes not four, and clattered south to Berkeley.

This was 1952. In Berkeley, Petard rented a room a couple miles north of the University of California campus, behind Lone Indian Rock a block up Milvia. A heavy dark wood door from an old ocean liner, embossed with the brass legend, Gentlemen, laid flat across two file cabinets below a bank of three windows. The windows opened over the bay, where he saw the orange bridge joining San Francisco with Marin County. His room was twelve by twelve and his desk doubled as his headboard. Petard liked the feel of books stacked overhead as he slept, books with yellow paper covers held together with glue that cracked when he turned the pages. Problem was, Petard couldn't read. He was illiterate and he'd come to Berkeley because Berkeley was a city of books. He learned the alphabet off license plates, starting with his own, 749 DAM. It took him most of a day to figure out that dam spelled dam. They didn't have vanity plates then and he'd never had an ID card, so he didn't stop to think it was unusual, his truck having the word on its front and back bumpers. Fact it threw him off for a while because after DAM he thought all plates spelled out words and went around for weeks thinking that most words he saw weren't in the dictionary. Numbers made more sense to him. He liked that you could think about numbers without using words. Petard spent his nights with a bottle of wine, steeped in the smell of the Berkeley Hills, a smell so thick, lilac, sunflower, rose, that thickness was what you smelled, both hands holding up his head like a compass in a sling, his eyes watering from the pollen, learning to read, not because he liked words but because words were used to explain numbers. Petard remembered the way the man in the pin-striped suit spoke of shear, friction, flow. He wanted to learn to speak that way. Most nights he stayed up late in bed trying to read, usually some hydraulics textbook, unfolding a pair of specs he'd bought off the rack at a drugstore in Emoryville. The big blurring lenses hurt his eyes and gave too much torque to the words. But he remembered the numbers, the depth measured in feet, the loss in g.p.m., the pressure in p.s.i. He wanted to use numbers the way real engineers used them, the engineers who built dams.

"During the early fifties," Petard said to me, "I played it safe and got into Cal on the second try. I showed up for class and did everything I was supposed to do. I got good grades, and around the Mining Circle, people knew who I was. Nights I sat alone in a booth at Brennan's, my sweatshirt turned inside out, balancing a beer and cigarette in one hand, looking at framed pictures of prize fatted calves at the state fair. I wasn't so fat then. I was blue and alone down there in the Berkeley flats, I knew what I had to do but it was taking too goddamn much time. I went for long walks at the marina at midnight when the Koreans, the ones who'd come over after the war, were out fishing with big white plastic minnow buckets and bamboo poles. Once one of them gave me some snapper wrapped in newspaper. The pier went out so far into the bay that sometimes I felt I was on a boat heading out to sea. I had the blues but I didn't call them that. I called them the flats because that's where I was. The flats."

"Did you ever go back?"

"Back where?"

"Home."

"I didn't want to."

"Why not?"

"I was afraid of myself. Home was the dam. I went back because I wanted to see the dam. I was becoming an engineer and I couldn't stay away from the dam."

Petard said he got away when he could; spring break 1954 was one of those times. Usually he rambled north, drawn but drunk, flooring it through the Sacramento Valley, windows down, feeling the gravel blast of the wind, stopping for ham and eggs at a redneck diner outside of Redding, but this time he'd shot up in a hurry, stopping only for gas. Petard pulled off the highway in the late afternoon, not too late to start up the mountain, not for him, because like the rest of the Diggers he felt closer to the land in the dark, having learned to measure days by nights, months by moons, years by winters. He left the keys in the pickup, hoisted his pack onto the tailgate, fiddled with the straps, and slipped right into the harness. He took a plum out of a Baggie, bit right in, and started climbing. Petard never took a map, hiking on trails he followed like sinuses through the woods to tree line, looking mostly at the ground, following water trickle round piles of logging slash where the trail disappeared into gum of stripped bark and branches. The air had fallen into the forties and Petard was clammy with sweat by the time he made it to the top of Ukonom. Below the mountain and to the east was the dam, white and incandescent. He'd seen it before. This time Petard thought the dam was beautiful. He couldn't take his eyes off it. The face of the dam was lit with xenon lamps. The siting was perfect. The great towers of Yokut Dam seemed to blend into the dry grasslands up the west slope of Ukonom. He watched the steam rise idly from the cooling plant; the clouds above the dam were also idling. They were nimbus, so they got close, but not too close. They were letting down long tails of rain but the air was dry and burned off the drops before they made it to the ground. It kept raining dry as Petard bushwhacked his way down to his pickup thinking about all that wasted vapor. Petard always hated the Bureau with all his might but now he had the same basic thought: he hated having it but he had it anyway: it was an engineer's thought but it was his and he couldn't stop having it: if only you could grab all that rain, bring it down to earth and make a nice shining lake of it.

"Wasn't the only time I had it," he told me now.

"When else?" I asked.

"Vietnam."

3

So, like my brother, Petard became a Bureau man. Before Nam he'd worked for the Bureau of Reclamation right there on the Klamath, south Klamath not north Klamath, running point for the Bureau in that matter of the Hupa nation. Ah Pah: it even sounded like Vietnam. He knew very well why he was there. 1957 wasn't 1944. This time the federal fist needed a redskin glove, an Indian scout to interpret the contours of the ground, to open the gates of speech with the Hupa tribe even though Ah Pah were the only words of Hupa he or anybody else in the Bureau knew. Petard was aware he was too late to do anything about Yokut on the upper Klamath but said he'd stopped them at Ah Pah Dam on the lower. He hadn't planned it but the whole time he was up there, tramping around the immense shrouds of the Salmon Mountains on survey, clambering over the bare abraded rocks, dampened with the strange dry moisture of the Coastal Ranges, he said he felt a favorable pressure gradient directing his every move.

The dam was already under way. The adit portals were up and the key shafts were down. Northern Sierra Power threw up a 132,000-volt substation on a rocky promontory near the canyon rim. Ah Pah was going to be the second dam in a triangle that would transform the Klamath from Upper Klamath Lake to the Salmon Mountains into a chain of western Great Lakes. The rock it sat on was solid but faulted. Petard wanted it to crack so bad that often he just closed his eyes and saw it starting to crack. But he was small and the dam was large. So he did what he was told and waited.

Every morning when he went to work he shoved a yellowfeather up the spine of his tie to remind him who he was. Below the dam site near the base of a jumbled rock slide, across a blaze of white paint marking the spots where the TNT sticks were going to be set, an encampment of Hupa now had a vigil going. Rumor had it they were praying for an earthquake soon, but the chief engineer Navier-Stokes thought the Hupa were beneath notice. He called them the Hoopla for all the noise they made, that low piercing nasal hum to be heard whenever the drill clatter let up. The Bureau let them be during phase one while the miners drove ringbolts, strung a cable-suspension footbridge, and hacked a shelf out of the cliff before beginning tunneling. But with the first phase over with, Petard was sent down there one shining silver morning to tell the Hupa to move, that the Bureau was going to blast the next day into dipole oblivion.

The air that morning was dense with omens. A wind

had come up and the little burl trees clinging to the cliff-side had blown clear down to lodge in the fluted sup-porting columns of the generator. The Klamath was still like sludge. The barracks where he slept smelled of am-monia. Petard dressed, mouth tasting of booze and coffee, and began to walk toward the Hupa encampment. It wasn't far. A tiny band of Indians was huddled with grief around a fire burnt down to orange embers, the circle marked off by cans of feathery water for making coffee or tea or soup. A few shivered with cold but did not ap-proach the fire. One shook with the DTs. Another was covered from head to toe with a dusty blanket. Petard looked into the wrecked face of the oldest, their chief, or so he supposed. The old man did not meet his eyes. He closed them, lids falling slowly as tears came down the ruts time had worn in his face. He lifted his arm, cutting the air to untie the winds and whip them against the dam. For a moment Petard thought he felt the pull of a prayer to still the river, to make of the river a wall and turn its waters inviscid around the intake valves at dam's base. A prayer directed against river and not dam. But no. De-struction did not shine gibbeting in his eyes. Despair did —a despair beyond despair that now came alive before him like dry wood on the near-dead coals.

"You okay?" Petard knelt to press close together the last embers of the fire.

"Just keeping warm," said the Hupa man. He wore a faded plaid shirt, jeans, no belt, a thin red headband. "The others are gone. I don't know where they went. Now you are here. That is good." The man opened the palm of his hand and Petard saw a tattoo a lot like the one that showed through the stubble of his own chin. The hand was arthritic. It only opened partway and it shook.

"I'm with the Bureau."

"I know," said the Hupa.

"Why do you pray," asked Petard, "when words won't move the earth?"

The sick chief told Petard that he was wrong. Words could move the earth. But had not actually asked for the earth to move. The chief knew well enough that for now the earth was going to stay right where it was. He stopped speaking, slumped back toward the ground, and then, for no reason Petard could think of, he said, looking up at the slate sky, speaking more to the valley than to him, "Thank you." And again, in a more distant voice, he said, "Thank you."

Petard tried to remember a line of poetry he'd read in Berkeley years before, something about the cities being destroyed but the mountains and rivers surviving. But he couldn't think straight. His thoughts tumbled together like sedimentary rocks. His father. Nina. The waters. The spirit of the Klamath. The open mouth of a dam caving in—

The Hupa chief was speaking and Petard heard him out. This is what heroism is, thought Petard, speech through pain.

That they were going to be destroyed, the Hupa knew. That the dam was strong and would last a thousand years was certain. That their small band had a hard fate prepared for it, a bitter thirst made the more bitter for being parched by water, was a truth evident in rock. And yet, the chief said, they did not want to be spared. If the red people of the three valleys shared a common fate they would share it too, though it meant the end of all of them. They knew of other dams, many beyond number. They were not certain if there was a future waiting for any of them. But they had asked that if there were, if such a time came to pass when the waters would fail and the people return to the valleys of rock and shadow and ledge that were their home, that they be given a true sight of the one among the many who would multiply the last of to-day into the first of tomorrow in this valley among all the valleys. They had not asked to see into the future. The Hupa simply wanted to know if there was one. And now they knew. To the sunderer of skies the Hupa asked if any among the peoples of all the Californias, among the cracked faces of the Yokut, the bright eyes of the Koyut, the dark chins of the Diggers, they had asked that if any among these ever come who can live inside the white man's magic and make its towers crumble and its waters fall, that they be given a vision of him before the waters rose and filled the mouth of the valley and took from them their ability to form sounds and speak words. And now he had come, they had seen him by the report of their own eyes, and now, when the waters rose, there would at last be calm in the valley of the blue rock. The time to come was to be a time in time and not a time out of time, and the Hupa were glad of heart at the full-ness to come that was more than full. The time to come was bound up, it waited like a new world, like a harvest, like baskets, and they paid homage to it by beating their fire-hardened sticks and laying them at Petard's feet. Pe-tard did not know what to say but he knew what they were saying. The time to come was him.

"What'd you say to that?" I asked him now.

"I told them to get out of there."

"Did they leave?"

"They left all right. They left because they trusted me. They just didn't know."

"Know what?"

"That I didn't mean to do what I did. That Ah Pah was an accident."

"Like hell it was," said my brother. He handed Petard a scrap of shopping bag filled with calculations of tensional stress. "I've been figuring. For Ah Pah to crack, the ground under the dam would have to have been read wrong. It's hard to blow up a dam. They only fail when they don't sit right on the ground."

I said, "Petard, the Bureau tests the ground before it starts building a dam."

"I know," he said. "I was in charge of testing."

Petard told us how he did it at Ah Pah. He'd invented a fault. It hadn't taken much. The earth slants, the ground's uneven, faults are everywhere. Preconstruction reports don't bother with faults unless the openings are more than an inch, but that's just an arbitrary cutoff. Petard knew that despite the index samples, the tunnel maps and core borings and test trenches, the tests were just augurs, that's even what they called them, augurs, drillings for signs in rock. He went on to say, "Geologists can't really tell you where to build a dam. They're not even sure where the faults are. But think about it. A fault isn't just an empty crack. A fault can be full of clay and silt and rubble, sludge of unknown specific gravity, unconfined compressive strength, unpredictable absorption. Finding a fault means seeing in the dark. Not just a hundred feet down, more like a thousand feet, ten thousand feet down. The people who can see this far down are the wizards of the Bureau. You know about Reclam R&A. That's why R&A exists, to do what can't be done using our technology. It's not magic. It's divination."

Petard called it divination, but as he explained it to me, it made engineering sense. To get them to build the dam wrong Petard got them to make a few errors along the way. The errors in computation were so slight they were almost imperceptible at first. The idea hit him, a chance opening, when at Ah Pah Petard saw that the left key trench had not been mapped. He knew there'd been a few problems beneath the embankment north of the spillway structure. A fault had moved, extending northwest along the margin of a caldera. The rock-core drilling and water-pressure testing showed a large fissure opening under the right abutment. Petard didn't do anything about it, but that was all he had to do: *not do anything.* He just let the fault go on extending till someone in one of the nearby access shafts picked it up on a piezometer. By then it was too late; the dam was half built; a million tons of concrete had already been poured into the fills. Navier-Stokes blew his top when he saw the core drills. It didn't take a genius to see that a dam was much too heavy to be moved once it was under way. The dam was dangerous and it was not going to be built.

"I didn't know what I'd done," he said. "Not at first. I hadn't wrecked anything. All those years I'd dreamed of ripping apart a dam. Watching it crack, watching the water run through it. Now I'd stopped them, but it didn't take dynamite. Just the shift of a couple of numbers."

He knew what to do now, plus how to do it. Everywhere he went, Petard started things that couldn't be finished, designing and building towers undermined, using the Bureau's own caution as a weapon against it. Cracks appear in all concrete, all dams have measurable seepage, temperature shifts, pressure increases. To cover his ass Petard had his workmen pack oakum into dry cracks to make it look like he was sealing off drips, sealing them up so the Bureau wouldn't notice. He got in trouble for that but it was the kind of trouble that put them off his trail. An infraction of the rules but they let him keep on building dams. Thanks to Petard the west was full of concrete monoliths wedged six hundred feet at bedrock, curving up and out, tapering to a thickness of fifty feet at top, smooth crests just under a mile long. Every last dam he had a hand in had over fifty tons of compressive strength, twenty over full-load specs, aimed maximally at transverse fault lines in the canyon floor. The dams were unfinished river pyramids, arc-lit tombs of incised concrete, too big to be taken down but plenty big enough to fall down of their own accord. Ah Pah was considered strong enough to be used as the bed for a highway joining Oregon with California. The rest were forgotten right-of-way, green with aztec moss. Around them the big rivers poured into diversion tunnels, bypassing dry miles of riverbed excavated down to bedrock, pouring out again in an explosion of sound and spray, swinging east, twisting south, rolling on down to the sea. They weren't the only dams. From '58 to '64, Petard's years with the domestic Bureau, he took out three more dams, all California dams, Tehama Dam on the Klamath River, Del Norte on the Smith River, Big Sage Dam on the Pit. He went everywhere, and everywhere he went, he built unbuilt dams, marvels of hydrologic that would have been marvelous and logical if only they'd been built in the right place. They weren't. Petard kept an eye on these dry dams. Every year during spring floods he returned to them, to crush yerba buena on the shelves of concrete, consecrating them as mounds to the memory of his dispersed people, and to check for cracks. He knew that one of these dams was slated to go first, which one he couldn't say. But he had a lot to say about the man who knew what he was doing and let him go on doing it, a Brit named Navier-Stokes.

"I hate that fucker," said my brother, rummaging around the dash looking for a candy bar. The dash was sticky with a hundred thousand miles of dirt, lint, cigarette butts, beer pop tops, and old ballpoint pens, but no candy bars.

"Navier who?" I asked.

"Charles Tillman Navier-Stokes was Under Director of the Bureau from '54 to '73."

"He was your boss?"

"He knew what I was doing and he held his tongue."

"Why didn't he get rid of you?"

"He knew I had some kind of power but wasn't sure what it was. What if those dams were a row of dominoes? What if I could knock them over?"

"Could you?"

"I don't know." Petard paused. "Maybe."

"I don't believe you," I said.

Petard was paring an orange with his teeth and spitting the strips out the window. He said, "Jimbo warned me you weren't the believing kind."

"I don't see what there is to believe in. You told me there were design flaws."

"Flaws? There were no flaws in my dams. I designed them to be the way they were."

"You're telling me you design things that don't work?"

"That's the American way," put in my brother. "Things falling apart that were never together to begin with."

"It's not the Digger way," said Petard. "My designs work. They're good designs. It's just that they're designed to serve other purposes."

I was all ears. "You're talking about sabotage."

"The Diggers fight back the only way we know how. Over time."

"And these accidents?"

"Remember, they only *looked* like accidents. It wouldn't have taken a genius to put two and two together. Wherever I was, a dam failed. I wasn't even the best engineer in R&A. It surprised me sometimes. Once at Koyut I ran a T&S, a simple test for tension and stress. The numbers were good and the dam should've held. But it failed just like the rest. Was it my being there that did it? I didn't know, but I couldn't get it out of my head they wanted me to do what I was doing. I mean, I was stopping the Bureau from building dams in the U.S. That was my worst fear. That they *wanted* me to do what I was doing."

"And this Navier-Stokes?"

"He's descended from a long line of dam builders. His father Clive wrote the Navier-Stokes equations regulating turbulent flow."

"I can't see how that matters."

"His family's from Britain originally. It goes way back. They used to have a sort of Bureau there once, too." Petard peeled himself more orange. "In Roman Britain."

"Roman Britain?" I said, shaking my head.

"That's right. Roman Britain."

"Petard, the Bureau of Reclamation isn't a dynasty. It's a bureaucracy."

"Only dynasties build dams," said Petard.

4

Outside the pickup the lay of the land had changed. It had risen steep and sharp, the green of pine and the gray of granite, now it fell flat and smooth, the brown of wheat and the red of clay. The mountains dropped off into the high flatlands of north-central California. I swallowed and felt the pressure drop in my ears. A river ran along the highway, dropping too, but it was a paltry coughing phlegm drip of a river. "40cfs if that," said Petard, who observed that dams made all rivers into creeks. So this was Petard's holy river, the Klamath. Or what was left of it, tailwater pissed out the discharge end of a dam. Petard said Witusa'a was twenty-two miles downriver from Yokut Dam. Upriver from Yokut were the ruins of the other two dams in the triangle, Ah Pah and Tehama. Yokut Dam itself still held; after a big court case his tribe had won back water rights; but these days the tribal council let very little water come out of the reservoir backed up behind the dam, save for a trickle spat out to the experimental Toad Development Farm, leased to an individual rancher in Weed, California.

"Travers," said Petard, smiling, the first time I'd seen him crack a smile all morning.

The smile went away as Petard considered Witusa'a. He said it meant the place of the last words. Witusa'a was a camp for dying languages, a hospice for tongues. This was the place where the languages of the river tribes came to die. The Klamath, working the earth from the junction at Trinity to the coast at Gold Bluff, was the river of the Yurok, the Karok, the Modoc, the Hupa. The names meant downriver, upriver, head of the river, river's end. The Klamath languages don't go in for north, south, east, west. They go for *pels* and *pul*, upriver and downriver. What about no river? The streets in Witusa'a were graded but not paved. There were a few houses, several trailers, plus some canvas tents with duckboard floors. The yards were full of old hoses, cables, piles. A stream bed running behind the houses was covered by a dense growth of marsh grass and tule. Visible north were the needle-nosed valleys of the Trinity Range, the pummeled flattops of the Basin Range due northeast, the foothill oak groves on the western slope of the Sierra Nevada due southeast, and due east, the Coast Ranges, with their series of small enclosed valleys, separated by gorges. Before Reclam got here this territory had been the drainage basin of the Scott, the Salmon, the North Fork, the Klamath. Now it was dry.

With a harsh grating of gears the pickup turned onto Seventh Street and headed up the hill toward the big water tank, the building Petard called the roundhouse, the biggest building in Witusa'a. The tank was empty, now a sweathouse. The road wound like a twisted argument and

Petard stopped talking to concentrate on his driving. It wasn't so much a road as a fishhook for jabbing trucks in their soft underbellies, and on such a road the Dodge was not much of a truck. The pickup had delayed-action steering that had a wheel-and-rudder feel. Slung long and low, the ass end of the bed was loaded down with everything, a corroded orange jumper cable, an old steel crankshaft weighing ninety pounds, plus Petard's portable drill kit, complete with NX diamond drill bits the size and shape of hot peppers, a long twisting wound corded steel shank he called a snake, some gadget for sinking the bit that looked like a subway turnstile, plus his own personal supply of spring water, weight indeterminate, stored in big leather sacks called ollas.

Petard never strayed far from his ollas. Back in Arcata, Petard was low on water, so, a ways up 96, he'd stopped to fill the ollas at wells drilled to order at roadside, drilled near sacred sites, near the terraced ledges of playas, on the braids of long-empty stream courses, by the wicker weaves of dry mudflows. These places he knew like lines in his hand. Once, on the road barely an hour, past Horse Mountain Summit and heading up toward the Siskiyou county line, he'd let out a yipping cry, the sound a goose makes, br-r-r-p, br-r-r-p, br-r-r-p, screeched to a stop on the shoulder, grabbed his kit, vaulted a barbed-wire fence, not caring if he cut himself, scrambling ragged across red rocks and blue distances toward Duzel Rock to douse an old Indian mound. Even capering he ran a straight surveyor's line. My brother followed him, no line pins in his mind, yelling just to yell and not caring why, and I simply followed, curious but cautious, using a dry weathered stick to flex open the sienna strings of barbed wire, lagging a hundred yards behind, my muscles aching. When I caught up with Petard he was rolling around ecstatically in a bed of flint flakes, flake scrapers, choppers, hammerstones, bone tools, pipe shards. "This place is thousands of years old! Can't you feel it? There were no dams anywhere when this was built! Just pipes." A mound's a well, Petard said fast, and the more he said, the faster he said it, a flexed burial of water, a tip-off that water's near, the dead have to drink or else they die beyond death, he wouldn't drink reservoir stuff, no fucking way, drink that shit and you lose your teeth, water piped through pipes isn't water anymore, it's blood. While Petard set up his rig and gradually filled his ollas with good clear water, I sat on the ground and gazed across great open airy flatnesses ending miles and miles ahead in walls of snowcapped mountains. It took the three of us half an hour to drag six ballooning ollas back to the Dodge. There wasn't much room but we fit them all in. Three hours later, the water that had bubbled up from that punctured mound now pushed the corrugated bed of the Dodge down to within a few inches of the ground. By the time we got to the top of the hill at Witusa'a the underside of the pickup was a nest of chaparral, cactus, oak, and conifer.

The three of us got out of the pickup and entered the roundhouse through an opening cut and cauterized with an acetylene torch so that its edges bubbled ragged and black. The Hupa man was there. Petard sat next to him. I waited while my eyes adjusted to the dark. I heard drumming but did not see drums or drummers; the riveted sides of the tank gave off a dull low metallic ring like a gong; someone was playing the tank from the outside. The inside walls of the tank were streaked with rust and let in light in many places. Bands of firelight shot up the sides. Blankets hung in the entries, front and rear. Angelica root burned as incense. The floor was covered with willow mats. A few figures stirred near the fire but the fire was not aboveground. A set of aromatic planks, seasoned cedar, roofed a deep pit where the fire lodged. A tripod held the water that heated the space with steam. I was in a temescal, a Digger sweathouse.

There were three old men here. The old Hupa man wore a blanket, tule leggings, and the high moccasins used by his tribe for mountain travel. The others were younger and they wore buckskin and simple rawhide sandals. The three of them eyed the three of us. With his sharp stabbing eyes and lips slumped in skepticism, a build like my brother's, big soft hands and a fast restless mind, the hairs on his chin not plucked but long and splintered, a sign of mourning from way back but it gave him a beat look, a honky-tonk look, Petard did not look like any movie Indian I'd ever seen, and neither did these three. The old man took out a pair of wire-rim specs, unfolded them, and put them on. The other two adjusted their skins like they were robes of state. They were clearly waiting for me to speak. Petard turned to me, hands on his hips, thumbs notching the belt loops of his baggy jeans. My brother turned away, abstracted, pulling his hair back taut with one hand and running the other gently across the surface of his scalp. I wasn't sure what to say, so I asked Petard where they lived, and Petard gave me a look to raise blisters, as if to say, you blew it, you idiot, but he went ahead and translated it anyway and the old man answered me.

"Nnappaquat."

"Dry weather," translated Petard.

There was a moment of resonant silence as the Hupa man timed his speech to fall between the beats of the drum. Then he spoke again and Petard translated.

"He is asking," Petard said, "if you have a hard time with words. He says the marks will help you to speak if speaking is what you want to do."

"Marks?" I said. "What marks?" But I knew very well

what marks: I'd seen the line on his chin. A flood line, not machined in the skin but picked in under the pigment, a line built up by a series of dots with no blood released, just lymph. Barreling east from Eureka, Petard had banked his talk in patterned circles around that line. He'd talked and talked around it. But still I said, "What are you talking about?"

The Hupa man continued speaking in the silences falling between drumbeats. This time Petard didn't translate.

"What about my brother?" I asked the Hupa man.

"Your brother already has the mark," said Petard, speaking for himself now. "On his scalp. He'd have to shave his head for you to see it. You can't see it when his hair is long."

"What kind of tattoo? That line? How long is it? How'd he get it there?"

"A mark isn't a tattoo. A tattoo is an ornament. A mark is different. I told you why it's there. A mark is memory."

The Hupa man must have been a mind reader, because he spoke again, measuring his words against the beats of the tank, and Petard said, "He's asking if you've come for the stories."

"Stories? What stories?"

"The flood line," Petard said. "It tells a story."

I still didn't understand. "What sort of story?"

My brother said, "It's not like they're written down. It's more like they're out there, ready for you if you're ready for them."

"So you know them," I said.

"Not exactly."

"You mean you've forgotten them?"

"It's not a question of forgetting," said my brother.

Petard took up where he left off. "The stories, they're not ours to give or his to forget. The stories are his stories.

You can only remember a story if it's part of you. The mark doesn't give you a story. It just helps you find the story you're part of. Your story."

"Then why can't he remember?"

"He didn't get his in a ceremony. I gave it to him but not for the stories."

He said the idea was to cut a little incision, pull the skin layers apart, the space between skin layers, squirt ink in, and sew it back up again. But first things first. The old man had inverted a tin coffee can over a kerosene lantern, and now he turned up the wick. The smoke built up at the bottom of the can. He scraped it out and added a little bit of water. He was making ink. Before the Ah Pah relocation he'd made ink the old way, collecting smoke from burning tree resin. But few trees grew at Witusa'a. Because he no longer lived in a place where masses of trees burned to the root, he no longer ground his own ink. But he still had the graver, the adz made from the bone of a bird. He made do and I watched him closely.

"Etah," Petard said, using the old man's name for the first time, speaking softly and with great deference. "Let me say it. I think I can say it in English."

Say what? I thought, but the train of my thoughts was cut short, cut off, cut up by a short sharp stabbing stinging sensation swimming up my right arm. My head dropped, I felt faint, I felt the light dimming, I felt my brother's hands holding me down, firm but fraternal, while Petard leaned over me, stretching my skin with one hand and with the other wiping the blood away using a damp cloth. My brother rolled me down onto my side. I glanced sideways at the tools on the mat. Different sizes for different marks. They looked like combs but the teeth were filed to sharp points. The mat was yellow but now I saw red polka dots. It was my blood dripping over the mats. I

fogged over and heard Petard saying, with a distant voice
like he was speaking to me through a long tube:

I have come with the bone of a bird.
I have come with the bark of a tree,
With an adz to push ink under the skin,
A sharp point that presses bit by bit,
The sharp beak of a once-red bird
That is now no more than a bone.

The mark strikes you like an arrow.
Do you turn away? Does the ground draw near?
Be calm. The adz runs steady and even.
That sound is the tapping of the mallet
Pushing the adz to make the wide line,
The flood line where the water stopped.

It stopped for just a moment.
But it was a long slow moment:
A morning with low sheeting clouds,
A dam stretched across a river,
A river running with blood,
Blood enough to fill a valley.

"How long will it take?" I overheard my brother asking
Petard.

"Depends," returned Petard. "There's a clearing in his
mind. I'm sure of that."

"How soon will he want to know?"

"About Vietnam?"

"I mean about the tattoo."

"You can tell him. Or I can. Whatever."

Coming clearer now, my cheek against the straw mat,

I raised my head and asked Petard, "And my brother. How'd he get his?"

"My what?" asked my brother.

"Your tattoo," said Petard.

"You tell," my brother told him.

And Petard told: he'd shaved my brother's head to save his life. Jump back in time, Petard said. He didn't go directly to Vietnam. Nobody at the Bureau did. Late in 1964 he took the Ogallala Trail, a paper trail of transfers that started at the National Records Center, Suitland, Maryland, went to the U.S. Army Records Holding Area, Okinawa, and washed ashore at the Vietnam Records Holding Area at Long Binh. His title was Chief Engineer, Headquarters, Second Office of the Division of Design, second because the first was in Saigon. Under him were a number of specialists, officers, enlisted men, plus some irregulars. Orders were to close wells in Quang Ngai Province. Days he sealed them with truckloads of sand, but the VC always dug the wells out again at night. It took him a while to figure out that well closings were a minor prelim to a major visitation of waters, an apocalypse of water, amounting to no less than the diversion of the Mekong Delta, drained and sent crashing into an inland sea. At first he didn't believe it was possible. He thought dams were skyscrapers, not warehouses. How could his job be to build a big dam, not the highest dam ever built but the longest one, a great wall of dams, a great zigzagging berm two hundred fifty miles long, stretching crescented from Cambodia to the South China Sea. And to do it quietly, incrementally, by shaping the earth into a long dike crossing the very back of Vietnam *without anybody noticing*? Someone, he didn't know who until later, was trying to win this war by drowning the entire country. The magnitude of the Long Dam project blew his mind. And to think how close they actually came to pulling it off . . .

"The dam was the biggest operation of the war," Petard said to me now. "Operation Reciprocal Altruism. Don't ask me why it's called that. Travers will tell you, if he manages to remember. But the core of it is that there was no longer a war in the Mekong Delta in '73. From January till the end of November *there was peace.*"

"Peace," I repeated, thinking I'd heard the wrong word.

"Peace," he said. "There had to be peace. You can't guard a dam with a war on. And this wasn't just any dam. Long Dam was the longest dam that'd ever been built. It wasn't just airlifted in. The dam was the debris of everything Vietnam had been. They built it themselves, that was the idea. You should have seen it. Old Japanese bombs were taken apart and used for chemicals. Rails were reforged into shoring. The wrecks of French half-tracks were dragged into the dam. Trash-compacted garbage from American bases went in. The whole country was the dam, the dam was Vietnam, and that was why the dam was going to work."

"And my brother?" I asked again.

"Riverine wouldn't touch the Long Dam project. Through channels I had to put out a call for someone, anyone who understood hydrodynamics. I got washouts from the engineering academy in Denver. They were smart and boy were they pissed. Your brother was the best of them. He knew rivers. Enough to fear the canals."

"Canals," I said. "He told me about a canal."

"It was late November. The dam was secure. It'd taken and was holding. His objective was three miles inland along the Kanh Xing Canal."

"That's not far."

"You don't know canals. You don't need mines to block a canal. A few fish traps will do fine. The canals were always against us. It was hard enough on the river but this was ridiculous. One low bridge and you were dead."

"So you found him?"

"Yeah, I found him." He let out a heavy breath. "He didn't know it was me till later."

My brother's eyes shot open to .50 caliber and he said, "I knew I was doing your dirty work."

Petard continued. "The diversion had just begun. I was up in a helicopter checking a line of dikes. Sometimes I couldn't get over how the Delta looked from the air. Trees grew on top of all the dikes. The dikes were beautifully conceived and executed, a low-pressure gradient across a long front. I mean, they were perfect for the place, they worked there. For a high dam you need concrete and iron. For a low dam dirt and trees will do. I was making a pass over a dike near the Kanh Xing Canal when I saw the smoke."

"The gunboat?"

"What was left of it. The UH-1 let me down in a rice paddy. The air was foul with engine exhaust and the circling dust of helicopters. Just over the tip of the embankment was your brother. He'd made it out alone, I don't know how. His gunboat was burning in the distance. He had only a carbine and two thirty-round clips of ammunition. He was hit bad. His chest was contracting every time he took in air, so there was less air every time and more blood, and he kept saying, 'The radio alphabet. I can't remember the radio alphabet. A is for alpha, B is for bravo, C is for charlie, D is for delta. But E? What is E for? Please tell me what E is for. I can't remember. Please. I can't remember what E is for.' "

"I wasn't a medic. I looked up. The sky was still there

but it seemed like a million miles away. Away at a distance an UH-1 Iroquois gunship flew at low gun, orbiting; the names, I couldn't get away from the names; the names of our peoples were following me even here. I radioed in for a medic but fire was heavy now and the ship couldn't land. I was on my own. All I had was a simple first-aid kit. He'd lost a lot of blood. I knew one way I could save him but it was an old tribal thing I wasn't sure would work. My father said it would work only if there was Digger blood in you, but maybe he was wrong, he was always saying things like that, in his mind he was always fighting John Wayne. I took the chance and lay down beside your brother. From my canteen I gave him a drink of water and then eased him up out of the paddy, where the dirty water might infect his wound. I wasn't sure if he'd stopped breathing but I knew I had to work fast, improvising with what I had on me. I'd seen hand tattoos done with homemade rigs, a pencil with needles stuck in the eraser, a motor from a tape recorder, an E string from a guitar, and I knew that the best tools were the ones you made yourself. I razor-bladed off a patch of hair just above his right temple. The hair was wet and came off easily. I cracked open a Bic pen, popped the sheath off my syringe, and eased the needle up the open vial of ink, drawing it in. I wasn't sure how toxic the ink was; a tattoo is a scar, so it has to be somewhat toxic or else it won't take. I started sticking the ink under his skin, not too deep, sub-cutaneous. I only had time for a few characters. Letters or numbers, I didn't know which to use, so I used the only combo I could think of, numbers first. 7–4–9. He couldn't feel a thing, that I knew. D. I botched the first of the last three letters and it broke into tributaries. A. I pressed more into the skin but I was pressing too deep. I was losing ink now, it was passing into his bloodstream. I had to stop. After I'd etched the last letter in, M, he looked up at me. There was no more bleeding. A column of white smoke rose in the distance, I thought it was napalm but then I saw the smoke was red, a Digger sign, trunk of the redwood, sign of strength. He had crossed over but he was going to come back. It was then I realized that your brother hadn't just seen death through a visor slit, *your brother had died*. He'd died and I'd brought him back. I didn't know anyone had this kind of power. And you know what? I could tell he still wanted to know what E was for. For the life of me I couldn't remember. I told him, E is for embankment."

This was before the dam broke. The embankment that grew into the dam that broke open the war, Vietnam's great wall. The dam that ran through all of them, Petard, my brother, Jenna, Travers, like a thick cable passing through the impassable needle of a hurricane eye in the Mekong River Delta. The dam that Travers ordered, Petard designed, Jenna photographed. The dam from whose waters my brother was drunk. The dam that darkened their faces and took each of them to a different depression in memory, Petard with his lipless sad wince, Jenna with a crease of the parentheses wrinkling her mouth, Travers with his heavy nose breaths and hands moving helplessly in magic circles, my brother with eyes closed and ears open to an invitation of noisome bells. The dam whose name was Vietnamese for the sad red earth. The dam at Da Trinh Sanh.

Three

1

Weed, California. The map spread out on my knees was Reclamation issue and Weed wasn't on it. Petard gave it to me when we left him at Witusa'a, saying the Bureau doesn't map what it sees, it maps what it wants to see. Maps are flat-earth wish lists, the ideal being your nice level alluvial plain, your river delta. The water jerked down the Klamath River, the truck banged along next to it on the river highway, and I propped up my feet against the dash and tried to figure it. The Bureau's California was a boomerang, a little thicker up north than usual, not drawn to scale but still ending right where it does at the 42nd parallel. This was because the map was a demographic map showing the sites of potential dams. It was one in a series of maps Robert Travers had commissioned twenty years ago when he worked as an analyst for the Bureau of Reclamation. On this map California was top-heavy with dams on the Klamath River. There were others in the series covering Africa and some places in Brazil, but the map my brother remembered seeing, the one Travers was known for, was the one showing the demography of dams in the Mekong Delta, circa 1973.

"Travers keeps copies of them," said my brother. "But

he's afraid of them now. He doesn't remember making them."

Travers was from an old family, old as they come. It sure showed, said my brother, filling me in while the truck rattled over the last stretch of road, the last light going from the sky, the mountains to the east bulked out like red plastic fuel cans, the big butte to the south a gutted black. He said Travers had this way of catching himself in the past that made you think history was a time line wound in a circle round his head. A great awesome headband of history, a time line that bent away from him, him losing sight of it as it wound round one ear beyond the range of his peripheral vision, going round the dark side of his head to come connecting back again sweeping past the other ear in a great flipping circle. Travers felt the ossuary weight of history more than anybody he'd ever seen. He felt outnumbered. More Traverses were dead than'd ever live again. The topsoil was a booby trap set just for him. He walked with his eyes pinned to the ground, afraid to slide his feet forward for fear the ground would rise in ambush against him. Step on a crack and break your mother's back: my brother said Travers's mother was still alive, he'd met her and she had a fine dowager's hump to show for it, but that he was afraid if he stepped on a crack he'd snap the supine snappable back of some previous mother, a dura mater dead but not quite gone, out to get him or so he thought, her sharp whitened spine lying in wait around him, worn by time into points standing upward, ready to jab him if he made a wrong move. Travers didn't want to make any more wrong moves. Since '73 he'd lived his life in constant fear of whitened trunks of bone sharpened into punji stakes, dipped in shit, hidden in grass, corded back with twine ready to snap at the right moment and drive a stake right through his heart.

"I didn't know him before Nam," said my brother, "so I don't know what he was like. Before."

"Before what?"

"He gets these—time slams. I can't describe them, so I won't. You'll have to see for yourself."

Travers came out to meet us when the truck pulled in. He had a big head, a high hairline, a thin pointy nose, and little hunched shoulders. His mouth was big, too, grossly big, a big catfish mouth pursing his lips open in a wide gummy O like they were made for sucking in water but they also gave him a look of nonstop astonishment, like he was always on the verge of saying, Ohhhhhh, so that's it. His cheeks were pink with acne scales. The lab glasses he wore were thick as prisms and added to the fish effect. An old white tux shirt he never took off had faded to the color of parchment. The shirt was a few sizes too small and when he leaned over it stretched over the ripple marks of his belly, the skin dry and loose but not fatty. He wore his baggy khaki pants hiked up high, Jack Benny style, and walked around in black flip-flops with white tube sox. Clipped to his belt was a transistor radio tuned real low to the weather channel, so low you couldn't make out the forecast, but it surrounded him with a standing wave of predictions. Over the forecasts he talked loud, too loud, the inflection always a bit off, a bit behind, his words never quite catching up to his thoughts. The strange thing was, while he talked Travers moved his arms like they weren't there, like they were stubs, like they'd been amputated below the elbow and he was only remembering the use of them. The hands at the end of his arms were gray, the color of flabby mushroom soup, and his fingers hung off them like string at the end of a mop.

Travers had been a biologist. A little big man who ran a slalom down the straight and narrow: Woods Hole, Harvard Bio Labs, Smithsonian Tropical Research Institute, Kelley-Roosevelt Wing of the Field Museum in Chicago, Monarca A.C., Ramsar Convention, Instituto Nacional de Investigaciones sobre Recursos Bióticos at San Cristobal Las Casas in Chiapas, on and on. Travers mastered biology, made the discipline his, unraveled his thoughts in egg string and made everyone grab onto them and shimmy up into his mind. When he had a thought it wasn't just a thought. His thought was always useful, zap useful like his brain specialized in converting its chemical energy into a DC voltage source. For a while everyone in America'd been interested in tapping into Travers, Harvard, Washington, the Army, the Agency for International Development, plus the Bureau of Reclamation's crack hydrology unit, Reclam R&A, R for research and A for action because at the Bureau R&A were considered the diodes of thought, your diode being double poetry, ode of thought plus ode of action. But the Bureau used him up. When it finished with him he was a wasted talent, stoned all the time just like the parable says. He used to be interested in insects; now it was frogs. Toads actually, Cane toads, but at the time they were all the same to me, with their short fat bodies, open broad heads, wide circular snouts.

The Toad Development Farm where Travers raised these things wasn't much of a farm and even less of a lab. Travers didn't give a shit about the local organisms. The small gray frogs with garnet eyes and yellow legs jumped about their business without any interference from him. Travers was into what he called mnemopharmacology. The here and now was cult bullshit. He wanted drugs that do things to your memory. Any fed using shelf chemicals could take apart the compound alkaloids that gave you a here-and-now high. He wanted to shred his way right through the ripstop pale of the present. These days he was hot on the trail of some new frog drug. Nothing mattered to him but finding a drug to take him back, back where he didn't know, just back. Out of this white frame house, he'd say, even though he lived in a line of five single-wide trailers laid out in a circle in the middle of a field, the side doors sealed off and the ends punched out so you could walk round and round without ever once turning to pivot on your heels. Travers'd worn a rut in the particleboard floors from so much pentagonal pacing. He slept on a rush mat laid out on the floor. A pot of cold chicken à la king was gummed shut on the stove. Layers and layers of silica dust'd settled over the white tile walls. The place was lit by rubber-covered droplights hanging from orange cords. Taped over the windows were a bunch of black plastic sheets streaked with faint blue-and-white blurs, skull x-rays. I made out the bulb line of a human skull but a jagged line tore through the brain like an indenture. The transparencies dyed the sky outside methylene blue. Outside, through them, I saw debris stacked in a big PX pile, clocks with bent dials and no crystals, some rolls of cloth tape with very fine brass wire woven into them, a glazed green elephant covered with dust, a hickory billy club, some aluminum siding, tin cans full of nuts and bolts, a black portable typewriter with a sheet of paper rotted right in the carriage. Stuff left over, he said, from his Bureau days. It was all part of the work he did then.

"What work was that?" I asked him now.

Travers didn't answer. He picked his nose and pulled at his gray beard stubble with his nails. A spasm jumped across his face. He curled his fingers and ran them over the shallow lifelines in his hands. He was somewhere else. Last time he was here, back in fall '82, my brother lent Travers Petard's truck. This was when Travers lived in a faded green trailer, rocking his life away in a black wicker chair, before he started to get interested in biology again.

My brother wanted Travers to get out of his hot small room with the punkah fan creaking overhead. He gave him a set of keys and a couple of freshly ironed shirts. Travers wiped his mouth on one of the shirts but took the keys and hopped in the truck. He shoved the clutch toward him and backed out the long dirt driveway, the pedal floored in reverse. The Dodge rickshawed off across the dry field toward the clove foothills, toward where the rice grass inched up the side of Shasta. As he drove away my brother wondered if this was it, the time Travers'd finally break the suicide barrier. For a few days he played chess against himself on a board Travers'd mounted on a lazy Susan. He weeded the little flower garden Travers'd planted full of orchids and yellow mimosa. Then he went out looking. He found him a week later on the highway near Grass Lake, breathing lightly in his usual tuneless whistle, half circles of cold sweat soaked under his T-shirt arms, the skin under his eyes creased into crepe paper, his pockets full of hard candies, his hands full of coins. When my brother pried open his hands the coins that fell out were from the same time, same place, *République Française 1937 Indochine.*

"I gave a speech," said Travers.

"You're gonna be okay," said my brother, arranging a blanket round his shoulders.

He was lying but what he said turned out to be true. Travers did get a little better. My brother sent him science books and Petard stopped by from time to time to take him for rides in the pickup truck. They took dirt roads up into the Klamaths, forest service roads that were passable enough summers but that dissolved like sugar during the rainy season. The truck stuttered up the mountain in low gear. The rides were uneventful for Petard but not for Travers. One minute, they'd be grinding down the side of a mountain through a shaft of trees, cedar and redwood and pine. The next, Travers'd feel his mouth dry out and see the truck plunging down to death, the brake line snapped, the gears stripped down to dowel, the two of them rattled to death sealed in a caisson, foreign matter expelled by the jade mountain. Then he'd open his eyes and see Petard holding the wheel gently, driving with a ceramic touch, adjusting his window from time to time when the air came in too cold. When they hit a bump the radio sometimes popped on and hissed between channels. They didn't talk much. Below in Shasta Valley the ground rolled to the edges of perfect little lakes. The fog was green and the rain, when it came, was soft in the late afternoon. Petard always took him home when it started to rain, but he always came back the next week to give him another ride just like he said he would, his engine muttering its way up the sawdust driveway. Whenever he heard the truck pull up Travers'd put on his dark red baseball cap with the H on it and go outside to meet him. He was ashamed of how he lived and didn't want Petard to see the inside of his trailer.

"I gave a speech," Travers said again, to me this time in the lab trailer at Weed. Turning to my brother: "You were there. Tell him what I said."

"I wasn't there. You were at Harvard. I was already in Vietnam."

"Did you give the speech for me?"

"No," said my brother patiently. "You gave it in L.A."

"Was there a good crowd?" asked Travers with sudden pinched-eye interest. "Were they appreciative? Was there applause?"

"The speech was so important that the Bureau destroyed every shred of evidence that you had ever given it. I tried to save the tapes but the Bureau beat me to them. Navier-Stokes and I had quite the chase across Pier 29 in San Francisco. That was in '74. Now nobody's sure what you said."

"Must have been some speech," I said.

"Now he thinks he told them about those—whatever the fuck they are—frogs."

Travers perked up at this. "We're not talking frogs. We're talking Toads. Big *bufo marinus* the Cane Toad. Ribbed, narrow-mouthed, thick-skinned. The czar of the Controlled Substance Analogs."

"The whats?" I asked.

"A CsA," said my brother, "is a drug separated off from an illegal drug. A derivative, a drug with a chemotype different enough so that it's not illegal because the feds don't know what it is yet. To make up their minds they have conventions and shit. They go to these big desert hotels where they sit on vinyl sofas and shiver air-conditioned to the ice point and stare at the plaster gold grapes twining up the wall, all to decide how illegal to make it, which of the three schedules to put it on."

"There are other CsAs," said Travers, cradling his fingers around his face like a catcher's mask. "Vine, leaf, berry, bark. It's important to remember them. For when I forget I make up ditties to remember them by. You may have heard them already. 'A is for alkyl, found in the eye, B is for benzil, compound of pi, C is chain alkyl, isomer high, D is dimethyl, black mushroom pie, E is for ergot, fungus of rye.' But none of these can measure up to the Toad."

My brother picked up a Toad, a hyperstill dull green with legs drawn up in zazen position, a fine compact Buddha with a patina. The Toad eyed my brother with suspicion from under its sloping cranial crest, inflating its lower throat like an elliptical balloon. The tip of the sac was wet and my brother touched it with his pinkie.

"See, this shit's bufotenine. The Cane Toad secretes it to ward off predators. It's toxic as hell. It definitely ranks with the best venom available, but in some ways it's better. It gives you cardiac glycoside poisoning. The bufotenine breaks both sister chromatids at the same time and you warp out right away. You lose total touch with the present once the bufotenine pale-stains the chromosomes. There's this almost immediate corrosion of the peripheral nerve. Your vision clouds over and you lose yourself somewhere in time."

"It's a natural toxin," said Travers.

"So is cobra venom or botulinus antibody."

Travers shot my brother an if-looks-could-kill look, and whenever he got angry, he got clear, least for a moment. This was why my brother did his best to keep Travers in a pointed state. In anger he was sharp again, like he'd been before '73. So my brother kept at him, needling him, prodding him, jabbing him with a long devil's spoon. And shit, it worked. Something inside Travers fell into place and now he was saying:

"The action of a drug is very important. Hallucinogens travel through your body in different ways. Your usual hallucinogen is potent simply because it's not very rapidly metabolized in the liver. Your better grade is more potent because it is more easily absorbed from the stomach and intestines into the bloodstream. Your high-quality hallucinogen penetrates more rapidly from the blood into the brain. Samsara-strength hallucinogens are the best of all because they go straight for the receptor sites in the brain."

"So if I get you right," I said, "the Toad destroys the evidence that other drugs leave behind?"

"A potent drug is potent because it's selective. It doesn't just tie. It binds. It goes straight for its target receptors on a suicide mission to bind with them. It zaps you no matter what, even when you take it in low doses. Bufotenine is one mean clean toxin. It knocks out the liver, sabotages the stomach, skips through the bloodstream, and strikes over the brain's receptors like bowling pins."

"A direct hit every time," said my brother. "No fucking around with the bloodstream, where shit drifts away."

"So the Toad sort of lays low in the brain?" I asked.

"It takes a while," said Travers, "to screen for a new drug. Sure, they'll ultimately figure out how to do it, but an adequate screening using intact lab animals takes about 25,000 milligrams of the chemical under study. It could take years to synthesize that amount."

"You mean to tell me there's no way they can tell if someone's wasted on Toads?"

"They can cut open your frontal lobes to check the condition of the neurotransmitters. To catch all users they'd have to lobotomize everyone they tested."

"Or," I said, "they would have to stop testing."

"You got it," said Travers.

Travers held the great charge in his hands. The Cane Toad hung upside down like a petty criminal grinning in the stocks of justice. He said this small creature was going to be the common carrier of American memory, the great liberator from the interdict on the substances that gave us access to the past. "This is serious shit," he said, and shifting the Toad into one hand and taking a mechanical pencil in the other, he drew us a diagram:

The Cane Toad molecule! Travers said that in outward form it looked like an ancient key to a forgotten door.

For him the Toad was going to open up an inside passage, a passage somewhere inside him, into the past his mind preserved in amber brain waves but couldn't remember waking if the future of the country depended on it. The blood of the Toad sure wasn't federal blood. No fucking way the Toad was going to allow the body to turn state's evidence against the mind. There'd be no more elemental analysis, no more litmus tests hung out to dry. The plain evidences of the bloodstream tolerating possession, the characteristic precipitates, the black stain of lead sulfide, the colorless crystals of silver sulfate when anions are present, the separated particles of tartaric acid moistened on multirange pH paper or mounted on a drop of water: these were the tests the feds used to detect drugs, and now they'd all be useless, obliterated by the unseen munificent burning of the Toad. The coursing of the Toad through American veins would defy magnification and the blood supply of the whole fucking nation would flow like a burning river you couldn't put out. Better watch out, Leviathan, Travers was saying. My Toad Development Farm is gonna turn your whale fins into leg sprouts and leave you a big fat tadpole bellying up onto the shore of a new American Caanan.

"He's been cultivating these Toads," explained my brother, "because they have special properties. They let you back into the past. Not the past as seen from the outside. The past as it saw itself."

"As it still sees itself," corrected Travers as another spasm jumped across his face.

"Bufotenine," my brother continued, "is a memory drug. It's the active ingredient in cohoba seeds. The Tupi and the Guarani in South America take them to fix past events firmly in tribal memory."

Sad and distant now, Travers said, "I'm using the Toads to try and find someone. A woman I think. I lost her in

Vietnam. I know where I lost her and when, Kien Phong Province, November 1973. But for the life of me I can't remember her name or face. I've tried everything and I still can't remember."

"So let's give it another try." My brother set to work on Travers's whole mad scientist rig, a big neon sign of a chem lab. He took some short lengths of fine-bore tubing and connected three glass columns in tandem. He isolated some sulfur trioxide as a reagent, poured a small amount of the yellow sulfur into the snout of an addition funnel, and sealed the ampule with an acetylene torch, all the while reading instructions off a 3×5 card he adjusted with his elbows when his hands were full. His face concentrated into a death mask because one false move and, wooosh, the triox flares and he's that film clip of the slow-burning monk in Nam. An even 4-4 rhythm hissed out of the vacuum pump and my brother tapped his foot absently to the beat.

"You're not isolating bufotenine," I said after a while. "You're making acid."

"I was wondering when you'd catch on."

"What happened to the bufotenine?" I said. "Aren't you going to make bufotenine?"

"Don't you get it?" said my brother. "You don't *make* bufotenine. The Toads *are* the bufotenine. You put them under a mercury-vapor lamp, they sweat, and then you lick them."

"Oh," I said. "So that's how it's done."

"Here," my brother told Travers, taking a Toad out of the hot cage, holding it down, and scraping its belly perspiration into a Petri dish with the flat side of a knife. "Take this."

"Don't do anything you can't undo," I told him.

"Nothing can't be undone," he told me.

"They're big," said Travers, nuzzling up to a benzo

brown, streaked from snout to vent with drab citrine mucus. The Toad flapped its tarsal fold wildly when he came near it and gave off a deep booming trill. "The size of a dinner plate. The best china available. Hotel china, in fact."

Travers was looking pretty schizo to me as it was, so I asked him, "You sure you want to take it?"

"Take?" he said, like he suddenly didn't understand that verbs have tenses. "Took."

No lie. Looking closely at him, I saw he was as still as a spinning top. It would take a while for Travers to snout back into the past and begin to find bits and pieces of what he actually remembered. The past was all somewhere in his mind. Where, though? He knew it was there still, and we knew he knew it. But it had been blighted and he had a hell of a time finding his way around there in the big convention-hall lobby of his memory. Problem was, said my brother, Travers remembered a lot of what he remembered in toad code. Once he'd crossed over into ravina nirvana he had a way of changing time zones. Every shift of his hips slammed him lateral into some new time frame. My brother said the Toad turned time into a palindrome. It sped time up, but not in your normal direction. Sure it shot you off like white light but then it 180'd linear time and took you careening back in reverse. Now Travers was off and running, running backward on the time line, his head facing us and his back facing the past, receding fast into the past. Imagine going at the speed of light *in reverse*. That toad load of the past took him in simple and uniform retrograde motion along one single given axis, retracing the line the past had taken when it had run flashing into the present. It changed everything, and I mean every little thing. Travers picked up a glass of water. "It's stopped evaporating." The age lines in the welted masonry disappeared and the walls were new again. Now his eyes moved up that dripping-wet red brick wall like they were following raindrops going up and not down. Then they followed a ray of light like the sun was retrieving its image from off the wall. Then they traced the motion of the sun backward along its ecliptic. I had never seen someone so totally thrown off. There Travers stood turning his head trying to see the past coming up behind him. When he couldn't crane his neck far enough he swung his body around so he could see what he thought he'd missed seeing. He kept at it like this, pivoting circles in place like a dog chasing its tail. The buffers had crumbled away, dividing the present from the present in the past, and the past from the past in the present. The hard glaring reflective surfaces of the lab, the polished floors, the glazed-tile walls, the white cork ceiling, were running together like lines in a lesion. What kind of light had been let into his mind? Opening on the walls did he see a green Krishna with thirty green legs on a spinning wheel, a byzantine Christ edging death with a wan green face, a Confucius with thin green lips, a pus-fatted green Buddha, a Quetzalcoatl with swollen green hands? I did not know, but I could see for myself that he saw and felt the fierceness of the Toad. This was clearly no dead work he was handling. The Cane Toad was a warrantable calling and it writhed in the field of Travers's senses.

"Oh God," said Travers after some time'd passed, I did not know how long, five, ten, fifteen minutes. "Oh God no." He saw it now. He saw the frame; the picture; the dress; the face. The face of a woman coming undone:

"Julia!"

He said it with a long ahhhhh, Juliahhhhh, his mouth held open like it had been forced by a tongue depressor. Very slowly he lifted his hands to his glasses and slid the clear heavy plastic frames off. His head bobbed a little, the ahhhhh aspirant then cut off as if his tonsils had dilated and sealed off his throat. His trachea was now a vacuum tube and Travers wasn't getting any air. He wanted more air but he'd lost the ability to gasp for it. He dropped his glasses and pressed both his hands against his chest wall like a tight bandage keeping his lungs from collapsing. His pupils shrank to specks, his corneas lost their transparency and took on a dull bluish-white color. Then his eyes closed and locked back inside his head with a summoning snap.

My brother was quick. Before I knew it he'd bounded past me in a fast leap, seizing Travers. He grabbed him vise-tight on the arm, jerked him hard against the wall, and pressed him there splat against it. He had him pinned, but Travers managed to slide his arms out of his shirt-sleeves and move them around in slow floating motion like balloons twisted into fat sausage arms. Up and down them I saw old black scars. His own hands free, my brother pinched the corners of Travers's eyes with his fingers to unlock them. They quivered a little but the twig of the nerve stayed right where it was. Then he took a flask of warm saline and splashed it in his face. Travers didn't even flinch. His face lost its specific gravity and his cheeks deepened into hollow bruised purple. My brother started giving him hard expelling short-winded slams to break the seal, to force the trapped air out so free air could come in. My brother was big and Travers was small and he was hitting him so hard I thought he'd snap his back like the spine of an old book. But he wasn't using his force against Travers. He was using it against time. He was ramming him to keep another century from settling into his marrow and tearing him apart from the inside. The two of them were bowed together expelling the past from Travers before it killed him. When his jaw fell loose my brother cupped his palm around his jawbone and shoved it back up again into place against its diptych plate, saying:

"I won't let go of you, you fucker. No matter what the fuck happens to you in that shithole past I won't let you fall down alone into it. I'll wire your fucking jaw shut if I have to. I won't let you come loose in time—"

But it wasn't helping. The rubber band holding my brother's ponytail broke and his dirty blond hair fell all over Travers. My brother didn't let him go but held him even tighter around the waist, so tight I thought his lungs might rip from the pressure. But damn, Travers began to go stiff, hard cold flat beat in coming rigor mortis. The cartilage in his arms was turning into cracked glue. My brother saw he couldn't stop it. He gave off slamming him sideways against the wall and instead took him around the chest in a Heimlich, using his fists to systole out the air remaining in his lungs. He heaved him up so high in the air and down so hard against the floor I thought he was going to crack the balls of his feet. It was no use. Travers had stopped moving. I moved closer, put my hand on his wrist, and felt a break in his pulse. His hands were almost white. Travers was up against the end. When my brother let him go he buckled friable to the floor. As he fell I thought I saw him falling through the floor down a long trash chute onto a dissection table, spent, alive but just barely, his skin pinned away from him in a thin scalloped line, dying for the sake of some botched experiment. Then I saw him in a white plastic garbage bag stuffed full with the carcasses of some lab dogs. No! The same image must have forced its way into my brother's mind at the same time, because just then, head back to neck crack, he let off one last viscerating cry:

"Traverrrrrrrrrs!"

Travers moved. His upper lip twitched. I saw him wet his finger with saliva, put it under his nose, and smell it.

His nostrils were asshole red. Waking, he'd expected to smell a woman but instead he smelled the sweet stamen tang of his nose hair prickle. A little expelled urine ran down his leg like lime thrown over a grave. Everything in him was lax and soft again. The dead were dead again, the past was past again, the present was present again, and Travers was alive again, clear again, clear enough, recalled from death to life, least for the time being.

"You're lucky to be alive," my brother told him.

"I didn't want to come back," he said. "You pulled me back."

"I didn't," said my brother, jerking his head in my direction. "He did."

"Me?" I said. "I just stood here with my mouth open."

"He's right," Travers told me, after considering it for a sec. "You brought me back."

"I watched you come back, but I wasn't there with you and I didn't bring you back."

"You mean you saw me back there?"

"Sort of. I saw you going back against the flow of time."

"No shit. What else you see?"

"The water going backward. But I only saw part of it. You were going too fast for me. I sure wasn't conscious of bringing you back."

"That's not what matters. When your brother was pulling me out I realized I had to come back to tell you what it was like. Why you, I don't know. But it was definitely you. How else could you see me if you weren't back there with me? So I stopped going back and let him pull me out."

Travers did not explain who Julia was. He couldn't. Whoever she was, the pain of remembering her hurt him so bad that he couldn't remember her at all, save for the name.

"I couldn't get her back," he said to me at last in a thin exhausted voice. "I went as far as I could but I couldn't get her back by myself. You have to come back with me."

My brother studied me with his lips slumped in strappado. "Travers is right. Usually he doesn't remember shit, even with the Toad. This time he got her name. Julia. I think he's remembering more because you're here. If you go with him into the past you might get it all. But this is your call. I can't press your tongue against that Toad. It's not like the tattoo. I have no idea what you might see if you take the toxin. You might die. Petard took it and said it was like death."

"Did you take it?"

"I took it," he said flatly. "It's not like death. It is death. You die and join the dead in the past that only they know. But more, worse. You start to recover the past that even they have forgotten."

"What do you mean, start?"

"You can't complete the recovery."

"Why is that?" I asked.

"If you do," said my brother, "you die."

I wanted to say okay right away, but I stopped myself. I didn't want to be pulled up off the ground and dropped halfway down with a jerk. I'd been untimely ripped before. Taking the wrong shit at the wrong moment rips the face off time and turns your mind into a polyp crawling through the half-life of a drug. Travers did not exactly strike me as your Dante-type guide to the low places. Seeing me hesitate, he motioned me over to a big tank, a Toad incubator. The incubator was a home rig. The cooling condenser was a coil of glass tubing in a coffee can packed with ice. To make the vat Travers'd cut open the shell of a 55-gallon water heater, removed the anode rod, and modified the fitting to accommodate a thermometer. For heat he'd pulled the element from a deep-fat fryer. There it was, under metal and glass, the whole terra infirma of the Toad, the America of shallow transient depressions, the America of open ponds in cutover roads, the America of temporary overflows and drenched cultivated fields, all to get your female Cane Toad to put out eggs, 24,000 a month gathered in small loose masses the size of a film can, each colony, like Travers said, a nation born in a day.

"I'll go," I said at last, "just so long as I don't have to lick those frogs."

"Toads," corrected Travers.

"Toads, frogs, whatever." I had this clear mental picture of two fingers of Travers's hand dug into the corners of my mouth, pinching it open into wide oviposition the size of a scream, the Toad sliding in backside up, let down slowly flat against my tongue, not actually touching my teeth, laying a double pipeline of eggs right down my throat—

"The best part," said Travers.

"Not for me," I said.

"All right, then," said my brother, more to allay Travers than to reassure me. "I'll rig up something."

My brother pieced together a very long straw out of many small segments of straw. One end disappeared into the Toad hot cage, a greasy sweating cardboard box, the other extended toward me. As the straw grew he tested it, breathing deeply like a respirator, making bubbling and popping noises, forcing up so much so fast that the straw caved in on him. "Goddamn paper straws." He crushed the flattened piece in his fist and shoved in a segment of replacement pipe. He did not bother to blowgun the paper sleeve off the straws, so each bit had a bunched-up slipcover. The straw was five feet long by the time he finished it. It sagged in the middle, reeds bending in different directions, but as a pipeline it seemed workable enough.

"Here," he said, handing it to me. "Drink from the past."

2

I sucked in and nearly passed out. I must have overdrawn. I was sitting in a certain place, a castered lab chair, I was conscious of my posture, my back straight, then my forehead was burning hot and I found myself thinking, gimme refrigerant, some nice crushed ice packed into plastic bags and knotted into a strong cap against the small veins of my temples. I was there and I wasn't. For a moment I felt colossally bloated, like I'd sucked an aquifer dry, water table dropping below zero. Then I swallowed and realized I was still withdrawing fluid from the straw. Clapping his hands around the straw, my brother had made himself into a pump station, squeezing out small priming doses through the straw and into my mouth in cut time. This was a zero-order infusion, delivering a fixed amount with each fix. Whatever this bufo shit was, it had a very high clearance and a very slow rate of elimination. Not much lapse of time between the alpha and beta phases of absorption. There was a sharp bend in a curve: was it a curve in the plot of the plasma concentration of my blood, the distribution phase rapidly falling, bending sharply toward elimination, approaching the baseline, or was it a curve taking me back into the past, not the past of my memory, the past of another order of memory, gradually reaching a point, a point waiting for me near the edge of a planar surface, a point laid out with graph-paper precision, a point punched in time? Where was I? Weed, California? I wasn't sure. Who was I?

I was Robert Travers. It was a bright day in 1967. I can't say how I knew the time. I knew it because Travers knew it without having to think about knowing it. I remembered it not as a date on a time line but as a day with morning and afternoon and evening. I was living life the way Travers had lived it, moment by pulmonary moment, a progression of moments in which time was transparent. What was was. Time was solid, compact, fixed, durable. Why question it? 1967 was the speed of light and the boiling point of water and the heat of the sun. With Travers I remembered the way the sun hit the Bio Labs at Harvard, the red brick catching the red light and glowing the litmus color of red with a faint blue tint. For a moment, pausing in the courtyard between the two rhino statues, staring at that tropical bend of light, Travers'd thought that it must always be there, bending across the window into bars, passing red through a very clear sky to land acid on alkaline brick. Red: time for a time had moved out of its place, the order of succession passing into the order of situation, a place in motion stopping to become for an instant an immovable place, entire and absolute in memory. This must have been a moment in '67 when Travers had sensed that time was more immanent than he'd been taught. Maybe he hadn't known what to make of it. Maybe it had been a pretty slight premonition, a thumb tilt in the balance of time. But this was the moment the Toad had chosen to let us back in, and there we were.

Travers was on his way to a faculty meeting thinking about suicide. Not his own, he'd botched that; altruistic suicide in insects. Bees and ants, that's all he ever thought about, all he'd ever been interested in, bees and ants. His life was one long series of meetings with remarkable insects. For six years he'd been collecting these insect Medal of Honor stories, tales of low-fallen bug heroes with no

cenotaphs to remember them by. His specialty was sac-
rificial attacks, insane charges, personal immolation, ka-
mikaze behavior, the nest wall broken open and the
intruder defiling and defiled, life that can only be thrown
away once thrown away once, the embedded sting pulling
out the stinger's entire venom gland and much of the
viscera with it, the banana smell of poison marking the
breach, the cry cried at the cost of the crier, the cry of
the warning call with death the rewarder met with the
call-giver's words, *grave where is thy victory, death where is
thy sting*. Travers'd spent a lot of time poking around in
honeybee hives and yellowjacket burrows but now he was
fixed on one species, *da mok*, the fire bees, those orange
stingless bees in Vietnam, the ones capable of pouring
burning glandular paste over the robes of their skins during an attack to die the jellied gasoline death of martyr-
dom. There wasn't much known about them. They killed
themselves to deter invaders. They lived to die death in a
warning brocade, the smashed folds of their robes flaring
sulfur covered with their own abdominal secretions spilling out in red and black characters over the ground. Not
much written about them in the usual places.

Travers'd had to stop reading journal articles and start
reading other stuff, veterans' accounts of these creatures
coming out of Nam in a sure steady trickle, accounts cir-
culating in manuscripts of crinkled bleeding carbon, not
your typical scientific accounts what with the weird witnessing going on, one grunt saying that for a moment in
the final flare of death *da mok* looked like embroidered
double herons, another watching one die and thinking,
all the sudden, he didn't know why but he couldn't get
it out of his head, not ever, the Emperor is the Son of
Heaven, Defer to Him, another having these dreams
about being baked alive in a clay oven filled with charcoal,
another going AWOL and making his way to Hanoi to

look for a street he knew the name of without knowing why, Kham Thien, street of the teahouses, street where the tea was so hot that it went down your throat with the momentum of acid salts, but never finding it and ending up mad in St. Elizabeths painting birds on a Chinese scroll. Travers knew that the sting of the fire bee didn't have any psychochemical properties to speak of, but these vets hadn't even been stung. The poor suckers'd just seen shit happening around the bees. Not much to go on but still he kept at it, trying to find everything there was to find on the fire bees. Turned up an old army field manual, FM 101-40, *Armed Forces Doctrine for Chemical and Biological Weapons*, that led him to the only other person in the U.S. interested in the bees, one Major H. M. Barton, arsenal information officer stationed at the Muscle Shoals, Alabama, Phosphate Development Works, operated by the Tennessee Valley Authority and constructed back in the early fifties on TVA's Wilson Dam Reservation. Travers went there once but came away with nothing. Barton'd given him a blood test before and after he entered the tower, a maze of pipes, furnaces, and vats that culminated in ten sealed stories. The Army kept bees there but for some reason Barton wouldn't let him see them. Back in the Bio Labs, Travers kept a small stalag of them in giant brown aerated jars. Here they stored them in thick steel drums. The sky outside was pale yellow even at night. The fenced storage area around the tower was under twenty-four-hour guard, the compound visible from the tower's clerestory, crisscrossed by sidewalks at odd angles lit dimly by low beam spread just like Harvard Yard.

It was nearly ten at night and Travers was almost there. He'd stuffed the invitation into his side pocket and, bulging, it chafed his leg as he walked. Travers'd never been to a faculty meeting at Harvard before and hadn't known what to make of the invite stuck in his box addressed to

Bio Labs 424. Tucked into the envelope was a small folded waxpaper figure of a woman cut off from the waist down. The paper was worn and dirty with age like it'd been dipped in water and laid out to dry. The date given was today's, October 26, 1967. The time was given, too, but given and then taken away, told like this, ten and not nine, ten and not eleven, ten and not eight, ten and not twelve, like time was going to begin at ten o'clock tonight and then, this was hard to believe but then again Travers was a Travers and was willing to believe almost anything, time was going to go back into the past and forth into the future from a zero point at which all time originated, a point at which all time's coordinates were zero, the lines moving off in both directions from a moment that hadn't happened yet but was coming up less than an hour from now. Must be some archaic Harvard custom, he'd thought, remembering that old Pusey the Prez always signed those black-rimmed death announcements "Your Obedient Servant," probably just preppy bullshit, but damn a lot of people here always seemed to be dying, no not just emeriti kicking off but people disappearing un-announced into death with these little tarot cards pinned to them like old Pusey was heading up the Americal Division over in Vietnam and the Yard was some kind of mass grave. Well, it was, Travers knew it was because part of the Yard'd originally been Travers's land and there were some Traverses buried under here somewhere, exactly where he didn't know, exactly who he didn't know either, graves registration being a secret combusted to ash in the pyre of his family's past. His family, always that shitty family of his, he'd never escaped their funeral fire even though most of them were dead as bedrock and nameplate. *Aqua Desertrum, Deserta Aquae*, ye olde family motto and yup that's why Harvard hired him yup he's one of theirs ergo he's one of ours and yup whatever he did, caught redhanded at a little low-grade amateur arson in the Andover chapel crypt in '56 and yup not even a reprimand, suicide attempt in '62 but at the bullet moment he swore he felt a hand reach out of the past and, yup, gently shift the barrel angle off to a tangent so that the shot'd barely grazed his skull osculate, his only memory of it now a nutmeg smell of powder, occupying Sproul with the FSM at Berkeley in '64 with everyone dragged out by the hair and beaten into a pulp, yup, everyone but him: whatever he did, he felt the vise grip of a strong dead hand reopening that healed crack on top of his skull, taking him back to the nation's infancy. He wanted out, he'd always wanted out of the Traverses but nobody in his family ever seemed to die, they just fell down into the ground through trapdoors where they waited in chambers for him to dig them out again. But every time he dug a hole in the ground to shelter himself against them, hoping to dig his solitary way to the South China Sea where there'd be no more Traverses, well, there they were, all of them, large dead stones placed in circles around him, all their skulls and ribs and jaws, gallons of dead Traverses buried in jars with their mouths turned downward to keep the insides dry. Sometimes when he was cutting across the yard to Harvard Square to catch the T he felt a pull, a down pull winding out of the ground in a lituus curve, the trumpet curve of judgment winding around him without ever seeming to reach him. The curve had a pull but it also had a beat, a muffled pulmonary beat, red current under white of winter, waver of blood under skin of snow, pull of platelets running slowly downstream at that temperature perfect for storing blood over time, four degrees Centigrade, the same temp now flashing from the bank sign on Cambridge Trust over the south end of the Yard. He was walking now toward University Hall, and the pull of the current made him think he was crossing a river in winter at a place where the river narrowed and the ice ran thick. The shallow crusted snow covering the Yard was hard to tell from river ice, and Travers thought at any minute he might run his legs deep into the hollows and cavities of some sick past frozen half dead under Harvard.

"The past has got to stop," he said to himself. "Someone's got to tell it: *stop*."

Travers steadied himself and shook his head. Like a lot of others he'd recently stopped cutting his hair and now he had the feeling, first time ever, of hair sliding along the back of his neck. For a moment the feel of hair kept his mind from bending secant into his roundhead past, but when he remembered how his draft board'd classified him 1-R, he was off and bending. The 1 was bad but the R was good because the R was for religion. He remembered standing half naked with a towel round his hips in the drafty old gym of Cambridge Rindge & Latin, the chill from the cold shower they'd made him take raising follicles on his arms, the light in the high windows dull and sunless, the bleachers laid out plainly like pews and smelling of new pine, remembered the board, six men at a table, remembered them telling him that, as a minister, he was exempt from the call to duty and, oh by the way, good luck with your work on altruism, it'll show the gooks a thing or two about the American spirit. Son you know we're expecting great things from you, great things. No matter you being a biologist. You're a Travers and that makes you a man of the cloth even if you wipe your ass with it. The board'd known that and so had he even though they hadn't said a word to him in that skeleton gym where the floors were made of planks wider than your usual gym planks, the boards warping loose underfoot, where the doors were held shut with two-by-fours crosslaid in a Z, and where, this not coming as any surprise to Travers, old portraits hung from wires guyed to the recessed basketball hoops, the paintings all glowing with the same dull yellow sheen as the old varnished ball court. On his way out, hands gripping the towel knotted a few sizes too tight round his waist, he'd thought he'd seen one of the portraits smiling at him, a long wide lipless over-bitten smile, a smile with no compassion in it, an elective smile that couldn't contain its delight at the foreknowledge that every Travers that'd ever be born would come away from every draft board ever assembled in every gym ever built classified 1-R.

University Hall had broken stone steps leading up to it with no locks on the doors. Travers went up. He climbed some stairs worn by many footfalls into a long slide. Up top the door to the meeting room was open and the first thing Travers thought going in was, this room is dark and full of people watching me. Bunch of dead fucks, dead fucks staring off the walls just like at home, another limed row of them. He felt like a little boy again in another room full of family friends, his mother taking him by the hand and him looking up at all the crumpled old corneas, their dead-oak hands holding steaming bowls of yellow and orange and white mush, pounded squash probably, her introducing him to them now, saying, Bobby, meet Increase Mather, Bobby, meet John Cotton, Bobby this is William Travers, your ancestor, you've never met him before but he knows all about you and is very proud, he was second governor of the Bay Colony, you know. The meeting room was like home, too, full of Windsor chairs and long oak tables. Over in the northeast corner was a small cupboard, a chest of drawers, and a headboard, headboard of a bed. Cornices came off the wall and seemed to define a little bedroom round the base of the portrait. Travers looked up at the woman, the pediment above her broken by a tiny Victorian urn. Who was she?

Just some Puritan cunt probably. Travers hadn't had much experience with women, just a few quick squirts here and there, but he'd always had this fascination with sexy pious babes, women who felt the driving waters of sex forced through them but knew how to pinch them convergent in a vena contracta of belief. He was examining her more closely now. Shit no she wasn't one of these, she looked well fucked to Travers, she had that dry pink flush. Sure was an odd portrait, full length not just breast up, no chopped waist, no flatness, no sheen, more like a woman checking herself out in a full-length mirror and ready any moment now to lateral out of it. Travers caught her eye and as he did, she moved. Yup she moved. A tuft of fabric swayed, tugged at the crotch center. Moved, no, impossible. But there she was ruffling that dress round her crotch again. She was beckoning him, he felt her beckoning him, calling him into the low folds now defining themselves yielding and labiate between her legs . . .

"Travers," he heard her say, not outside him but speaking from somewhere inside his head.

Huh? He looked round him but the sound left no dying fall in the room. The voice had resonance but no echo. He wanted to back off from her but there was nowhere he could back off to. Her voice was his voice. Her voice spoke to him in his voice but he had the perfect awareness it wasn't his. It had a perfectly regular quality that made him think of a beehive, an army, a strongly organized religion. It came over him now that the name she'd spoken inside him wasn't even his name. It was hers. It was his name spoken the way it had once been spoken, the way she'd said it, inflected with a tenet strength he'd never heard in any living voice. The woman in the painting was speaking to him, pronouncing her name, and that name was Travers.

Travers was sweating now, mopping his forehead with

a red terry-cloth jogger's headband he wore around his wrist as a sort of bracelet. The lab at Weed had grown dark with cool blue night. He bent his knees a little and they cracked with the motion. Coming for a moment out of the past he felt the Toad moving him but not along the time line, along the spectrum. He was moving in the blue direction, light blue, blue, light purple, purple. He wanted to speak but before he spoke he found himself thinking, a cell can't stay alive indefinitely. Stick it in a Petri dish and it turns purple. Give it a little buzz though with a microelectrode and—

"Pull me out," I overheard him pleading with my brother.

"I can't," said my brother. "You're going at break speed down one of those anion canyons in your brain. You can't be stopped till you hit a synapse."

"What should I do?"

"Find that Julia woman."

"How?" said Travers, not really knowing what he was saying but saying truer than he knew. "She's in her grave."

"Then," said my brother, "find out how she got there."

"What if I can't?"

"Don't fight it. The past is still there. Just let yourself fall."

And fall he did, and me with him: right into the arms of Julia Newton Travers, Travers's mother nine removes away. We were back in University Hall and Julia was luring him upstairs into the past of her portrait. She shook the side of her dress in a fast dancing snap. The dress moved up her leg. The flesh wasn't pink but gray, same flab gray as his own Travers skin but somehow beautiful when pulled tight over the skeleton of a woman. I saw Travers move closer to the portrait, unbuckle his belt and step out of his shoes, place his hand on the rim of the painting. The portrait had no birth date, no death date. I tried to look up at her face but all I saw was a passing of shadows in a space white with zero color. What was her face like? Was she pretty? His forehead bunched into a dry furrow, Travers tried to remember. He said he saw a lot of things, a large standing vase full of dead flowers, an inch of rusty water at the bottom, an arm with the sleeve delicately rolled up over a wrist absently turning the pages of a book, not a bound book but a sheaf of loose pages, a woman with brittle white vase skin leaning a little forward, smiling a little but not much, the wrinkles just creasing her nose like splinters, her dark blond hair newly washed and done up tightly. The face above the dress long and straight and colorless. The neck a long vertical. The hands a little twisted like they'd broken and healed. But the eyes, the lids were wide as if pinched and held there by pins, her eyes had hardly any sockets to them, open dark dry bowls instead. Travers made eye contact with the gravel in her eyes. There was a faïence tint to the crumble and he remembered thinking, Your eyes were blue.

"Watchet," he heard her say.

"Watch what?"

"Watchet eyes," said Julia. "William used to tell me I had watchet eyes."

"What are watchet eyes?"

"You have them, too."

She reached out for him. As she did he knew who she was. She was the only one of his ancestors everyone in his family called by her first name, Julia. She'd done something bad, unspeakable bad, anathema bad, something called the Altruist Heresy, and died young, braziered for it. Her body hadn't been dug up and moved to Mt. Auburn Cemetery in the 1830s to the family plot everyone called The Amulet, those two words soldered into a black iron gate in early Victorian fishhook, because the fence strung around it was like a high choke collar round a throat of graves. Travers saw her dress just crumble away and fall to her feet. She opened her arms to him. She wanted him to step into her portrait and he was about to, then this image forced its way into his mind, image of him stepping into a body bag, sliding in next to, oh shit no, and hearing the zipper pulled up and over him. But he went in anyway because he saw her green bodice was off and she was down to white linen and graywacke. Was she a mirage? He couldn't see her now but he felt her trying to lead him to some kind of narrow preserved place. He felt a pull and a pall, a peace coming over him, a sense of security like he was wound in a sleeping bag on a cold night. He was in the world of the dead now where death was as familiar as sleep. Then he had a sense of following a paraffin torch down a blackened corridor, his feet cold, the stone floor warm, her leading him deep down a shaft ending in a sealed doorway. From the lintel down, the door was mortared shut, but Travers knew where it led. This was the door to Julia's memory.

"There was some kind of past Julia was trying to get me to remember. This past, it was wonderful and horrible at the same time. At first I figured it was horrible for her because everyone who'd lived then was dead now. But then I realized that Julia didn't mind being dead. She minded what the dead had done when they were living. Something had happened in the past that was permanent that shouldn't have been permanent. Something that had to be undone. And I saw that the only way to undo what had happened was to remember it differently, to enter into her dead mind and retrieve what only she remembered."

"What is that?"

"A trial. She remembered a trial."

"Whose trial?"

"Her trial."

The last moment of her trial. One man was speaking. He'd seen him before and knew where. He was mounted next to Julia in University Hall. Draped in a hanging garden of dark green cloth, chain of office ringing his neck, ears pricked up for invisible commanding voices, he held his sin-purged body like a peel twisted of juice. He exuded patience. All the time in the world was his and he was time's tightass proctor. Travers felt the tension in him. It wasn't in his jaw but in his lips. His jaw he held like the mandible plates had opposing valences and had never touched. But his lips were pulled rubber-tight over the space between his teeth in a wince that said, Don't fuck with me, I'm munching on the grapes of wrath. For a sec Travers lost focus on him and as he did his face fragmented into a pentangle blur, five faces with ten eyes. These loose roving eyes were for everything in the Bay Colony, twisting the world he saw into a single pendant cord of perfect severity. Dare to be more perfect than God: a shudder rippled through Travers when he saw that this man lived by these words. No wonder nobody in the courtroom looked directly at him when he spoke. Occluded he sat off to one side, alone in his body, his head too big for him, his torso below used-up-looking, stretched and flabby at the same time, making Travers think of urine voided into a heavy plastic bag. He knew him, always'd known him, couldn't remember a time when he hadn't. He was Julia's husband and his father nine fathers ago, fathering him through one hard direct line of fathers. Travers felt his nose. He'd inherited that narrow nose held up by joist of bone. Nose of William Ludlow Travers, second governor of the Massachusetts Bay Colony.

The trial had been going on for a long time, weeks by the look of it. Travers heard Travers speaking. There'd already been a slew of other incidents involving her. Seems that the committee that'd met for six years in rooms at Harvard College in Cambridge had never been of one clear mind about what to do with the Governor's wife. They'd run out of the usual options. Hanging, branding, the ducking stool were for people other than Traverses. This freethinking bitch was the cross the Governor was carrying. He was willing to do just about anything to get rid of her, but the committee held him back. No question but she was an enthusiast of some sort but you never know, maybe there were some marital problems, Travers wasn't someone you fucked with but there must be something behind her going around saying men cared more for one another than for God. The committee wanted to forget the whole thing, they wanted him to shut her up, he was her husband before he was governor, wasn't he, that'd've been a lot easier to understand than his bringing his own wife up for trial, and worse, deciding to try her himself. But Travers had insisted it was time for Julia's dissent to be put to an issue. "Altruism is a word she is using to wreck us." He could no longer wait on God to set her straight, so he'd gone ahead and dissolved the Charter Council and left it for him to judge to his own satisfaction what to do with her. For something had to be done. Man is not the author of altruism, he told her. Only God is perfectly altruistic.

She interrupted him. "William. I'm not saying that man is *perfectly* altruistic. Only that altruism works. That it's the best way."

William Travers didn't slam his fist on the table, though that's what he felt like doing, saying, You bitch, it's not the New England way; he knew nothing untoward would rid him of her. Instead, he said, "This altruism of yours, I know what it means. It means you believe men are better than God."

"No," she said. "It means I think men help one another for the common good. That their love is reciprocal. That love *can only be reciprocal*. And that society, that life, is formed on this."

It pissed off Travers to see his wife facing him unbending. She must have been spent to the null point. Eight months she'd lived in a holding cell, spooning corn and beans boiled together into a parched mash. She was effectively silenced, her pamphlets burned, her followers dispersed, cut down over six years to a small number, and now, far as he knew, cut down to the second smallest number, the number one, slipping from there down to the final extinction of zero. Julia was up against the zero barrier, the wall against which intolerance jammed tolerance in a last crush. Did she really think there was anything waiting for her on the other side of the zero wall? She sure acted like there was, like there was a kind of reverse underground life to be had on the minus side of zero tolerance, a parallel world suspended in virtual contact with the length and breadth of the America the Visible Saints of Massachusetts Bay decreed tolerable. In her cell a small window had given her a view of a bunch of trees lying fallen over each other, one, two, three feet off the ground. Beyond, a field of wheat sat untended. When her husband cried down judgment on her she sat very still and looked out beyond William Travers onto the familiar bare field, ribbed now with November's first snow and abraded at its far edge by broken river ice. At that moment, hearing her sentence passed, the seal of her fate torn, her exile pronounced, she felt her mind open into a perfect vacuum of calm and float detached from time, and she spoke.

"Our children," she said to Travers. "What have you done with them?"

Travers watched Travers watch Travers. He knew there was more going on here than he saw transcribed. "What am I seeing?" Travers remembered asking Julia.

He didn't expect her to answer but she answered all the same. "You're seeing what I saw."

"Why am I seeing it?"

"You are seeing Altruism. You found me without knowing it. Now you know what you have found."

"Reciprocal Altruism?" asked Travers.

"Even so," she said.

"But I'm a biologist," said Travers.

"Altruism is the reason I am with you now. It's better that you know. Know that I am speaking through you."

"Then why can't I hear you?"

"I have always been speaking through you. *Travers, you have always heard me.*"

It was there in the void of University Hall, spent and crumpled around Julia's portrait, the other portraits pulled off the wall and scraped down to white canvas, that Travers did all his quiet thinking about time. He'd known what to do. He'd killed her, silenced the voice he couldn't stop hearing inside his head, killed the family of others, too, all of them there in that room. With his nails he'd ripped them apart with a hatred he'd not known was in him, peened them down to durationless blanks. The paintings were gneiss in his hands and they'd fallen apart foliated into flakes. Now his hands were covered with spall. Julia he'd saved till last. He took one last look at her, hoping to see jell in her recessive eyes, but all he saw were two white nicks. She made it easy to do, took the reality out of herself, bared her neck to him, turned her head a bit off to the side. Still Travers cried, cried for the relict of her in him, his lungs shaking for air, thinking, oh bitter God I can't see her eyes, just can't, her answer then sounding back inside him, sounding in that voice not hers, not his, maybe not anyone's, sounding for the last time impedant in his ears:

"You have my eyes now."

Julia was down off the wall now and Travers had her in his arms. The rip he'd made in her took the life out of her in an instant. The rip across her face hadn't aged her. The rip across her face was a rip across her face. It had returned her to what she once was. The portrait was pure American naïve. An old comic-book face, the lines set first and the color filled in later, a face with surface but no inside. The canvas drooped in its frame and Travers smoothed out her dress with his hand. Julia was back in the world she'd died in. That was her world just as this was his. Then now and then then were closer than he'd ever thought possible, but the people then and now were centuries apart and it couldn't be otherwise. She and the other faces in the room, torn faces from the seventeenth century, were now impossibly near and far. The mystery was too close, too immense. It was like picking up a rock and thinking, This rock is millions of years old and here I am holding it in my hand. Julia dead again, Travers felt more empathy with the portrait of the current Harvard Prez, Nathan Marsh Pusey, than with any of the old stone faces rubbed on the wall in University Hall.

Travers made eye contact with Pusey and knew he was back in 1967, but it was a different 1967 than before. There were new memories, old memories that were not his but now a part of him, too. He wanted like mad to pinch them out of himself, put them on a slide, shine light through them, and project them opaline against the white wall of the present. During the trial he'd sat next to her on the stand. She had a bag of seeds on her lap and she'd taken them out and counted them out one by one during the trial. Out the seeds came like beads slipped on an abacus. That was counting, and somehow Travers had always identified with counting. Numbers strung out time on a long straight line. But this counting was like a circle bending off to connect with itself again, a curve like thread, a circle like breath, a counting not for the sake of counting but for the discipline of keeping track, watching but not waiting, watching just to be there watching. He'd watched her watching. He'd seen the seeds shift. Each seed was an oval grain, almost round. He had never really looked at one before. The seed was soft and fat. On one side there was a ridge like the cut on top a loaf of bread. He'd given one seed a nice incisor bite-down and it broke easily into two lobes. When he came to that morning, Julia back dead on the wall and him curled under the Doric leg of an old Empire table, he'd found these broken seeds in his hand. They felt warm in his hand and he smelled them. They smelled like coal tar, like varnish, like creosote. Much later he took them to the Peabody Museum on Divinity Avenue, right across the street from where he'd moved, for carbon-14 dating.

"Where did you get these seeds?" the stunned lab technician had asked him. "They're hundreds of years old and *they're still germinating*."

"You mean they can reproduce?"

"Can? They already have. Look in your hand."

But back that October, when the snow was on the ground in Harvard Yard, the seeds cupped fresh in his hands, the thought dilated in him that Julia had done more than open his eyes. She'd scooped out his latter-day eyes and given him a new pair to see with. These eyes were first eyes. They were the eyes that saw this land before too many Travers eyes'd seen it and worn it flat with too much seeing. Seeing was eroding, and now he had new eyes to scour the world with. Tramping down the stairs, dropping his legs one after the other in a dead heavy shuffle, each step a shinsplint, Travers caught sight of himself in a speckled old mirror. Gone was the dilute blue adulterated by too many generations. His eyes were shades bluer, like a canal'd been cut into his retina and filled with fresh blue water. These eyes were going to show him more than a few monadnock remnants. They were going to take him back to zero and show him the America around him for the very first time.

Back now at ground zero, feeling the retinal whiteness of winter, Travers pulled on his gray woolen overcoat, left University Hall, and took the 72 Huron bus to Mt. Auburn Cemetery. He knew she wasn't buried there. He just wanted to be in a place where the creep of time was no strain. The cemetery was a silent city on the edge of Cambridge. He remembered the snap and tug of the wind as he stood facing the pale calcites, white and green and rance. Across the street were signs of life, a supermarket, a greengrocer's, a shoe-repair shop. A few feet away on the other side of the street were signs of death, cornices, copings, moldings. He crossed Mt. Auburn Street. A berm of minor dead rose scarping around the whole of the cemetery. So much design here, but for what? Some architect had put up a wall of dirt and wood and flesh and bone so that those who were living could not see how many had died. Crossing over, Travers had no idea that death had undone so many. The land of the living was a few short steps away, if he ran he could be back there in ten seconds and yet, no, here there was no running and time ran down. Time did not stand still here. Out there time clicked in a toothed wheel and ratchet. In here time moved in the wound mass of a spring getting tighter and tighter. The dead were tightly wound in a past that got tighter and tighter the longer it curled in the past. The more past the past got, the tighter it pulled. What agony:

he knew it was agony because he knew how it hurt Julia: that unbearable tension: to be wound and wound and never snap, never shorten, never slide into the flat even line of release. The poet fuckers were wrong, death wasn't a release. The dead wound and wound and couldn't snap. He was walking in the middle of a stone forest of monuments to a past that wasn't petrified but coiled up like the inner spring of a clock. He had a sudden craving for a strong cup of black coffee. He wanted to feel the force of his heart at work, to feel that coronary flow, burning myocardial oxygen, tensing the baroreceptive walls of his arteries. He started to run; he wanted to lift his weight against gravity; to feel strain; to make his heart give velocity to a mass of blood; to activate muscle; to flex living tissue to show what made him living and them dead. He wanted to show off how alive he was, and, running, he felt it wasn't enough, he wished he'd brought some decent drugs along, something to fuck with the homeostasis of his blood pressure, something good and strong like serotonin or vasopressin. Just a little bit, 0.1 mg. or so, would turn the color of his blood from red to black and make his veins sing the heavy burden of life.

"Julia," said Travers, winded and gasping for cold air. "Julia."

Travers was so weak, so shaky, so wound up in a dead coil, that he barely made it back to the T stop and into Harvard Square. He knew what had happened. Julia was dead again and could never come back to him but he was alive again.

The Huron bus let him off in the Square, where there was a large white church. He went in and sat down in a bare heavy pine bench and closed his eyes in a dead seam. He saw himself there, he had been there before. Not in this church but in this place when it had been a different church, the church before this church that had burned down. In 1658. In 1658? Now it folded over him with full clarity: that trial. That Altruist Heresy. The trial had been in a church. He remembered a lot of windows, curtains of white sheeting run on wires, a reedy organ, a lectern, a plain pine table, rows of benches. Julia had not once taken her eyes off him when he spoke in her defense. The feeling ran chills through Travers that Julia'd spoken three hundred years ago so he could hear her now. He wondered what the trial had been about, if there even had been one.

He had to find out. Travers ran straight out of the church and over to Widener Library. He didn't know his way in. He bounded up a wide balustrade, swung around a corner so wide he knocked over an exhibit case full of old Radcliffe report cards, pausing for a sec at the circulation desk, unvelcroing a flotation wallet out of which tumbled a deck of ID cards. At the stack entrance he had a hard time remembering who he was. He looked at the crimson block of his Harvard officer ID without any shock of recognition. He pulled out an Institut-Max-Planck Berlin pass, an old postcard of Grand Coulee Dam colorized to look like there were cracks twigging across it, a buffalo nickel with the date effaced under the Indian, a page from a book by Konrad Lorenz he'd rubbed in goat shit, keypunch library cards from Institutes for Advanced Study in this and that, expired driver's licenses each with different expiration dates, Mass exp. 3/67, Cal exp. 5/67, New York exp. 7/67, all with photos of Travers, his hair combed shiny and flat like water film on moss, blurred photos of him reaching out to shake the camera, front and side and even rear, including one meteorological closeup of Travers's hurricane bald spot. In he went, but Travers was losing it, he was forgetting who he was and whenever that happened he got it into his head to snatch him some snatch, he'd heard there was a rapist in the stacks and he thought maybe he'd punch himself a hole in some grad student hymen one of those frail arching willow virgins with lots of brown moles around the soft dripping mouths of their cunts just waiting to sire some more Traverses for some incomprehensible sick fuckup of a future. Maybe that was what Julia wanted him to do; find some innocent and drag her by the hair into this prison of misprison, find a living woman at random and rape her raw then make her bite off his balls and swallow them so this could never happen again.

"Is that what you want me to do?" he yelled down the gray setback of a stairwell.

He knew Julia was not down there. For a second he really hated her, hated how much he loved her. In a thousand ways she was telling him that she wanted him to undo something. But what broke him was the idea that something done then, done in 1658, had to be undone now, undone in 1967. He wanted like mad to do something that couldn't be undone. God fucking damn it all: *What if there was nothing in this world that couldn't be undone?* What if the past could always carry over its irresolution into the future? What if the past was never past at all? He understood her now: Julia lived in the darkness of what could have happened but didn't, her dead life was not an abandoning, an utter leaving, but a coming closer to what might have been. Life extended after death only when life before death hadn't completed itself. Life after death was an irresolution of life before death, and his life was heading that way fast unless he resolved to remember what only she and a few other forgotten dead had not forgotten. For a moment he wished he was dead and done with, but if he had been, he'd have left this undone and he'd be dead the way Julia was dead, undone with, and he didn't want that nohow.

Travers heard his voice echoing down the stairs, "Is

that what you want me to do? Is that what you want me to do?"

He knew that Julia could not hear him, not now, not ever. He looked around him into the uprooted air. There were winding flights of stairs and an elevator that didn't work. He was left without her inner voice directing him, and the next step had to be his. He knew what she wanted. Julia wanted him to find a lost past, a past that lived hiatally, interrupted by a thousand synapses but fixed somewhere in lodgement of American memory. If Julia was right there'd once been an apostate altruism under America. In Widener there were shattered bits of a story. Something called the Altruist Heresy. It blew him away when he found out what it was; it was what he'd been doing in the lab for years; it was where he came from and who he was. The heresy was this: Julia thought human society didn't require the love of God. People loved because they had to, because they lived better when they loved, because love was cooperative and the basis of human society was cooperation. They tried to shut her up by telling her altruism was earthly love, but she had an answer ready for them. She said that God gave altruism, that altruism was God's perfect love. A bird calls to sound the alarm and save the nest; the predator hears the call and kills the crying bird; but the nest escapes and the colony lives on. The bird was the type of Christ on the cross; the colony was His church. Altruism was God's most perfect love. That was it; any fucking with their typology was too much for Puritans to bear; they went after her with a vengeance. Julia said after a period under house arrest in Cambridge she moved along the coastal preaching circuit, not publishing a word, just speaking in her quiet convinced voice, letting her words fall where they may. Travers knew from his family that the Puritans saw words way before they heard them. They saw them coming at them like divisors, and what they hated more than anything else under creation was the cumulant bend of the spoken word away from the word of God. In the sinking curvature of the oral they saw the origin of all things discord and deviate. God for them had no mouth. Their lives were stays against the sibilant first fall of speech. Travers knew how quick they were to fix what they heard cusped and recursive in print. He also knew they were worse than Nazis when it came to keeping records of those they'd banished. If Julia'd finally been kicked out of Massachusetts you can bet your last piaster there'd've been some record of it, some checkmark in some court of record somewhere, but now, a little over three hundred years later, all he had to go by was the spoken word of Julia, the soft fade of her voice telling him at the end before he shot her over into another death (may the earth be light upon you, Julia, you were only a lamina away from peace), telling him in her voice speaking with the sound made blowing out a candle, the Altruists are inside you, let them speak to you, Robert, let them find you and let them speak.

Coming out of the library, Travers knew he'd crossed some kind of line. His eyes were drifting, and the peripheral clarity he'd always felt in the world, the keen edge of sight, was losing its borderline sharpness. The muscles of his eyes were pulling his corneas upward with his lids still open and he was seeing the world in strobe. It was then he saw a headline flickering in a yellow newspaper box chained to a street lamp on Mass Ave. His eyes barely made out the shapes of the letters and his brain didn't really put the words together. The date on the paper was today's, October 27, 1967. A group of antiwar protesters in Washington, D.C., were claiming they'd levitated the Pentagon at exactly 10:53 a.m. Eastern Standard Time. Lifted it up. Uprooted it. Jacked it up and let it down.

The article went on to quote General someone or other who said, "Jack shit. You can't tell the earth to move."

That winter Travers moved out of his family's house off Brattle Street into Div School digs at 14 Divinity Avenue, which was where Navier-Stokes found him five years later laid out on a mattress smelling of fungus and dead rubber, a pile of Christmas wrapping paper next to the bed and Travers folding intersecting lines into the red-and-green holly till it fell apart tesselated and torn. When he first moved in he told himself he wanted to be close to the Bio Labs but he'd known that wasn't it. It was the joint architecture of biology and theology that pulled him there and kept him there. From his room on the second floor he saw the red brick Bio Labs bending in a quadrangle round the Georgian rectangle of the Div School. Between was a muddy courtyard with a volleyball net strung across it. Across, flanking the entrance to the Bio Labs, were those two Dürer rhinos, big bronze armored sentries with horns pointing outward like they'd been there for three hundred years keeping out the Counter-Reformation, waiting to come unsculpted and charge blindly to punch a horn in whatever bit of it happened to come their way, haunch–ready to die for an idea, not just any idea but the only idea worth dying for, the idea he'd seen Julia put to trial for, the Altruist idea: the credo that life is deviant, separation the source of diversity, division the only surety against hard winter, faction the only guard against predator, variation the only stay against extinction. Getting up in the middle of the night to pee, Travers half expected to see Julia riding one of those rhinos like a horse. But he never did. The windows in his room were parabolas that let in a heavy pendant light even on cloudy days, waking Travers on his mattress laid on the floor, the light white in his eyes, the sheet drawn to his chin, waking always with his head lifted a little from the pillow to hear Julia's words annunciate in his ears, "Altruism is God's most perfect love." Sick with sleep he'd set his coffee on its hot plate, the grounds whirling around the fringe of the pot with quick axial torque. Then he passed over to the other side, the Bio Labs side, where he ate a cold lunch and a cold dinner over his books. He took baths in a big stainless-steel sink, always filling the tub too full, so that when he hoisted himself in, a table-cloth of water napped over the edges and onto the floor. The place got wet but he didn't care. He lived in a pit, and after a while his clothes shaled into a heavy damp crust like tent canvas, giving him that smell he still had, the yeasty smell of mildew rising.

It went on like this for years, and for days on end, Travers felt her trying to tell him something in a language he'd learned in childhood but forgotten. He had an old typewriter in his office, a Royal made of black stucco iron. He spent days in there typing across the frozen carriage of centuries. He'd transcribed what she said best he could. She'd talked about the Colony and he knew she meant the Bay Colony. But for him a colony was a group of insects living together, an isolated group living in a new place, and that was what he wrote about. He wrote; published; he began to get famous; got bought off. Harvard promoted him to associate professor late in '71. Travers saw a trailer attached to the letter saying his appointment carried with it a position in the Bureau of Reclamation, GS-5 engineer. He didn't tear it up. He took the letter and hid it under a little box of ice cream in the lab freezer. The Bureau was his prime funder, and after a while his sole funder. Navier-Stokes, the Brit on the phone with the Midlands accent, said just refer all offers to him. He'd double them.

Travers knew he was being kept, but for a long time there was nothing he liked better than being kept. He was still working on hard-core altruism, not insect altruism, human altruism. Why do people kill themselves making worlds they'd never see? Travers'd written some articles on how ants built nests, the scouts submitting proposals by dancing a little administrative dance of report, queen and parliament taking their sweet time deciding, though, always running a few more tests just to make sure, sending out a few dowser ants to tap the ground and compile field data, trends of pressure and drainage and impedance, the decision coming last and almost as a neural afterthought, it being a vote-with-your-feet where the nest ups and moves to its chosen site, digging tunnels, laying summer eggs, building up brood cells and stocking them floor to ceiling with provisions. Travers wrote how up and down the great chain of beings public works always come first; how you can get a society to do almost anything if it thinks its work belongs to the first work, the groundwork, the plebiscite work of a society digging its own nest. Travers went back, read some history, and started to see that altruism was the oldest con in the world when it comes to getting something for nothing. Shitloads more than something. How does getting everything for nothing sound? Twisted logic, but if you want freebie labor, promise the ultimate in high-end benefits, the higher end. Pharaoh needs a house, man. If he doesn't get his house the dam holding back the sky'll break and the stars'll fall and bash your head in. Is that what you want? Way back when this do-or-die altruism almost always fed into some kind of big public-works project, and your first public works were waterworks. Menes, first ruler of united Egypt, laid a dam of stone blocks across the Nile to divert the river and build Memphis on the dry riverbed. Amenemhet III cut the oldest canal in the world, Canal of Joseph, to collect flood runoff in an excavated lake, Lake Moeris, sunk in the marshy Faiyum depression fifty miles outside Cairo. The original Suez Canal was a blank, built by nobody knew who, a channel forty miles long connecting the eastern branch of the Nile delta to the Bitter Lakes, cut wide enough to allow two triremes to be rowed side by side. Old Herodotus said that the Egyptians invented slavery just to dig canals and shadoof the water out of the Nile afterward, and over the phone Navier-Stokes told Travers the Pyramids were part of an unfinished wall of dams. Travers hadn't believed him at first. He told him the Valley of the Dead wasn't anywhere near the Nile and that it wasn't no fucking saltierra either, but from wherever he was calling, the Reclam labs at the Denver Federal Center, the Gulf Coast Hydroscience Center at Bay St. Louis in Mississippi, the Asian Institute of Technology at Bangkok, and, lately, from Reclam R&A Saigon, Navier-Stokes was always ready with answers. He'd said these dams weren't for holding back water. They were for holding back the makers of water.

"But who made the water?" Travers'd asked.

"Same outfit as now," said Navier-Stokes.

3

January 1973. Late in 1972 Navier-Stokes'd sent him a plane ticket, Boston to LA, with a short note saying, Come talk to us. He wasn't in a position to say no. The 707 took five hours to cross the country and for most of the flight Travers sat next to the window with his eyes closed, his mind blank, his hands flat and trembling on the little tray that folded down onto his lap. His eyes opened when the 707 began its long bevel down through the tempered California sky. It cut down over the San Gabriels into the Los Angeles basin, the dirty rug of smog stretching flat to the horizon. The mountains were a long dam, the longest Travers'd ever seen, a reclamation project walling off the Mojave from a dry brown lake of air flooding the basin all the way to the Pacific. Could Reclamation dam the air, too, and send it convected where it willed? Travers didn't know but he knew that Reclam had the rep of not paying overmuch attention to the laws of engineering, especially when dams could be built without them.

With his ticket Navier-Stokes'd sent him that small pocket book of hydraulic tables published by the Bureau's Coefficient Press, unlike any tables he'd ever seen. The intro said a table was nothing more or less than the side of a gem, round and brilliant, bounded by eight star facets. The formulas given had a table-cut exactitude all their own. One called for a nail to be driven through a shale to the spoken command, Return to husk. A gloss said science turned names into numbers and that, to recover the powers originally mixed with earth, the numbers'd have to be turned back into names again. Words were more than labels. Buried below the scattering layer of every word was a real word, a first word, a word that made a telling of the earth, both a count and a command. The real words had been covered with tabular ice. But strip away the labels and you see how shale comes from OE *scealu*, husk. Usually shale's so indurated it won't fall apart on wetting, but when you tell shale to return to husk, *the shale hears you* and the hard detrital surface sheds its fissile membrane as easily as green skin peels off an ear of corn. If this book was the hip flask every Bureau engineer carried around for on-site swigs, shit, what kind of men were these, these grimoires who ruled over all the earth, not the ten or so feet above the surface, that was mammals' play, thin vitric lamination compared to the magic circle of the great globe itself, a circle wound to its core with words.

When the plane was on the ground Travers flagged

down a taxi and found out that the plane'd landed not at LAX but at the Torrance Airport in the lee of the Palos Verdes Hills. "Venice Beach," he'd told the cabdriver, a black guy with an Afro pick stabbed in his falx of hair. Driving north on the 405, they passed rivers that were dry and full of bunch grass. Travers saw big drain outfalls and small flood-control dams. But he also saw bridges missing arches, mud washed up over the doorsills of houses, highway culverts clogged with red brown mud. Travers smiled his sagging truss of a smile, happy to see a bit of America unreclaimed. Right then and there he made up his mind to move to California, but he had no idea when the time would come, or if the Bureau would let it.

"How much do I owe you?" Travers asked the taxi driver, who'd pulled the yellow cab up under a dull pink awning.

"L.A.'s a desert town," returned the driver. "The Bureau rides free."

The Oasis Hotel had dirty stucco walls with little sugar-cube air conditioners butting out all the windows. Travers went in. Five grand stairways twisted down into the delta of the lobby. Travers ran his finger along the brass railing curving around the lobby like a swollen coronary artery. A rococo motif of fountain water dripped down the wallpaper. The domed top of the lobby was blue, not sky-blue, water-blue. It fit right in. To give the Bureau boys something to jiggle their dicks at, a big wave tank had been set up in the lobby, a 300×30×3 foot River Processes Test Basin, complete with sub-exhibits on spillways, sluices, fuse-plug levees, penstocks, diversion works, stilling basins, dredges, cavitation-free baffle piers, floodway structures. Very impressive far as it went, but this was water-palace stuff compared to what was coming. These days Reclamation had a Defense Department feel. Navier-

Stokes had already let him in on the open secret that the war'd diverted most BR jism into pontoon design and pneumatic floats, breakwaters at naval air stations, harbor piling, and get this, *prefab dams built in dry-dock!* Wha . . . You could see the engineers jittering with ambition and the free black speed the Bureau was troweling out in Baggies to pick up the pace of thought. So the Bureau was out of its Dead Sea logjam. It made no sense to Travers. All those major dam fuckups, so many he'd lost count, Travers knew about them, everyone did, those big unbuilt river pyramids, a strike-anywhere scandal of California politics what with two in the Klamath quadrant alone and theories and speculation mounting, public interest flaming in all directions and every month or so a new dam on failure's brink. Old belly-scarred L.B.J. said the thing was an act of God and maybe it was because, look, the wave men and the river men in the Bureau never got along and now they were all working together on something so big that it was like God, you didn't dare say the name.

Going into the Oasis lobby, Travers kept an eye out for Dominy and his right-hand man, that fat Indian Petard. Navier-Stokes said don't even look at him, his eyes suck the life out of you and spit it back in your eyes through the spitoon gap between his yellow teeth. Dominy was his slave and there were rumors about Petard and the Valley of the Dead, which was what the *L.A. Times*'d taken to calling that string of unfinished dams up on the Klamath. Every spring there were these hauntings, not skeleton & scythe stuff but mangy honky-tonk haunts with big Petard in a rough sweater, his long black hair blowing out straight behind him like a pirate flag, steering an old dented rowboat right toward the high-tower abutments of Yokut, Ah Pah, Tehama like he thought they were spreads of soft reeds. You didn't need a slide rule to figure that the outflow discharged at the bottom of those dams was enough to snap a coal barge. Yet when Petard went out at night, trolling slowly with his good arm stretched back steering the outboard, the Evinrude popping out deep bass notes like a river Harley, he didn't go round the dams. Shit no he passed right through them, right through the great deep keyways to come out motionless and unbroken on the other side, the cold side, the reservoir side. River rive: he said the word and somehow the word was enough and the concrete just fell back to let him through, no ra ra, no ceremony, just the restored uninterrupted drift of the Klamath and the sound of Petard's outboard not breathing too well, chuffing along. His left arm was numb, useless from some accident in '57, but mister that right arm of his could sink a shaft into the silence of death and Navier-Stokes was trying to keep him a dowser's distance from the new DOD projects. On his way in, Travers thought he'd seen him out by the curb mailing a letter, eyeing the blue box with hatred of everything federal, then shoving it in, in it went then shit he shook the mailbox till the iron plates holding it to the concrete ground cracked loose man alive he was plating it open with the weight of his rage, crushing the federated earth like he was anointed of God . . .

"You said it was a mailbox?" Navier-Stokes'd asked him on the convention floor a few minutes before proceedings were due to begin. Delegates with pink-and-blue litmus badges moved this way and that across the floor. The temperature was dropping and the few women he saw were wearing fur coats.

"Yes. A mailbox."

"A *blue* mailbox."

"Yes, blue."

"Sorry. Where I come from, mailboxes are red. I wasn't sure. But I've been watching him for a long time, since Ah Pah in '57. Everyone wonders about him but it may be he's really nothing more than a dowser. Britain is over-run with them digging around. I come from a village called West Kennett, north of Beckhampton. There was an old woman there who could find water by shaking a stick at the ground."

"What did the stick look like?"

"I don't know. Just some piece of wood probably, but she never let anyone see it up close. Emma Boothby was a recluse. On rainy days when nobody else went out I often saw her scrambling over long barrows, burial mounds located at places where there is a peculiar complexity of underground streams. Emma once told me that a mound near Overton Hill was crossed by four converging streams at a depth of 433 feet. A peculiar person. Our Petard must be like this, his mind half underground, witnessing the earth. This blue mailbox: I think every little thing he sees aboveground has some kind of analogue under the earth where he plants his feet. The red he sees is sympathetic to iron, green to copper, orange to gold, violet to silver and pure water, gray to lead and foul water, black to coal and sewage, white to voids and chasms. Blue means electricity and tainted water. There must be an old electrical main under that mailbox. An old foul disused main from long before this place was a hotel—"

"So you think there's something to it," said Travers.

"There's something to everything," said Navier-Stokes as he got up out of his seat and walked to the podium to blurb the first speaker.

The first speaker was Dominy, an incontinent old fud who told some frontier stories so bad they must have come from a spaghetti Western. Travers paid no attention to him and neither did anybody else. Next was an old contractor from Bechtel who'd built coquina roadbeds under highways in Cuba back in 1929 using mestizos siphoned off the sugarcane lots plus leftover Jamaicans who'd dug the Panama Canal. Then came an AT&SF rep who talked about railway beds, said they're there and why not use them, nice ready-made bench terraces, embankments slooping across fields complete with varnished copal ties and steep compact drops on both sides. Then came a lady from the Argonne National Laboratory who said tree roots held together the Dutch dikes, said the Bureau could dike up the Delta real good with little baby Xmas trees C-5A'd in from Minnesota. Then a fat guy in a white Panama suit and a yellow straw hat who talked about what everyone called berm perm, the problem of berm permeability, and the way he joked about it you'd have thought the soil profile was a Freudian slip in the ground. Then a physiologist from the UCLA Fatigue Laboratory who got up, hung a few charts on a tripod, and rattled off stats about heat prostration, and said the Bureau ought to salt the shit the gooks ate and make them drink more water with their IR8 miracle rice. When he dangled a little white plunger for forcing water down throats, the men in the hall laughed, the uncorked future sizzling aghast in their old dry throats like air bubbles in seltzer water.

From his seat down front Travers saw what they were all getting at. Labor problems. Long Dam wasn't going to be just one dam. Long Dam was a TVA of different dams, something for every riparian lecher in the Bureau. The headache was getting someone to build them all when twenty thousand grunts a month were taking freedom birds home. The dotted line that was Long Dam stretched across 262 miles of Mekong Delta turf, most of it technically Republic of South Vietnam, but it didn't take much brains to see that the Delta was already VC property. A dam 262 miles long? He eyed the wood-and-plaster model wheeled into the hall on a steel hospital cart. He couldn't figure it. It made the dam look like marl, looseshit soil good for nothing but crumble the second it hits the air. The fucking gooks called their nation *da nuoc*, earth and water. How on earth was this lame grouty old rice paddy of a dam supposed to hold back a nation's worth of delta water?

Travers was next. His was the paper everyone was waiting for. He mounted the flatbed truck of a podium. You could feel sphincters tightening all across the floor as he took the twenty or so blue typewritten pages out of their manila folder and laid them flat in front of him on the podium. Travers knew that his audience was full of geologists, that they knew less than zero about ant cant, that he'd have to pitch it to them in lingo they understood. So he slid the slurry carbon back in its manila sheaf and started talking, saying whatever came into his head, first things first.

"Your basic gook," he began, "is an insect."

The old men laughed, their throats jiggled and the change in their pockets rattled. Travers waited till the last snorts spent themselves and then he said:

"Not just any insect. A specific insect."

That had them. A hush fell. Somewhere a rheostat dimmed the light on everyone but him. Travers then, the Travers of January 1973, went on to give that speech in the half dark. Back with him, I saw the crowd waiting for him to speak, their faces stretched taut like clear vinyl pulled across skin. In the plastic silence I waited, too. But Travers, Travers now, was losing the thread of it.

"Don't let go," I said.

"It's not all there," he said. "Part's gone."

"Part of the speech?"

"Part of the room."

"Missing?" I asked.

"Emptied," he said.

This is what he remembered: the room emptying out

as he spoke. He thought it was a bad sign, but he felt zero impedance opposing the current of his thought. The longer he spoke, the more people, mostly engineers, low-ranking GS-5s and 6s, were ushered out, forced out the rear by plainclothesmen, past the trays of convention food, past the right triangles of orange cheese and the perfect squares of mottled meat, past the dull green sofas and gold-flecked Leatherette chairs and fluffy tutu drapes. In that padded auditorium he was saying something that wasn't meant to be said, and if said, then not meant to be heard by just anyone. His words were for the box seats only. The lights kept dimming. In a couple minutes only a narrow band of top Bureau operatives were left congregate in civil twilight, the two hundred empty tables behind them flickering with votive candles. Navier-Stokes'd called them the hanging judges because these were the ones who'd dropped dams down the steep gallows of America's hanging valleys. In the nightclub dark they looked like fat bald swollen old infants with glasses on. Travers never forgot the blotchy red sheen of their faces, but the speech, the speech he gave, was not where it should have been in his memory. He said he remembered not the speech he gave but the speech they'd heard him give. The two were not the same. He remembered what they'd taken away from what he'd said. He remembered that their listening was like a ransacking, a curtain rip in the crushed interior of what he'd said. They heard something in it he hadn't meant for them to hear. Them hearing it turned it upside down and it became something else, something he hadn't counted on, something he couldn't've foreseen, something he hated.

"All in one speech?" I said.

"It wasn't the speech. I told them we were losing the war. What they heard, what they did with what they heard, was more important."

"What was that?"

"That we could end it."

"The war?"

"More than the war."

This, he thought, is what they must've remembered hearing: We're losing the war, said the hotshot Harvard professor just turned twenty-nine, losing it bad to a bunch of insects. Ants, ants everywhere, ants pressed between the walls of the war effort. The gooks are swarming all over the landscape following odor trails our eyes can't see. Most of them are wingless, ragged, and blind. Looking down at the Ho Chi Minh Trail from the air, our choppers can see them moving in chains along the edges of hills, tapping their antennas along the steep trails like blind men feeling the edges of tables. Spray them with every pesticide in the book, spray away, for all the good it'll do. Sugar water doesn't throw them off. The tips of their stings are pens inking a thin line over the ground in invisible pheromone ink. They go by scent and move in the dark through vapor tunnels that evaporate before we can get a fix on them. They carry a hundred times their weight. Life for them is a bivouac on a death march. You've seen the overflight photos. The ant columns of the NVA are moving south, clamping their mandibles round the hind legs of the ARVN ants. Pull up the tarmac and this country is one big nest of invading ants.

"And they went for this crock of shit?"

Travers almost bit his lip in two. His head flinched and his eyes recovered some of their old focal clarity. He was pissed, his dirty mouth trembling with fuck this and fuck that, saying, "Think this's some fucking metaphor? Some fucking ant fable? Think again. Why do we call gooks blue ants? Why do we call ourselves wasps? It's not fucking metaphor but the way things fucking are."

In the lumen strength of anger Travers was calling up

more of it now, hearing more of what they'd heard, seeing it come out of the clouds through the general novocaine haze of his memory. He still had no idea what he'd said but he was coming clearer and clearer about what the top ops in the Bureau'd heard. At Harvard, they'd heard him say, right there smack on Divinity Avenue where Leary went bleary, We're finding social forms no one knew existed. These forms are beyond existing political sociology. We're talking something much deeper in the entrails of man than the intestine tunnels of human institutions. We're talking about instinctual social forms, *biological* sociology. It's going to be called sociobiology and this is what it means: we can wage sociobiological warfare. Forget what you've heard about biological warfare, sending a few measly strep viruses over to wipe the Delta clean. Why kill them all when we can get them working for us? We can wage sociobiological warfare against them, building their societies as service societies annexed to our own. Sociobiological war isn't adversarial war, it's cooperative war. The perfect war's an uneasy truce between like and like, an ant war where the war survives intestate no matter how many ants die. Under Diem, Vietnam was ants versus ants. Looking down at the nest of Nam in August '62 you'd see a red ant pulling at a black one with a hind leg clamped in his mandibles. Looks uneven to us but it's not. The red ant stings and the black ant sounds the alarm. Problem is, though, we heard the alarm and came and then it wasn't ants versus ants anymore. Americans aren't ants but high solitary wasps. Ever seen a flanking column of wasps? Your solitary wasp can do almost anything, mate, build a nest, dance the waggle, nab prey, sting and paralyze it, lay an egg on it, and seal the nest. Lone insects like wasps've worked out a high-tech battery of chemical and mechanical defenses. Wasp honeycombs are small and elaborate—too small and too elaborate, like our fire bases at Khe Sanh and Song Ny. A wasp can always napalm a few ants with venom shot out through the sting end. But a wasp can't fight all ants at once. Zap one ant and there're still fifty million left in the colony. Zap a colony and there're still fifty million colonies left sending out sappers for fifty million Tets. Not even a colony of ants can defeat a colony of ants. Only extinction brings defeat, and there's no force strong enough to bring extinction on a species. A species can only bring absolute death on itself.

Travers now told me, "You can't get ants to do shit unless all of them, every last one, winged or wingless, thinks, feels, knows, it's in the interest of the whole colony to do it. But if you can get them to think that, then *they all do it*. And being ants, they can't do anything else but the one thing they do because they can only do one thing at a time. It's the way they are. Ants are nature's CBs, insect construction battalions, doing everything in parallel not series, concurrently not sequentially. Every move a colony makes is systemic. If one ant fucks up, you can bet another'll make good."

I was beginning to get the idea, and I knew if I was getting it, the old boys in the Bureau'd gotten it better and faster. In the Grand Ballroom of the Oasis Hotel they'd contemplated the trays of shrimp swimming in small inland seas of cocktail sauce. Ice cubes melted in glasses with no water poured in them yet. In every mind every table became a Delta map, the meatballs were mounds, the hams were hills, the goulash was swamp, the salad was rain forest, the gravy was brown water in reservoirs of mashed potatoes. The crease in the white tablecloth was the outline of a diverted river. They were all thinking in streams alongside Travers, keeping up with him as he Huck Finned along, carried by the current of his own thought, following it with nothing particular in mind, just heading toward the next bend in the river.

Travers was all worked up now, talking up above his usual middle octave, breaking for a bit into his tonsular falsetto, toed up high and ventral behind the podium for extra stature, shifting his weight from foot to foot like a mime walking in place, so excited by what he was saying he spilled half his water over himself trying to take a drink. He'd stopped giving them his ants-are-a-Confucian-society rap. Now they heard him say something offhand, something Travers just came on, but it ended the evening right then and there and made the Bureau see the future burning long and yellow in Travers's filament eyes. The future: Reclam'd almost forgotten that the future was anything other than a pipe dream full of the perfect liquid the chem-lab boys said they'd come up with one day to replace water. He was piped into a different future. They heard Travers tell them to put the past to bed in its bed of dark rock. The Bureau was the turbine behind America but it could be the turbine behind the world if it re-oriented itself in a revolving searchlight swing from zero to 180. The cupola on top of the Bureau's LeConte Building in Denver could become the third canopy over the rain forest's two. Tired of scale models? Sick of the loose grainy small change that passes through the 65-mesh sieve of the House Appropriations Committee? You can do whatever the fuck you want without Potomac cash and piss smoking into the cold federal wind and tell Interior to go shit Tootsie Rolls. So what, let Nixon put on some flat alkali pancake makeup and veto the dam appropriation. It won't mean shit because we can do it all, because we know what infiltration means. It means water moving into rock and soil through joint and pore, it means an upwelling current where a wind blows out to sea and away from here, it means doing it all without the sidle suck of bureaucrats and their soft-water hands, doing it all without federal tollbooth approval because we'll be

doing their will without them, without any of them, by
acting with the will to act that they've lost and preserve
only as intention . . .

Aggregate in Los Angeles the Bureau of Reclamation
saw Travers pause, take a deep breath, reach for his water
glass but think the better of it. There were rill marks in
his face like he'd lost the clear flow of his thought. Had
he reached the final breaking point they'd massed for, only
to drain seaward back into himself? For a sec, turning up
his lip against the vent of his nose, he looked ready to
stop. Then with an opposing reflex the words came rolling back over the parapet, rolling over the low wall of his
mouth, opening into the auditorium, the Reclam men
lapping up every word, hearing and remembering. I don't
know why I know this, they heard him say, but I know
that they want to build it as bad as we do, maybe even
worse. Long Dam is the future the Vietnamese want for
themselves. They'll think we're crazy to give it to them
but once they see we're serious they'll help us build it.
Give them a taste of that good old American tit-for-tat
altruism. Send them a beacon flash from the Great Society
and see if they flash back. Call off the ground war, send
the Navy back to Pearl, turn the war over to Interior, use
the Bureau by land and the Coast Guard by sea. It doesn't
take many of them to work with us but we need only a
few. The pyramids were built by slaves who hated being
slaves but it didn't matter because it took generations to
build one. No way we have that kind of time. We have
to compress a couple centuries of slavery into a little under
eleven months. We're not talking forced labor. We're
talking elective slavery. Long Dam has to be built by slaves
who want to be slaves. I don't know how this'll happen
because the cooperation will evolve, but when it does, it
will surprise us. The dam we want to build will go to
hell. But the dam they build for us will store up water

like grace in heaven. They'll build our dam better than we could've ourselves, and whatever they do, they'll do it with determination, the big grim D we haven't seen in America for three hundred years. I tell you, you wouldn't be here now unless Long Dam was already waiting in heaven to fall built on earth . . .

When Travers finished, the silence in the hall was electric. Really electric, he thought, not diode electric with the current of thought passing one way from him to them, not flowing one way through wires like water through pipes, but shooting both directions at once in a freeway of force. For a quiet moment the liquid-tight eyes in the room sparkled like headlights with one thought, this thought: *They want the dam.* There was no applause, no cross talk between tables, but that was all right, he didn't expect any. But he hadn't expected this amplitude of fear. The old men looked dazed. From the podium he watched the flabby pink faces in the hall blanch. They were scared, no not for themselves, not for their country, not at what they were about to do, but at the terrible prescience of the one man who saw the roll of white butcher's paper laid out so straight down the bloody carpeted aisle of the future. Pretty flat in the summary, but in that hall you could see the old farts taking off their bifocals and squinting blindly at the coaxial clarity of the future unwinding before them. So this was the tape of the speech Travers had forgotten. There was more, there was magnetic signal on the flip side, too, but this at least was some of it. It was the most famous thing he'd ever written and, shit, he'd never written it down and never remembered it, not till now.

"Any questions?" he remembered blowing into the mike.

After the speech at R&A that night, Travers and Navier-Stokes drove off in a federal limo, a Cadillac with lots of doors, and spent a few hours at a hamburger stand on La Cienega Boulevard. The limo idled outside while they sat sucking the grease out of crinkled french fries under a buzzing red neon sign. It was an L.A. winter night, wet and dry at the same time, the trees lashing around in the wind, big Altec speakers hung upside down blaring out country rock to the four corners of the room. Travers screwed the top off the shaker to dump extra salt on his fries, while Navier-Stokes, that thin bitten lip of a Brit, dumped vinegar on his. Navier-Stokes wanted to talk about the dam but Travers was sullen and turned his face up to look at the television images snapping by. Over in Pasadena the Dolphins and the Redskins were playing in the Super Bowl. Travers heard grunts, ref calls, the clatter of hard plastic against plastic. Then the picture cut to a parade dirging down Pennsylvania Avenue in Washington, where Nixon was swearing himself back into office on wooden bleachers outside the east front of the Capitol. The inauguration branded the date hissing into his mind, January 20, 1973, but mostly Travers remembered drinking some gin he carried around with him in a mason jar and not touching his red hot dog in yellow onion grease.

"What a shit-train," said Travers, drawing some gin. "It's never-ending."

Navier-Stokes held off, making a pause. "It will all be over soon enough."

"Like hell it will."

"The war will end on November 29, 1973."

Travers's eyes shot open to zero darkness with the fucking exactitude of it all. Ten years, he thought, almost exactly ten years of war. Navier-Stokes handed him an 8×10 glossy of Long Dam in the early stages of construction. Not a deep hole of a dam—a shallow trench.

"This some secret plan I don't know about?"

"You already know all there is to know."

"Then how come I don't know I know?"

"Because," said Navier-Stokes, "you thought of it."

"Thought of what?"

"Sociobiological warfare."

"I thought of it to amuse myself, not to end the war."

"To end the war? If by the end of the war you mean us winning and them losing, no. They will win and we will lose. That has been clear since Tet. This project is intended to bring about an ending."

"The end of spring flooding?"

"No. A different kind of end."

"The end of what?"

"The end of Vietnam."

Navier-Stokes started to explain but Travers leapt so far ahead of him that the voice he heard explaining Long Dam to him was his own. In the collapsing space of a second he saw the lines extending into their alignment and rejoinder: the weapon of American innocence exported abroad. Lay on, Billy Budd. Send our reps over like it's babes in soyland. Give the gooks some small is beautiful, a little harmless low tech to rebuild their country with. Ferry over the Bureau to reclaim the land. Win the war after it's over, just like Marshall did. And do it as an irrigation project. Dig and level, always the excuse for your western dams. Now, how many of your gooks know about slopes and slants? Not many I betcha. Gotta keep them chinks away from the dam, though. It's got to hold for six days before we rest easy. Long enough to drain the paddies and snuff the crop. The famine'll have to be finessed but hell it shouldn't be a prob. Turn the ARVN into a *guardia civil*. They'll hoard supplies for the black market they'll assume'll develop but won't. But by the time they figure it out there'll be nobody left in the country to figure anything else out ever again. When the water drops go into panic mode, declare defeat and Dunkirk out. Withdraw, blockade, lament a little, then sit back and take it all in. Minimum 24 million dead in under four months. Only 34 million in the Delta anyway; that's fifty-six percent. By April of 1974 the count could top 33 million. Ninety-seven percent. Better than ICBMs wiping out the Ukraine. The greatest grim reap of all time.

"We're not talking about victory," said Navier-Stokes at last. "We're talking about revenge."

"I can understand wanting revenge," said Travers, "but you can't make me plan it for you."

"Plan it for us? You've already planned it for yourself. Before the war even started you had already thought of how it must end. Those articles in *The Biologist*. Your ideas on the sociobiology of insect societies. I don't know how you got them. If I weren't such a skeptic I'd say that some voice planted them in your ear for us to hear."

"I'm not your instrument," said Travers after a pause of he did not know how long. He tried to take another swig from the jar but he saw his left arm shaking and his right arm holding it down and Navier-Stokes looking at him funny and distant.

"You are your own instrument," Navier-Stokes was saying. "The Bureau simply recognized your plan for what it was. You see, dams have always had—other purposes."

Before Navier-Stokes could explain anything Travers had already bypassed him again and leaped those eleven months ahead. He saw beyond what Navier-Stokes saw to what he did not want to see and could not understand. Long Dam would fail. It would be built because it could be built, it would be built the way they wanted to build it because it was possible, just barely possible, to build it that way, and it would fail because it had to fail. The idea, it hit him the way ideas always hit Travers, in hard levered impact like his forehead was being split in two by a mallet-driven wedge. He scrunched his eyes as the black-and-white circles of a concussion widened and dispersed in zebra waves across his field of vision. Circles pounded inside circles until it came clear to him what he saw. Long Dam would be a Vietnamese dam. It had to be that way. They'd build it and we'd lose it. He'd recovered enough from the blow to see Navier-Stokes watching him. He saw three of him, then two of him, and when he saw one of him he knew that Navier-Stokes did not know what he knew. He did not know it was the Great Wall of China all over again, a wall built against invaders, except here the invaders were the ones building the wall to kick ourselves out. Navier-Stokes thought that what had hit Travers was one hit too many of gin. But what he'd got was one hit too many of the future.

4

Back in the lab at Weed, Travers was waiting for the next light flash of memory to hit him. He wanted more, but the more he wanted more, the less there was of it. During the dark interval between flashes he felt the grain of the past fading against a silver background fog. He knew he was back in the lab. His memory was failing him again and he felt himself trapped between the sheets of the present. Later, when I came out of it too, he told me what it'd been like for him to find Julia, to find his way into the mind of Reclam R&A and find his way out again. Travers told me there were two sheets defining time, one stretched out in front of us, one in back. Two white sheets. The sheets moved with us whatever direction we moved, usually forward. But when you slide back in time, he said, the sheets slide back with you. Even in the past those sheets are there, cutting you off from the past's past and the past's future. You get to see what happened, but only so long as you forget that you once belonged to some other present. To go back into the past, to really go back, for the past to be more than a spectacle to you, the past has to be your actual present. The second you think, Hold on, I'm remembering, don't I belong to some other present, you lose the presence of the past and before you know it, you're back where you started from.

"Except that you're a little further along," I told him.

"Depends," Travers said. "The sheets are like curtains, dividers. They mark off the limits of the present in the past and the limits of the present in the future. The present isn't really stationary. It doesn't have a fixed duration, so it lasts a lot longer than you think. It's not just the chip of a second. Those sheets can be close together or far apart. The present can be short or long, short as the skip of a heart, long as the time of a life. When I lost Julia my life became lost in a long present and I was trapped. Those twin white sheets walling off the present ought to be thin loose transparent gauze blowing in the wind. They should let in other time. But mine became opaque. I couldn't see anything. The lines of time took on blurred edges and space lost definition. The best I could do was watch the past and the future tracing out shadows across the twin sheets. If you think the past and the future can be vague, give the present a try. The past and the future have nice hard sharp lines because that shit's happened already. Only the present, which hasn't happened yet, is slack."

"So you were trapped in a short present," I said.

"The present is always short," said Travers, "even when it's long. At some point, when you come up against the limits of the present, you figure out, like I did, that time is a perfectly designed prison."

"That you got out of."

"That nobody can get out of."

Not even the dead can escape the morgue sheets of time, Travers went on to say, but then, in that lab at Weed, the Toad'd released Travers but still had a hold on me. Travers was right about the sheets. I felt the isolate whiteness of the present, the colors shifting under the cream of all colors combined. I thought I was back in the present but then I saw some images shifting behind the gelatin white in low solvent folds. A curve in the sheet rippled and broke. Another scene was slowly unbleaching in my mind. An exposure was appearing, the outlines defining themselves more and more sharply against the glare of the present. For a sec the lines looked like broken sticks and rotted leaves frozen under a winter blanket of snow. Then I saw blue, a whitewashed blue sky overexposed above and cloudy below. Then I saw Travers. He flew in the sky. He wore a tan suede collarless jacket and fogged plate sunglasses. A basso voice spoke next to him but not to Travers, though. "Digger One I'm breaking off to the left." Petard, Petard's voice. "Roger, Digger Two," said Digger One, my brother's voice. Travers and Petard were sitting side by side in the cockpit of a Bell UH-1 Huey. Below was the putty of the Delta. I was watching them, but alone this time. I was back in Travers's past, the past he'd dropped out of because he'd forgotten it. Without Travers the light around me had hard sharp sure edges. The high fog level through which I'd seen the convention was gone. I wasn't seeing the past etched negative on Travers's eyes. I was seeing a different order of past, a past internal to the past, its internal image. No memory'd dyed it maximum black. I was in some kind of place beyond the reversals of memory where I was seeing what Travers'd seen more clearly than he'd ever been able to. The Toad had taken me out of Travers's black-and-white memory into the cyan yellow of the Mekong River Delta.

The sun wasn't more than six degrees above the horizon, the sky a pale orange. When Travers closed his eyes he still saw the red cockpit lights. The ship'd slowed to 90 knots, normal cruise, and the VSI was showing a slight climb. The altimeter read 4,000 feet. The blades snapped the air and the nose of the mule tilted a slight jut forward. Travers felt a slight down-pull and remembered they'd strapped a fiberglass seg of prefab dam to the belly hook. The pallet of dam swung below them like a weight at the bottom of a pendulum, and Petard kept both hands steady on the grip, correcting for drift. Petard wore a black cotton T-shirt, tan shorts, no shoes. Some stanched blood had bled through a bandage on his shoulder. He smelled like wet-tent mildew. His thumbnails were smashed black. He didn't look like any official Cav pilot Travers'd ever seen, the esophagal cord from his flight helmet dangling severed behind him, his flak vest unzipped, a Beretta holstered to his chest in a sling, no wire sunglasses bridging his nose, brown eyes shaded by crushed brown skin, but then again, like everyone else in the Bureau, he wasn't officially anything because, to keep up deniability, the Bureau wasn't officially in Vietnam.

Travers opened his eyes, sipped some coffee from a thermos, and pressed his thighs tight against the clacker that'd fire the gas they were carrying in the aft cabin. No side gunners rode with them anymore. A few spools of concertina-fence wire lay coiled around the empty gun posts. Travers felt vulnerable without the door guns but Petard said they were safer without them. First time Petard'd flown unarmed he said it'd been a Swiss cheese run and he'd barely made it back to Binh Thuy, the femur tail of the mule broken and leaking gas. That'd been February. It was now late September. These days the air corridor between Can Tho and Cao Lanh was called poodle shave. The gooks were only shooting at gun bristle, which was an OK start. The week before, Travers'd said as much in a briefing over at Reclam's Long Binh Cavitation Center, formerly the Sandbag Hilton, windows covered by grenade screens, nice roof-garden cocktail lounge up top, fleet of white Mavericks parked out front, the one with Reclam's logo, sheet of a dam, set in a big coin of raised white intaglio. Since he'd landed at Tan Son Nhut in Saigon on the fifteenth, Travers'd wanted to take that coin down, flip it, and see if it broke on the ground. With the Bureau always designing designs inside designs, you never knew. If he threw it up in the air it might bend like a pizza. But maybe not. Travers'd always loved maybe-nots, the infirmities of chance. When Navier-Stokes'd asked him about the odds of Long Dam succeeding he'd rolled three clear red Lucite dice across the big teak conference table in Denver, calling the toss, saying, "Five, one, two," but then, get this, Navier-Stokes writing the numbers right down on top of each other, 5, 1, 2, then adding them up, $5+1+2=8$, then biting his bit Brit lips at the 8 like Travers was an augur who'd just given him the birth number of the dam and 8 was the tenacious wayward cipher of the thing itself. Maybe it was. Travers made up all the data he gave them, hashed it up into his own personal Hebrew, but when he did they took out black mechanical pencils and wrote it all fucking down like they were adding all his figures together and repeating the process until they reached a single determining number. Did Navier-Stokes know about Julia's voice? About her telling him that truth was always in deviation from the covenant wind of the norm? No, he was not one to hear voices in the wind. In the guessing wind of chance Navier-Stokes saw only the abscissa and ordinate of determination. He knew Travers made everything up and had wanted to keep him safe in the Bureau's Los Alamos outside Denver, but the old butt-falls in the Bureau wanted zero deviation from the future they'd seen in

Travers's eyes back in L.A. and so they'd sent him out into the great quadrat of Vietnam.

Travers was too valuable to leave to unappeased chance, so natch Navier-Stokes'd arranged to have him paired with Petard, that Crazy Horse no bullet could kill, for a little firsthand riverine recon. R&A'd said the first phase of Operation Reciprocal Altruism was pretty much of a success, but not a complete success, because it was hard to tell who'd decided what when the Travers idea was to let the truce evolve. Navier-Stokes told him to try and find out what Petard was up to. The Mekong had eight reaches, driving water from the gorges north of Vientiane, passing through the broad flat valley of Savannakhet, turning through the high drops and forested islands of Sandbor, opening into the four arms of Phnom Penh, and extending into the sea via the six distributaries of the shallow Delta. The river's reach exceeded the Bureau's grasp but not Petard's. The man was a cantilever who didn't need Bureau support to extend operations. He did things in dream time, and now all eight reaches were fine cracks in the dream surface that Petard called the crazing of the Delta. The upper Mekong was a wild river and upriver were Montagnards, indigenes who said the river was a sleeping giant and who were now, far as Reclam knew, running a clandestine generator at Khone Falls in Laos just north of the Cambodian border. Not one bridge'd ever crossed the lower Mekong but god there were rumors of bridges being built everywhere, nothing concrete yet but recon photos showed groins of landfill, check and jetty and base, extending into the water from a hundred cofferdams strung along the basin. Travers'd been there a week waiting for a break in the monsoon rains before Petard'd said fuck it, the wet won't break till November, and took him up anyway, telling him, as he took the mule down round the cloud table, that if I can fly in it you can too, you have to take your chances same as anyone, chance is a personal god and you never know till you break cloud cover whether the little roulette bullet'll take that chance fall into the empty chamber of a muzzle pointed your way.

"We're heading for the sea now," said Petard. "The clouds end there."

"Then what?" asked Travers.

"Down to the Delta."

Petard began a turn to the left to U down around under the table's end of clouds. He picked up speed fast as he put the Huey into a near-90-degree bank. Two Gs pressed Travers buckwheat flat into his seat, him watching Petard, thinking, shit what a crazy drunk Injun, but then he remembered that Petard'd stopped boozing, that the war was booze to him now, that he could land a mule on a balance beam if he had to. He felt his ears pop and watched Petard smile his slow earthworm smile, the tunic of his lips turning out then opening up to show the wet red fold inside. When at last the Huey broke cloud cover they saw the Mekong Delta all at once. The Delta was not like a valley, not even close. No fist of ridge broke the vast alluvial tract of land at the mouth of the river. The bending river had the even stagnant sheen of a swamp, the wide cursive scroll of a floodplain. It seemed strange to Travers that anyone'd go build a dam in a swamp when the swamp was already a sort of dam. From the air the Mekong Delta was a thin sheet of puddles separated by low fissures of clay. The water in the rice paddies caught the yellow tropical light and gave off a dull fungal glare. It reminded him of wet pavement after a rainstorm, a film of surface water balanced evenly over a flat surface. "The earth wants to be flat," Petard'd told him, saying how gravity forces water downward through land to sea, carrying a crust of land with it as waterborne silt and sediment and bed-load. The earth's one big erosion crap, wearing itself down to an overall flatness, hills and mountains sliding through the intestinal sluices of rivers down to the oceans, filling them up with sewage of land. He said the Bureau was just doing its bit to speed up the future, greasing the gradual skid of the inevitable, the day when all the land'd slide into the sea in a slow landslide, not quite filling it, though, so that one day, not too many million years in the future, the final surface of the earth'd lie settled a few feet underwater in fine colloidal clay.

"Fucking gooks oughta thank us," said Petard over the beating of the rotor, "for showing them how the world'll end."

But to Travers the Delta looked uninhabited from the air, like the world'd already ended here, so he asked Petard, "Anybody live here?"

"Half the country."

"Then how come I can't see them?"

"Like you say," said Petard, "they're insects."

Travers felt his stomach tighten. He was sorry he'd ever let out that line. He didn't know shit about politics. He knew about arthropods, enough to know that the gooks weren't actually insects. They lived in a land that'd never produced a Hobbes, a society in which dominance and subordination were not imposed from the top down but'd evolved from the bottom up. Things got done because people sensed a larger design working itself out among them. Call it what you want, call it sharing, altruism, communism, trophallaxis, whatever, call it a covenant that's only halfway there, it's all the same behavioral biology at work. Work now because the present is a void and the past is a mass grave. Time is later, not now. When they see that we are part of an unfolding design, a turn in the great page curl in their patient book of changes, they will do us no harm. They will wait for us. Least that's what he'd said in L.A. Now Travers was afraid that America'd go gonzo waiting out our part of the wait, waiting out the terrible dripping interval between now and then. For Americans time was water torture. Every drop was a long loud forehead bang that said, *Wait you sucker, the payoff is later, the payoff is near, the payoff is coming, wait for it, just you fucking wait.* America'd always been a country couldn't sit still in its seat without squirming its ass in the hiatal void between nomination and election, U.S. elections being what they were, all part of one big election, not one every four years but one each at the beginning and end of time. What do the elect do to fill time till the end? They hurry up to get there before anyone else does, and sure nuff, when Nixon was President but also President-Elect he'd sent word, in his flush of double election, to hurry the fuck up. Just hurry up, dam the Delta and close the gates on November 29, 1973. Travers knew that wasn't enough time, but he also knew that nothing he said now'd abate the compressive force of what he said eight months ago.

He also knew never to underestimate the Bureau. Look at Petard: Petard'd told him he slept less than an hour a day and that he was pushing the zero barrier of sleep, that it'd come to him there were hours on the other side of the twenty-four that could be used to build the dam if only he could figure out how to get at them. At a few minutes of sleep per day he'd felt near collapse and needed to pop Dex tabs to keep going, but at zero sleep he'd found that what was near collapse was the scaffold of time separating the contiguous twenty-four from a circumparallel twenty-four. Looking over the day's edge he said you saw the day had sides, walls, faces. Round the day was a fixed derrick braced and guyed from the other side to keep time stable. He knew there was more time to time

than what he'd been told in the spec sheets and he was
determined to reeve in those extra hours and use up every
last measure of moment, linear, liquid, cubic, dry, to build
this dam. Travers didn't know if he could do it, but if he
could, if Petard learned how to turn spirals inside a day,
why then the Bureau could go slow and fast at the same
time, and Long Dam would come into being accelerating
along the raceway turns of the tipped 8 of infinity, with
November 29, 1973, arriving on schedule, eight weeks
but also eight generations away.

"Digger Two, you in position yet?"

"Almost," Petard told Digger One.

Petard settled the Huey into a hundred-foot hover directly over what he'd said was a nick between two dikes.
The hover was motionless like zero buoyancy and a lot
of time seemed to pass in a few adrenal moments. Travers
leaned out the door, and over the whip crack of the rotors
he heard Petard's voice asking him, See anything? A foam
of haze covered the ground. A line of high trees broke
the white to the north. The sun fell burning to the west.
Travers turned up the visor knob on his flight helmet and
checked the haze for thin spots, but no go, so Petard eased
the belly of the Huey down a little into the top layer of
fog so they could get a closer look. Still nothing. When
Travers pulled himself back inside the mule his eyes darted
over to see what Petard was doing. A few tracers of rain'd
come out of the sky, hitting him through the open door
on the pilot side. Petard wasn't ignoring the rain. No,
he'd closed his eyes, tilting his head back to let the raindrops hit his face in full random scatter. The sweat'd dried
in his hair but the rain ran down his face in tears. The
rain, thought Travers, watching the monsoon clouds
gather on the red horizon, the rain, he's listening to the
rain, exposing himself to the pain of the air, waiting for
the right drop a few hundredths of an inch in diameter

to tell him, now, down with it, this is the moment of release and I do release you from low cloud paste into this my Delta. The sky was a god speaking to him through its medium, the water in air, the same water hanging around them everywhere, awful hundred-percent humidity to Travers but an invisible reservoir to Petard, a low directive push coming at him from all directions if only he stopped to listen to it. He was listening now. In barometric trance Petard'd switched hands on the grip, giving over control to his dead arm, the left one with fingers that went up and down but didn't exactly close, restricted in motion, Navier-Stokes once told him, like the distal joint of a bird. The fingers of Petard's left hand now closed on the grip. The rain was awakening the nerve endings to grip strength and now Travers felt the ship going down, the rain lowering them, winching them down, the clouds streaming in. He watched Petard's pinkie snake round the grip and press the cargo-release switch. The dam fell into the foam. From below, a muffled trampoline sound. They weren't rid of it yet; the overhead hook at the bottom of the cable still held them down; it had to be unhooked from below. Stuck in mud, the dam tugged at the ship and rocked it from side to side. The turbulent downwash of the rotors took a lot of the lift out of the mule, and spinning in its own dirty air, the machine began to sink to ground drag-ass with the strain. Travers smelled the citrus of burning kerosene from the turbines. The low-rpm warning buzzer went off. Petard didn't flinch. His eyes still closed, his dead arm reduced the collective, the ship drifted down closer, the turbine wound up into a high hovering scream, and just when the skids'd almost touched the high grass, the rpms returned and the Huey stabilized. When the load released, the ship shot up suddenly. Travers heard a voice cry out, *Di di mau, di di mau,* gook for get the fuck outta here, and the sec Petard heard it he pulled back the grip and the ship rose, carried by a sudden updraft into the free air.

"You know gook?" Travers asked him once they were well away from the ground and the rpms'd slid back into the green.

"Not much," said Petard. "But there's this photographer flies with us nights. She does."

"A woman?"

"She wears black pajamas just like a gook. Carries a camera slung around her neck like some scapular. I don't know why, but that empty camera scares the shit out of them."

"How do you know it's empty?"

"I don't. It's just that I've never seen her take a picture with it."

Travers fingered the 1973D penny, one of two Navier-Stokes'd given him for good luck, D for Denver, the Bureau's headquarters. The other was an old French penny with a liberty head on it and a hole drilled through the date under the Phrygian cap. He gave his knees a light bongo pat and leaned out. Below the river was a muddy yellow band and the rice fields dotted green in all directions. Not many people around; sure wasn't the termite hill down there he'd said it was. A few thatch huts steamed in hot air at the palmetto horizon. Peasants moved along the little dikes, two in a team, pulling a harrow, with a woman wading behind, guiding them with a stick. The fields were already flooded a couple feet deep. The work was more dredge than cultivation. The two men'd hitched themselves to a big wooden rake they scraped along lightly in the early-evening sunbake, one pushing from behind, one pulling in front, hitched to a strap. Petard put the mule into a low hover and Travers took a look. As he did the two men slipped back their mill-wheel hats to look back at him. Their eyes were brown but the whites were pink, weary albino pink with mended-china wrinkles under them.

"Almost there," said Petard, breaking the mule down toward an island not more than a mile ahead, a finger crooked and atrophic in the middle of the Mekong River.

The place was called the Grand Hôtel des Ruines. Not much of a hotel anymore but you could still see the triple-deck balcony, wickerwork of black iron shoved up against the Alamo façade of brick and stone. A small atrophied tower capped the building, which was coated with a paper glaze. No paint on the walls, no glass in the windows. Out front was a courtyard that had dried up, a broken fountain, some tree stumps, a park of red trees with crinkled candy-wrapper leaves. A yellow earth road led away from the hotel into the jungle. No sign whatsoever that the place was the gut center of Reclam Vietnam. He pressed his ass tight against the armor-plated seat, waiting for Petard to make his recon pass over the island, the blue under them turning green. But the mule dropped down without a pass, racketing low across the water toward the hotel. They were too low now to see it at all. A mist trailed above the water, giving off a bark-rot smell. Travers figured they were seeing it from the ferry approach. Water-bugging low in, he waited for the firefly flashes to sequens out of the island's green blanket. He waited and waited but nothing happened. He knew there was a truce, he said there'd be one, but he only half believed it, so he braced himself, waiting for the gooks to mass-fire, shooting green and red tracer bullets ahead of them to gauge the length of lead and angle of approach, watching the mule fly into iron hail. Travers waited for a tracer hit to inflame the Huey's hot joints, or worse, those mortars needling in. But he heard nothing, just the blender beat of the rotor and the suction pressure of a voice in his headset, my brother's voice, saying, "Digger Two, clear for landing."

Travers asked Petard, "Is this the place where Long Dam is going to begin?"

"It keeps changing," said Petard. "It was upriver at Pa Mong. Now it's downriver at Da something or other."

"You mean you don't know?"

Petard answered under his breath. "It's their dam now."

The mule flew low over a tree line marking a dike. Travers knew that slow landing was prime shooting at an H-21. Petard had the machine in his hands and was wagging the tail from side to side with the slight limbic slither he always used to signal his approach. The sun was low in the sky. Travers made out low rows of rubber trees broken ahead by a red smudge of a clearing.

In the clay courtyard a man in a white drill suit and silk foulard was waiting for them. One of his arms had been shot away. His sleeve hung loosely from his shoulder, the cuff turned up and pinned closed. He said his name but Travers didn't catch it. Petard said it was Defosse. Low dams were his specialty. He'd made a name for himself working for the Compagnie Nationale du Rhône, digging the canals for the Donzère-Mondragon diversion back in the early fifties. He came here in October of '52 to clear the upper reaches of the Red and Black rivers for an outfit called Travaux Cochinchine, lost his arm to mortar fire at Dien Bien Phu, joined Reclam as an *ingénieur attaché* two years later. He had a handmade map in his hands with deep nail marks sickled in it and a copy of *Agence France Presse* tucked under his good armpit. Petard and Defosse went way back to '56, when Petard prepared Reclam One, the Bureau's first report on the Lower Mekong. They walked together like they were used to walking together. Travers followed them toward the veranda of the old hotel. Defosse's polished shoes cracked as he walked. An old Spencer carbine was slung over his back. He had a wet bandage on the back of his neck that was coming undone. He smoked those Doan Kets, gook cigarettes made of black bitter tobacco.

"Any progress?" he heard Defosse ask Petard.

"Some," said Petard.

Travers looked down at his feet as he walked toward the hotel with its yellowing white walls and red roof. A few blue ants scrambled over his shoes. By the door to the hotel a woman was parking a bicycle below a window box full of pink and white flowers. The windowsill was crumbling and a little loose stone flaked off the wall where the handlebars touched it. He heard her voice break into a soft alto to say "*Bat tay*," gook for hello. A radio crackled inside. With her one hand she opened a coarse lidded basket slung between the handlebars and took out a smaller basket filled with uncooked rice and a pineapple. With her free hand she took out a Vinh orange and balanced it in her palm like it was a big diamond. Not much food there but she handled it lightly, gently, with deference almost, just like a gook.

"Mme Coulton," said Defosse.

She put the food back. The toe of her foot gave the kickstand a light tap and it clicked down. Travers saw her from the back. She had long gray hair wound in a braid and tied at the end with a red cord. Weird the way gooks never went gray, their skin just pruning up on them instead. This woman wore the pajamas they all wore, but her black tunic had a high Chinese collar and thin lines of blue silk sewn into every seam. Her sandals had wooden soles and plastic straps, modest even by gook standards, but then again Petard'd said she was a photojournalist and maybe dressing down was part of the deal.

That was the way it worked in his family, dress like you're on a mission but make sure you take care of business, and he thought she might be from a family like his own. Funny, he didn't catch her name. Petard hadn't mentioned it, and Defosse made it sound so French, saying it like cool-tone, that he wasn't really sure what it was.

The woman turned to him. She put out her hand. Travers took it, looked into her eyes. When he did the hand crumbled in his hand. It flaked into rice paste. Her arm was a knob of bone. Her hair dried into a green mosquito net. A crack zipped down her neck seam. Her frame was a palisade of bamboo poles. Her eyes socketed empty. He was in University Hall. He was in Vietnam. A drain'd carried away all the water in her and she was thin as a wraith, strong as a ghost, fell as a desert. You: you are: are you:

"He's fainted," said Jenna.

"Must be the heat," said my brother.

"He's been hot before," said Petard.

"Better take him inside," said my brother.

Travers took the glass of lemonade Jenna handed him but didn't drink from it. The pulp was the color of blood. He turned away a bowl filled with upright burials of dried salted fish with a lemon cut up in it. The bowl was wood lined with tin. He was on a ratty old couch in the lobby of a ratty old hotel. The floor was a checkerboard of old mattresses. Patches of dull blue silk rotted off the walls. Tacked to the silk was a rubberized linen map of Indochina that said, U.S. Army Air Force, November 1943. On his lap he saw a white cloth napkin folded into a right triangle.

"Travers," Petard said to him.

Travers heard Petard say his name but it bled away from him before he could take it in. Where was he? He was in a room. The walls were mattresses. He tried to move his hand. The fingers moved but not together. He wanted to lift his head but he did not have the strength.

My brother took Travers's hands and laid them one on top of the other. He looked at Petard but Petard turned away abstracted, his fingers dug into the roots of his scalp.

"Where is he now?" asked Jenna.

"I don't know," said my brother.

"Gone," said Petard.

Travers did not hear them. Sweat rolled down his forehead in rivers. Crickets beat tambourines. Smell of glue, cloves, hot ink, cigarettes. Where was he: by a skeleton of a town built on a river as a resort, under a crinoline of trees, rocking in a barge lit with paper lanterns, under a ceiling fitted with a turning fan, in a place where men ate dogs. Who was she: a guest at a dinner party singing a song to amuse a king, dressed not in black but bound now in the white robes of mourning, singing tonelessly, "In the daytime I am in the north, in the nighttime, the south." Her face wasn't Julia's but it resolved itself into Julia's. It came within a fraction of being hers but wasn't. It was her own. He knew it was her own but he couldn't keep them apart. One face was suctioning down over the other. Julia over Jenna, Jenna over Julia. One on top of the other like two sheets. Two white sheets.

Four ●

1

The Sacramento River Delta. Our pickup was off the pavement now, bumping over the frontage road, taking us into canal country. A delta wasn't just rivers. A delta was canals and that's what my brother said we were seeing, a shallow nation of canals, a lithography of them scratching the surface of the great central valley of California. Before I knew it the fields, which had turned a metallic brown in dry season, were a vast zinc plate of them. One canal led to another and it was strange because first you thought one canal was one canal, each canal a line between points, till you figured out there weren't any points, just lines. Canals led to canals led to canals, just like in Vietnam.

"A lot of them don't even have names," he told me. "Just letters."

Ahead I watched the San Joaquin River break into an alphabet of canals. The canals irrigated the rice paddies, though they weren't called that anywhere near the San Joaquin. Here they were rice checks and all around us I could see the rice seedlings standing in a few inches of water. There were fields of sugar beets and marsh grass and milo, but mostly there was rice. The ground here was perfect for rice. Not too low, not too high, it was level all the way across the great valley to the Sierra. There wasn't a dip in the land that hadn't been righted or routed into a canal. One of them was the fastest way to Turlock, the irrigation district where Jenna Coulton'd lived since she made it out of Vietnam in 1975.

"Jenna was the last one out," he told me.

My brother wouldn't talk about his last days in Vietnam, he almost never did, but he started telling me about how she got out last. He had it indirectly, through Petard, but indirection didn't matter to my brother. He started filling in details like he knew what'd happened from the inside till I thought maybe he'd been there with her after Saigon fell. He said Jenna was the last American out of Vietnam, that it hadn't been easy for her to get out, but as he spoke I kept thinking she might have been second to last, that my brother was really the last one out even though I knew for a fact he wasn't. Saigon was already six weeks fallen, Travers two years mad, my brother six weeks discharged and living with me in Fontana, not saying a thing about Vietnam, not even breathing the word, not even the vet version with the Viet chopped out of it, just passing time on my couch getting fat dressed in his plain blue overalls with back pockets big enough to sink a book into, wearing white clean collarless shirts, carrying spares with him in a droopy leather bag and changing them every time they got even a little dirty. His hair was getting long and stringy, though then I didn't know he'd never cut it again, letting it dwindle down his back till it didn't grow anymore. For him the war in Vietnam was over and now he was at war with himself.

For Jenna there were six hunted weeks in Asia burning. Choking in her lungs she made her way through the dream hallways of a city she once knew. She took pictures then, lots of them; she'd hidden her camera in a wrinkled brown bag and hardly had time to set the focal length; *The Fall of Saigon* would be her last book. In those last weeks she'd dyed her hair black, pressed her face against window glass to flatten her nose whenever anyone was looking, shuddered across streets and counted tanks till the tanks were like stars and she lost track. Standing by the docks near the Port Authority Building, Jenna looked down at the river. The river reflected nothing back at her, nothing at all, not even her own image. She knew she was in a place she loved that no longer loved her back. The people in the south knew she wasn't one of them, that old geomancer with the cane tapped it like a gavel whenever she walked by him in the market, his shop was open to the street like all the shops and he knew she was sleeping in an oil drum, combing a small field back of the old Reclam building on Duc Thang for green onions. She kept her hair in a dirty strangled ponytail and went look-ing for her house in Cholon. Cholon was Chinatown in Saigon. She knew it well, it wasn't far from the bus station taking you west into the Delta, that long dusty lot full of old De Soto buses hot and windowless with water tanks up top for watering the engines down. She wished she were in one of them now, inching her way west toward the river and out of the city, even though she knew she'd never make it through a ticket line without getting picked up by the police. So, ticketless, she made her way to her house, the only house on the block with windows in it. She shared it with five other journalists and Defosse, a French engineer. The others were Americans and were gone now. It took her most of a day to get there, she'd had to avoid long columns of soldiers but she knew right away that Defosse was there. A perfectly pressed clean white suit with an arm missing hung on a hanger outside a straw house. And there he was next to it, clean-shaven, sweat collected above his lips, face a little burned by the sun, khakis dusty but otherwise not much disturbed by the American exodus, raking the dirt in a garden that wasn't a garden but a plot of arranged earth. The rock garden was a calm place, the sand the color of pears and the stones laid out like cups, but the man she knew didn't have any of this arranged calm, he had a different calm, the reworked calm of opium.

When she saw him Jenna took the *non la* off her head and laid it carefully on the ground. The point of the hat settled delicately into the calligraphy of the rock garden.

"Defosse," she said.

He put down his rake and turned to her. Eyes dropping to the ground, he was stiff with surprise, not at seeing her, but at seeing the hat where the hat had to be.

"You put it in the right place," he said.

Jenna lowered her head.

"The others," he said. "They are gone." Defosse meant it as a fact, not a question, but Jenna answered anyway.

"Yes, they're gone," she said.

"I knew you wouldn't go," he told her.

"I wanted to," she said, "but I couldn't."

She'd wanted to leave Saigon when Saigon was falling but what she told Defosse was right, she couldn't. Not that she hadn't tried. A few weeks back she had a special pink passport from Reclam R&A, it was called a rescind document because it rescinded anything anyone wanted to do to her. Still it hadn't stopped the bus from stalling on the way from My Tho. Everyone and everything was going to Saigon. The road was jammed but there was no safety in numbers. White starving ducks filled the hollows off the road. People shuffled east in black rags. She walked the last twenty miles feeling something had passed and hoping the passing would be final, complete. On the shoulder she went by a monk bowing at her, bowing and praying in high monk quiver. She didn't know who she was anymore but he knew who she was, she was an American and he was praying, not at her or for her, he was telling her to pray, *nam mo America, nam mo America,* pray for America, pray for America. Jenna made it to Saigon on an empty stomach, most she had was a cup of tea with an aftertaste of dirt to it. It wasn't cold, the streets were shaded by tamarind trees and the shade was warm as ever, but the city was shivering with fear. The sky was scratched with flares. Guns thumped in the distance. Jenna followed a bleached row of palms to the U.S. Embassy. The marine at the door didn't ask for anything, he just pulled her in and pushed her up a stairwell. The stairwell was dark and someone handed her a rough blanket. A little boy dropped his lunch box and started to cry. A voice started to calm him, and other voices piped up. Headed for California? Lots of lemon and orange trees in California. Date palms, too. There was another life at the top of this stairwell and right then she knew she wouldn't make it up. She hadn't known it till then, and even then she didn't know why. Word shot down the stairwell, last helicopter, it's a Reclam bird, one of those water vultures and they're only taking Bureau people. A Marine filtered through the quiet expectant crowd, saying in a clear careful voice, Is there a Jenna Coulton here, a Jenna Coulton?

"I'm not going," Jenna said weakly.

"Sure you're not." Clenching her upper arm, he lifted her up the stairwell and into the bay of the waiting helicopter. The UH-1 shuddered uneasily on the roof and the rotors beat out a thin scream.

"She doesn't want to go," he shouted to the pilot.

The pilot unclasped his helmet and turned around. "You don't?" he asked her.

Jenna shook her head.

The pilot said, "She stays."

The pilot was Petard. He'd come back for her, he knew

she'd be the last one to leave and he'd waited till the end of April 1975 to be the one to come get her. It'd taken some doing. Reclam wasn't officially in Vietnam anymore, and in the aftermath of Da Trinh Sanh, Reclam wasn't really even officially in America anymore. If he'd stopped and asked why he'd come back, he would've said it wasn't to get her out but to see her one last time in her adopted home. He knew she wouldn't leave without Defosse even though Defosse was French and wasn't in any danger except from overdose. Seeing her now, resting against a wall, letting her weight slide gently down the wall until she was squatting, he was satisfied she knew she had to go. It was now just a matter of when. He'd go home to California and find a place for her, not near him, she was a New Yorker and he knew she couldn't live where he lived up his black cut of a mountain road, knew she'd never get used to the sky and the high clear air, but he'd find her someplace where the rivers were leaping with fish and the fields were flooded for miles in every direction with tracings of rice. Until then, then: the slicks were off the ground now, and pulling back the stick, Petard picked the Huey up into a four-foot hover, turning it one full swing so he could see her one last time. Blue-burning kerosene came flooding off the turbines and into the air. He still couldn't see very well, so he turned up the visor knob on his helmet and looked down at the Embassy roof. Jenna was still there. He felt like he was leaving her stranded on a gutter, but he left her there anyway because that was what she wanted. Petard sat in one of two metal seats, the other was empty because it was to have been Jenna's. He'd set the sliding armor panel on the seat to protect her but that didn't matter now. The helicopter cut trellises in the air, slashing the vines between him and Vietnam. Jenna was calm. She smiled and waved at him with one hand. In the other she had a plastic bag with some small strawberries in it. Saigon was falling, Petard told my brother, Vietnam was lost and Asia a vast tangled garden of barbed wire and Jenna Coulton was carrying strawberries. He said he tried to imagine her picking them that morning at the marshy edge of the city where the reeds began, but he couldn't. The strawberries had thin threadlike green vines on them. The bag they were in had water condensed near the top. He said he just couldn't imagine where she got them from.

"She grows strawberries now," my brother said to me now. "You should see them. Some are as big as your fist."

"So she's a farmer?" I asked.

"Not exactly," said my brother.

"I thought you said she was a photographer."

"Not anymore. She works for the district."

The district, he explained, was Turlock Irrigation District, and Jenna was a manager in the district. Turlock was the biggest irrigation district in the valley, so Jenna had a big job. Here she oversaw the irrigation of a rice check. Actually she spent most of her time searching for weak spots in irrigation ditches near Turlock, bumping over dry dirt roads in a pickup. Jenna's house was off Lateral 1, which ran west along the Tuolumne River almost as far as Ceres, one of your typical Bureau towns, a river town without a river running through it anymore, a dry town, all flying dust and cracked paint and bleached wood, named after the Roman goddess of agriculture. Laterals 2 through 6 ran east-west as far down as the Merced River, the district's southern border. Her job was to keep things even on the laterals. Every day she'd run her truck up and down the banks of the main canal, her eyes following the strain of the water, stopping every bit to set the boards and gates. The roads were long and straight and usually empty, but the real roads were the laterals shooting off the canals, neatly cut and lined on both sides by a fringe of trees. She had a regular crew she brought in when she needed to replace flumes with fills, knocking down the old aboveground aqueducts and carving out new laterals in their place. The laterals fed into great greening fields of rice. There was nothing like this kind of green anywhere in America. The other greens I'd seen didn't come even close. Corn was a stunted green. Grass was uneven. Spring in the Monongahela Valley was more like brown. My brother said Jenna didn't know what to call this green in English, so she called it what she'd heard it called in Vietnamese. *Mau xanh la ma.* The green of new rice.

Jenna lived in a field station in the middle of all this rice. She had a farmhouse just outside Turlock, off a ramp within grinding earshot of a highway, past a cluster of truck stops. My brother pulled up the driveway and cut the engine. Parked next to us in the driveway was a white pickup with Turlock Irrigation District stenciled on the doors. There was an old frame house, a garage, some outbuildings, and a high antenna with a blinking red light up top. The house had two stories, and from the second, facing north over a garden full of hard tomatoes grown for ketchup, and beyond, toward a row of strawberries lining a dirt road leading to the main canal, you could get just enough elevation to make out that the Great Central Valley really was a valley. Fifty miles wide and four hundred miles long, it wasn't a snug place. With June coming, the grasses were turning brown. In the distance a railroad track was lined with packing sheds. Everything in Travers's place'd looked like war surplus and probably was; Jenna's house was older and so was she. Pushing fifty was what he would have guessed, but my brother said she was born in 1937. She covered the war for thirteen years, he kept saying that, for thirteen years, though after we'd parked the pickup and gone into her kitchen through the back door, there wasn't much to show for it. Not much

Oriental around except on the wall next to the sink beside a leaded amber window, a Chinese hexagram done in needlepoint. My brother interpreted it for me. It was the hexagram Fu. Six lines, five of them broken in the middle, signifying Return.

Jenna was at the kitchen table, an old camera with a light meter beside her on another chair. She held a pair of scissors in her hand, cutting some film so it'd fit into the camera. I took her in. Her face was a long oval and her nose narrowed to a point. Her arms were thin and hard. Her hair was almost gray and she wore it pinned up. A few pins above her ears held up most of her hair, and when she unclipped them and shoved her fingers through it, which she did a lot, you saw the hair brown at the ends and gray at the roots. She'd once had brown hair, but one thing hadn't changed. She was small as ever, five feet two if that. Standing next to her with his hands plunged in the deep square pockets of his overalls, the blue bib clipped with pencils and pens he never touched, my brother must have weighed near three times as much.

"You look different," said my brother.

"Different?" Jenna asked. Her nose flared a little as she spoke.

"Different from that picture you sent me."

"Older?"

"I don't know. Different."

"I'm not," said Jenna.

"Maybe the picture changed," he told her.

"Maybe," she said.

Jenna's voice was dry and a bit raspy and she talked from the center of her mouth, not out the side like Petard and my brother. I heard the New York in her voice. She wore a windbreaker but the jacket was white and the bleaching sun of the great valley gave it a silk sheen like she'd taken one of those Vietnamese *ao dais* and sewn it

into something American-looking like a nylon windbreaker. Jenna seemed to accept this explanation about a
picture changing. But it was late in the afternoon and my
brother was getting irritable, the way he did whenever he
spent too much time with anyone. He sat down at the
kitchen table and laid his hands flat on the table. He began
scoring his thumbnail into the Formica.

"So what have you got waiting for him?" he asked.
"Petard had a tattoo. Travers had Toads. That camera?
You gonna take his picture?"

"Not exactly," said Jenna.

"He passed out for three days after that last bit. Travers
says he knows enough now. When he woke up he told
Travers what happened to him. Travers was grateful. So
grateful he took out the lease to the Toad Development
Farm and offered to sign it over to him. To Gailly." He
laughed his high short snarl of a laugh. "Can you see my
little brother—a *Toad rancher*?"

Jenna ignored my brother and looked straight at me.
"What was it like?"

"What was what like?"

"What you saw. The past."

"It wasn't *like* anything. I was in Vietnam. I saw what
he saw."

"Was Defosse there?"

"Where?" I asked.

"In 1973," she said.

I had to think for a sec. "French, right?" I thought a
bit more. "Yes. He was at a run-down hotel in the Delta.
Petard was there. So were you."

"What about me?" asked my brother.

"I told you. Your voice was on the radio. You were
somewhere else."

Jenna continued. "Defosse told me something once.
About Dien Bien Phu. About what he did there. He said

he built a dam. I never knew if it was true. I didn't believe
him, I don't think anybody did. The story was incredible.
He died telling it over and over again. Before he died he
made me swear I'd never forget it. He said his story was
the story of reclamation, the real story from beginning to
end. He made me set every word to memory. I've never
forgotten it but I've never known if what he said was
true. I was hoping he'd appeared to you."

"He did," I told her.

"What did he look like?"

"Pale like a ghost. Strange translucent skin. I didn't
know why he was there. He wasn't building the dam. It
was like he came with the place."

"Did he say anything?"

"No. Nothing."

"I was afraid of that," she said.

"Afraid?" I asked.

"Yes. Some things never come clear. I always felt Defosse would come back to me. He told me to tell it again
when the time was right. He said his story was part of my
story. He said that's why I'd remember it."

"Do you?"

"Every word. Just the way he told it."

"I don't want to hear it again," said my brother, un-
lacing his boots with a Baltic frown.

"You don't have to," said Jenna.

"Good," he said.

Jenna set the table with mugs and spoons, a spoon di-
agonal in each mug. She turned the stove on. When the
water boiled she sat straight up pouring tea with fingers
stained green from the tea leaves. My brother said she
could read them if she wanted to, but she no longer
wanted to know what the leaves at the bottom of the cup
told her, so she gulped them down before she could see
them. Why she should be so cautious about not using

some predictive power of hers I didn't know, but I watched her section an orange and put the pieces on a plate.

"Want some?" my brother asked when she was finished, scooping up the oranges.

After a while he told Jenna he was tired and asked if he was going to get his same room. There was nothing in this room but an old iron sagging bed but my brother liked empty rooms with nothing on the walls. The room he slept in actually wasn't so empty, it had pictures same as the room I slept in that night, but before he came Jenna always took them down for him because she knew he liked it that way. He walked to his room down a hallway past some windows opening onto a row of shirts on a line. The line wasn't rope but white insulated wire braided between two poles. The shirts had dried stiffly in the wind.

"You still do laundry in the canal?" he said, turning around in the hallway on the way to his room.

Jenna smiled. She said he asked her that every time he came. She did that only once, she told me, once in '76 after she first came back, before Petard pulled some strings to get her the Turlock job. She said my brother liked to think of her as Vietnamese, a refugee in a far country who didn't know she wasn't supposed to do her laundry in an irrigation ditch, a girl from the Delta slapping her shirts on the stones and wringing the water out of them in knots. That one time she'd done her laundry the way she used to do it in Cholon, laying the wet clothes out, not on lines, but flat on dried stalks of rice back of her house. Jenna didn't like the way the wind filled her shirts with amputated ghosts of herself, her arms flapping about without hands, and besides, it reminded her of Defosse and his arm lost at Dien Bien Phu. She didn't like to call that up so much if she could help it.

"He's been dead eleven years now," she said of De-fosse. "He died in San Francisco but the funeral was in France. They buried him in a dam there."

"I didn't know that was allowed."

Jenna didn't say anything to this but pointed to a photograph of a man set in a red frame, the glass a little above the photo, the photo warped underneath. In the picture Defosse didn't look well. His eyes were puffed half shut with the cancer that was about to kill him. Jenna took a rag and wiped the dust off the glass. Defosse trusted me, she told me, trusted me with his story. I didn't know what to say to this, so I stared at the carpet and waited until she showed me my room.

2

The next morning my brother slept in and the two of us took the Toulumne River highway out to Coulterville, Jenna driving. Fog hung over the ground and blew through the open windows of the pickup. Jenna pulled off the road under some trees. The highway forked here at Window Rock, one road going on to Yosemite, the other heading back to Turlock and I-5. She opened the door but didn't get out. I knew we were up pretty high but I couldn't see farther than fifty feet. Jenna told me it took a couple of hours for the fog to burn off. She settled into her seat, zipped the windbreaker to her neck, and started to talk. I pulled my coat closed and listened.

"There isn't a day goes by," she began, "I don't think about him. There's a dam on the other side of this fog, La Grange Dam. It's about a thousand feet ahead. If you listen you can hear the rush of the water and the hum of the generator. But if what Defosse told me is true, that dam is a kind of demon."

Jenna laughed.

"What's so funny?" I said.

"God, I don't know," Jenna said. She wiped her eyes and laughed again. "It's just a story."

"Then why bother?"

"It's such a perfect story, from beginning to end. If you believe it, it changes everything. If you don't, it gnaws at you anyway because that's the way it is. Petard believes it and your brother doesn't. I'm caught in the middle. I don't believe or disbelieve. I think Defosse wanted it that way. He knew I'd try to be objective. You see, I was a journalist, a photographer."

I already knew Jenna had been a photographer, maybe the most famous photographer to come out of the Vietnam War, but that after *The Fall of Saigon* appeared in 1976 she'd never taken another photo again. She told me now she'd begun in '59 with a studio on the top floor of a three-story building on Ninth Street in Manhattan, her bed in the corner, a dirty skylight over her, a telephone on the floor. She'd done a book on circus freaks, attracted some attention but not much because the pictures were strange. It took her three years to take them. Days she taught civics at P.S. 47, nights she drove out to the marshy plain in Passaic, New Jersey, where the circus set up every spring. She didn't take many pictures, not at first, and those she took weren't even of freaks. They were of their children. The parents were painted and deformed but the kids were normal and wanted to be like their parents. Jenna saw them trying, she caught the purpose in their eyes, the agony of their voluntary deformity, the pain of them trying to be what they weren't, and that's what she photographed. There were pictures of a tall freckled boy standing in an S, a girl wearing a backpack under her shirt to thicken her back, a pair of twins swimming in the Passaic River, their hair soiled by industrial scum. The book was called *Circus Freaks*, and it won her a job at the Primus Agency on Spring Street. The editor there was convinced she'd make a great war photographer because that's what war was about, deformity, wasn't it? Jenna sat quietly in a wing chair while he praised her work; the kids weren't freaks but they all had that same circus smile, the muscles too strong at the edges. His name was Janssen and he gave her an advance of two thousand dollars and a one-way ticket to Tan Son Nhut Airport, Saigon, Vietnam.

"I didn't know much about Vietnam," Jenna told me. "Nobody did then. But I went anyway."

The year was 1962. Ngo Dinh Diem was President of the Republic of South Vietnam and Petard Davidson, Chief of the Division of Design, Bureau of Reclamation R&A, would not touch down at Tan Son Nhut for three years yet, surprised by the tobacco he saw growing around the airport because he'd thought tobacco was our slavery, not theirs. It'd be eleven years till Robert Travers touched down there, a colonel with a fat neck in the next seat telling him the gooks called the Mekong Nine-Headed Dragon River and Travers thinking, chop off six heads and you get the Mekong Delta, chop off three more and you get nothing at all. Jenna told me she didn't remember any specific first impression. As her plane broke cloud cover on its final approach to Saigon, she remembered looking out and seeing women weeding the rice, pulling the weeds and piling them on the dikes to dry. Tombs in faded pink and blue stone sat untended in the middle of rice fields. Miles of fields were shrill with rice. On the ground she caught a cab straight into the center of the city. One look at the hotel, a copy of something in Paris, and she told the driver to keep on going till the streets narrowed and the heat shot up into three digits. She didn't know the names of the streets but wished she did already, wished she'd known them for years. Shaking her hair out

of its braid, she stepped out of the cab and into the war
whose eyes she would become.

"I remember that first hotel," she told me now. "It had
a disco with red twirling lights on the fifth floor. A lot of
young girls were waiting in line to get into a Saturday-
night dance. Some dropped their shoulder straps when I
passed them in the stairwell. They didn't care I was a
woman. They thought I was American and might want
them, too. When I said the words for photographer, *nguoi
chup anh*, one dropped her blouse."

"Not that kind," I said.

"Not at all. I took her upstairs and had her run through
her routine for me. I paid her well but didn't tell her what
to do. A few of the poses were porn but most were theater. She'd lift her leg over her head and balance on one
foot. It was like watching a ballet dancer practice at the
barre. I used four of them in *Annam*."

Jenna made her reputation fast. She was fearless, didn't
mind the heat and didn't brood about the war, didn't care
who won or lost or why. She didn't care about stories
either, just images, and images are what she got. She used
a zoom and her pictures had almost no depth of field.
She'd catch faces and leave the rest in blurs. But the war
was in those faces, face of a village elder, a thin man with
thinning hair, tugging at his fingers as he spoke at a re-
settlement meeting, face of a groom cutting his wedding
cake with a machete, face of an American sailor trying to
serve rice to a row of villagers in brown baggy pajamas,
rice they wouldn't eat because it was cooked our way,
white and light. Back in Saigon she'd let an assistant develop her pictures, deciding on the final valence of light
and dark, while she headed off to a bar she knew, settling
into a cool corner to catch her breath, sending her soup
back to be reheated when she went too long without
touching it. Her best-known pictures were distance shots

taken from a boat drifting in the middle of the Mekong River. In the Delta she'd rent boats with flat bottoms and sides sloping steeply upwards. In August of '68 she took that photo of the tiny coal barge, not much larger than a canoe, a small man on the tip of the stern rowing with double oars, the oars locked in a cross; it made the cover of *Time* and made Jenna Coulton the most famous war photographer since Robert Capa stepped on a mine at Dien Bien Phu.

"I was like Capa in a way," she explained to me now. "Everything I saw was a potential picture. For a while I switched to color to get a lot of bright red details, things black-and-white couldn't pick up. Like a woman with a red comb in her hair. Red teacups, sandals with red plastic soles. Huts with red tile roofs. I got attacked for *The Color of Happiness* because I used a pool of blood in the series. The reviewers said it ignored the violence of war. But it was beautiful. The color was perfect scalding red."

Jenna said she soon grew to hate fame. Fame took her away from the war. For a while *Time* picked up her credentials and sent her to do a photo bio of President Thieu. Jenna hadn't liked Nuygen Van Thieu. He dressed in blue suits but still thought he was some kind of emperor. Thieu sat very still while she photographed him; he leaned over from time to time to brush the static off his socks and pull them up over his ankles. On the way out she'd taken some pictures of the massive reflecting pools he'd recently had installed in the presidential palace. That came as a relief to her. A camera was a kind of gun, not a snub-nosed .38 but a long-bore rifle with a scope, and Jenna was a sniper who liked to shoot at a distance. She knew her picture of Thieu tugging at his socks was going to be pure character assassination; one click and there he was, a big man caught in a stupid little gesture he'd never be able to explain away. The picture would define him forever and he'd hate her for it. She knew what would happen next. From now on, every official in Vietnam would stare at her cold as a statue. Thinking it over, she found herself wishing she could be invisible behind her camera. If only the camera could take pictures on its own; if only it could bypass her entirely. She was already known for going it minimal. Filters were definitely not her style. She didn't use flash-guns or flood lamps. She had one lens, a simple $f/2.8$ Schneider she never changed. If she couldn't get good light she tilted her camera and made do. She knew she had a good eye; her pictures had balance and proportion, but these were not the same as truth. Jenna wanted truth. Was truth making Thieu into another circus freak? She wanted her camera to see, but not with her eyes. She wanted her camera to have its own eye and its own heart.

"Supposing," Jenna said to me now, "that it was just possible. For a camera to pick up things you couldn't see. To take a picture of everything something is. Not just the past of it and the present, but its future, too. What then?"

"I don't think anyone would believe it," I said.

"I saw it done once. Only once, back in '62. Diem was President and one night this incredible picture of him appeared all over Saigon. He must have seen something in it, too, because his goons stuck it up everywhere, in markets, temples, shop windows. But the power of the image wasn't in what he was wearing. He wore the usual blue suit with padded shoulders. It was in his eyes. You could tell in his eyes that he knew the lost war was already lost, that fifteen months later November 1963 had already come and gone and he lay dead and crumpled at Cha Tam Church in Cholon. It was like he understood that events moved independently, without reference to time. In the picture he was perfectly aloof and imperturbable. I read that before he was assassinated he'd had to be shown how to bend his head to fit into the personnel carrier;

that he thought it was unseemly for a president to bend his head. I swear you could see that in the picture. His life was completely there. I never found out who took it."

"You saw all that?"

"I never saw anything like it again. Not till it happened to me."

It didn't happen right away. Like she said, Jenna wanted to be invisible in Vietnam, and for a long time she got away with it. She was tight about being known. Even this morning, bumping along a lateral road on the way to one of her dams, she'd scrunched her eyes closed and clenched her teeth rather than talk too much. Her face never re-laxed. She wasn't a photographer anymore but she still liked to know what was going on around her. She was full of casual gestures intended to put you at your ease but they didn't work, you'd see her smoking but then she'd grind out her cigarette in the ashtray like a drill, she'd run her fingers through her hair but then pull out some hairs by the roots. None of them was convincing, the whole time you could feel her fixing your image in her head. She admitted as much to me now. She'd go on like this for three or four hours at a stretch, watching you with a bit too much inattention, but watching you closely all the time, and just when you thought you were free, just when you relaxed, let down your guard, *revealed yourself*, out came the camera and in you went. She said this was the one thing she never missed, the pretend innocence of photography, the lie in every image that it wasn't stolen, exacted by fraud and a kind of torture.

Jenna was good at hiding behind the camera and getting away with it, but every once in a while someone smoked her out. In Saigon she haunted the fish markets. Half a world away from home she'd pick her way through the stalls spilling over with fish, finfish and shellfish from all over, pausing to look at the abalone and tuna and great swollen flounder. The Vietnamese in the market noticed she came a little before trading began and didn't shrink from the writhing fish like the other blue-eyed American women. The stands had roofs extending over the sidewalks and sometimes, working her way through the market, she thought she saw her mother's face behind one of those stalls, impossibly pale and dusted with flour. But no, she wasn't at a pier at the foot of Pike Street near the East River; the man here didn't wrap her fish in white wax paper and mark the price with a grease pencil. He had narrow observant eyes and could tell she was used to being around fish. When he handed her fish he tried to ask her where she was from. Jenna waved him away, pretending not to understand. When he kept at it she pointed her Leica at him. He let her take his picture but never talked to her again, not even at the end, years later, the day Saigon fell, when he shoved her under his stall to hide her from a passing squad of NVA regulars.

"I didn't have friends," she told me now. "I had assistants. For a long time I had Engh. He was a boy of fourteen I picked up on the street back in '67. I taught him how to run a darkroom. He was good at it. He was the one who started to notice."

"Notice what?"

"That something was wrong."

"Wrong with what?"

"Wrong with the pictures I was taking."

Jenna said she'd installed Engh in a small outlying hut behind her house in Cholon. Every day he'd leave a manila envelope with a contact sheet in it. He'd tie the envelope with faded red tape, a touch she liked. One day, though, there was no tape. Just a 5 × 8 mounted on cardboard and stained in its lower half by water. The photograph was of a dam. One of the dams the Bureau of

Reclamation was building near a village called Da Trinh Sanh.

The picture was one in a series she'd taken the week before on a quick trip to the Mekong Delta. There was a strange peace in the Delta that year; everyone noticed it but no one could quite figure it; peace since February of '73. Remembering Tet, Jenna had gone upriver thinking the VC were getting ready to spring something big out of the general quiet. The trip had come to nothing, or so she thought. Still she made it upriver boatwise, the motor rattling and the boat rattling with it, thinking that the Mekong River was narrower than she thought it would be. She made it upriver all the way to Da Trinh Sanh, a village on an island six miles inland from the Cambodian border. Around the village the Mekong River split in two, and down off the south shore was where the river was narrowest anywhere in Vietnam. A row of fishing scows, sampans probably but they looked like old boxcar floats, lay strung across the narrows of the river. A string of blue buoys, plugged Clorox bottles with red cord tied between them, held the nets in place. Some kind of dam was going in but she hadn't paid much attention to it. As usual she went straight for the little details. An old bulldozer tread laid out as a footbridge. Farmers tilling the land using U.S. Army bivouac shovels. The banks of a canal lined with big concrete urns with *Reclam R&A* stamped on them. She'd even taken a picture of Petard before she knew who he was. He was busy directing work at a very low dam off the river. Jenna said she was struck by the cold focus of his work; half circles of sweat under his arms extended down to his belt and he didn't seem to notice or mind. She didn't even mean to take a picture of the dam he was building. Waiting in the morning fog for a gunboat to round the bend and take her back, she'd also been struck by the water buffalos straining away in the fields, heads lowered, the thick bosses of bone between their horns set against the yoke of the plow. They were preparing some fields for rice just below the long white dam. That's when she'd snapped the picture Engh had blown up for her now.

Jenna almost never took pictures of technical things, so now she had to strain to remember what the shattered thing she was looking at had once been. She remembered wading out into a rice field toward the dam. She'd wanted a particular angle and a peasant in floppy black pajamas had led the way. Jenna followed half capsized, her clothes getting heavier with each step, dragging her feet in the green mud. Maybe she'd held the meter too close to the dam's white, but then again, maybe she hadn't.

Back in Saigon she kicked Engh out of the darkroom and blew up the pictures by herself. Elbows and all, she stuck her arms in the shallow developing tray, diving in there like it was the ocean. She ran through the procedure over and over again, waking every morning to the picture stuck in her mirror, always with the same result. The lines across the dam were braided into it. The dam was cracked in a hundred places. She'd gotten it wrong, she thought, she must have gotten it wrong. She'd always thought photography was an act of absolution; picturing life meant she wasn't part of it. She wasn't the little girl handing President Diem a bunch of severed white orchids, she wasn't the guard standing at terrified attention in the main corridor of Gia Long Palace, she wasn't the orphan at the Nam Tha School running a three-legged race to the finish line to win a Hershey Bar or a No. 2 pencil: every picture she took absolved her from what she saw, saying *I wasn't the one doing this, I was outside it, the one behind the camera, the one you can't see.* This absolution had worked so long as her camera had kept her out of it. But now that same camera was pulling her in. It was showing her something that wasn't there. She was in the mirror, too, and she didn't like what she saw. Every morning she woke up and looked in that bedroom mirror to see some black skin flaking off her lips and her hair long and stringy and unwashed. Sometimes she wanted to take her brush off the dresser and rub the glass till it was so scored it couldn't throw her own image back at her. But she knew erasing an image wouldn't solve anything. Not if the image was real somehow. She had to find out if it was.

Jenna told me she tried a lot of things, talked to a lot of people, before she managed to track down Petard. She didn't find him right away; when she went back upriver the low dam was finished and the Reclam people were vague about his whereabouts. For months she was off on her own, lost in a city she thought she knew. Even now, years later, when she knew it like a book, she said Saigon was still a marvel to her, a pop-up book pushing dragons in her face every time she turned the page. Jenna was brought up streetwise on the southern tip of Manhattan; it was hard for a city to surprise her, but this one did. The Vietnamese weren't skeptics. They believed everything she told them about her pictures. They took it for granted that her pictures were windows to some other reality. There was a strange consistency among the augurs. *Of course the cracks aren't visible. They're not there yet.* Most of them were nutty but they took her so completely seriously she had to wonder what they were about. One handed her a bowl of dyed eggs and told her to pick one. When she took a red egg he said the dam was going to be a boy. He told her not to worry. "Boy very good." By the time she found Petard in Can Tho, holed up in a hotel room overlooking the Mekong River, she was almost ready to give up.

Petard sat waiting for her on a rattan chair in his hotel room. The floor in the room was made of six plywood pieces painted white and coated with shellac. She took in the rest of the room. The window was half open. An end table had bottles of Ricard, Vermouth, and black rum on it. A sleeping bag was rolled out over the bed. Petard had a phone receiver tucked into the ridge of his shoulder and a cigarette burning down between the second and third fingers of his right hand.

He put down the phone when he saw her.

"You're the photographer?"

"Yes."

"The one who did *Annam*?"

"That's right."

"You wanted to see me?"

"You or someone like you."

"What's that supposed to mean?"

"Just what I said. You're an engineer. You have to know what's going on."

Petard finished his cigarette and put it out. "It doesn't work like that. Engineers aren't interchangeable."

Jenna brushed her hair back from her ears and tried again. "I saw you upriver. Directing work at a dam."

"You're not another one of those—"

"Don't worry," she said. "I'm not trying to stop the war. I'm even not sure there is one."

"Then what is there?" Petard asked her.

"You tell me."

Petard said nothing. She watched him go over to the sink and sponge his neck with a wet towel. He had strong small hands with thick fingers and a full flat face coarser than the faces she'd seen on Saigon streets. He only shaved twice a week, and under the scruff on his chin, she made out the black faded welt of his flood tattoo.

"A dam," she said finally. "There's a dam."

"So what? Vietnam's a country of dams."

"This dam's different. I don't know what's wrong with it, but I think it's going to fail."

"What makes you so sure?"

"I've been upriver." She reached in her bag and handed him a manila envelope with a contact sheet in it. "I took these."

Petard wanted to say, you're from New York, what the fuck do you know about dams, but when he slipped the sheet out of the envelope and saw the pictures, saw the cracks spidering across them, he stopped and looked at her closely for the first time. She was small and thin, her hands and feet not much larger than her wrists and shins. One of her eyes looked bigger than the other. She squinted at him and wiped away the sweat from her forehead with a blue terry-cloth wristband.

"Where did you get these?"

"I told you. I took them."

"When?"

"Last month. Listen, I've been going out of my mind trying to get someone to tell me what these mean. I mean, I'm just a photographer. I take pictures. It's not that hard. I point the camera, adjust the focus, hit the shutter, and let the light in. But these aren't just pictures I took. None of these dams has cracks in them. I went back and checked. Not one."

Petard was getting his stuff together now. He put a couple green oranges in a plastic bag and tied it with a red tab. It was clear he didn't want to talk to her here but was talking under his breath about everything in this place being so fucking extreme. The Extreme Orient, that was what the French had called Indochina, and at least they got that much right.

"Take a walk with me," he told her.

They walked that day. Jenna wasn't a walker but Petard

was and he took her all over Saigon; that day it was his city, not hers. Petard walked through the city like he was retracing old lines. Jenna followed him past the Hotel Continental, moving down the street past windows filled with ducks hung upside down, past bars with 33 Bière Export on tap, past old women carrying baskets and monks in orange robes with shaved heads, past an old man who sold towels and a little girl holding packets of cough drops, so little she didn't really know she was selling anything. He moved quickly into the side streets, threading his way through the stalls piled with sacks of rice, baskets of fish, boxes of fruit. He didn't look back to see if she was there behind him. He just pushed on through the crowd, turning into one of the cool alleys off Catinet and disappearing into a dark narrow market. When she caught up with him he was standing in the frame of an open green doorway.

"Where are you taking me?" she asked.

"Somewhere we can talk."

"We can't talk here."

"We're not going to talk here."

He turned into the doorway. He had gone a few steps when a woman reached out for Petard from the shadows, her reach wasn't quick, it was slow like she knew him, but Petard tensed up when she touched him. She was a girl and she was blind; her teeth looked too big for her mouth; her parents, small shrunken people, smiled anxiously at Petard from behind the shutters in the doorway. Jenna wanted him to take his time, but as soon as Petard saw her watching him, he broke away from the girl. Almost pushing her away he took Jenna's arm and they walked on past the side entrance to a pagoda. But Petard's hands were rummaging in his pockets and when he found what he wanted, coins and a few bills, he told her to wait while he doubled back down the alley to come on the woman from behind, almost running, but there was no surprising her and when she turned her face to him he bunched her cheeks in both hands and kissed her on the nose. Then he said something low to her in Vietnamese, not the right words, but somehow he got the uplift of the accent just right, his word order was mixed up too but Jenna heard him say the words for devotion, *sung bai*. She was blind but she blinked like a seeing woman when he kissed her again. White in the eyes she stood next to him, trembling in her patched blue clothes, but Petard was so big it was like she was standing under him, she wasn't after food or money, that was clear, he was protecting her and when he gave her a handful of dong she pushed them away, she didn't want them, she wanted him, and said, loud enough for Jenna to hear, When, when, Petard, when? *Khi, khi, Peytar, khi?*

"Tonight," he told her. "I'll be back tonight."

She seemed to know what tonight meant because when she heard the word she let go of him and let him force the money on her. Every journalist Jenna knew kept a woman in Saigon. But Petard's woman was different. She was an ugly stupefied girl with chipped teeth. Jenna continued to follow him through the market to a little noodle stand he went to a lot. Petard turned into a dark corridor leading through an old house. It led to a backyard garden surrounded by a fence made from bamboo stalks. They took seats at a table next to a small pond with brown fish in it.

"How'd you find this place?" Jenna asked him.

"Leni's sister runs it."

"Whose sister?"

"Leni's the girl in the alley. Her sister runs this noodle shop. You can see her over there by the cooking pit. She's the one with swollen eyes. She's afraid. They all are."

"Afraid of what?"

"The end's coming. They feel it, too. Last week I watched her father burn photographs. Family photographs. He says he's afraid they'll come after his children."

"They won't," said Jenna.

"Maybe. But he feels the end coming same as us."

"So you've told him," said Jenna.

"He knows there are NVA in the Delta. Everyone in Saigon does. It's only sixty miles from here."

"Do they know you're building a dam?" Jenna asked.

Petard didn't answer; he waited for the sister to clear the table. She brought them tea.

"Can you get her out?"

"No."

"Why not?"

"It won't help," he said.

"Don't you want her to go?"

"What I want doesn't matter. My father told me I'd meet a woman here. He saw it in a vision. And now I've met her."

"How'd you meet her?"

Petard spoke slowly; Jenna remembered how slowly he spoke—slowly like he was reading aloud. He said he sniffed out this market when he first came to Saigon. Open-necked in a wrinkled white shirt, he'd come here to get away from the other Americans, squatting on the ground before a small brazier with a fish or two grilling on it. He got to be a regular there, showing the guy how to cook fish the way he liked it, the fish buried under the coals. After dinner he'd roll a cigarette from local tobacco and smoke it down in a few pulls; sometimes he'd play chess with an old man, using stones on squares drawn on the asphalt. Whenever he was in town he'd come back to the same market, same stall, same spot, sometimes staying into the evening, always till the time they got out the oil lamps to light up the market, till one evening he was tapped on the shoulder and invited to a movie. The movie was shown backward on a sheet stretched behind an open-air stall. Petard watched with his eyes closed. He knew the plot, all his people did. The movie was a Western; the Vietnamese loved Westerns. A convoy of covered wagons was moving West. The people in them were about to take his people's land, and when they did, they began killing them. Petard went through the film in his head all the way to the final scene, the massacre, his people pushed into a natural dead end defined by high bluffs, their horses trapped and bucking, their nostrils steaming in the cold mountain air, picked off one by one by white riders in blue cavalry pants and stained white undershirts, their own horses rearing, holding onto their hats with one hand and shooting with the other, no way out, the chaparral visible in the distance where the bluffs ended and flattened out into plain they'd never make it to, his people falling but the camera not stopping to watch them hit the dust, just falling, always falling and never hitting unsaddled ground. Petard clutched his knees and held back from vomiting. When he opened his eyes the movie was over but nobody in the theater had moved. He had not said anything but they knew. He knew they knew. They knew who he was.

"You?" a woman jabbed at him in English, pinching her own skin and pointing at the white sheet.

Petard nodded, and as he did people all around him in the makeshift theater began reaching out to touch him. An Indian, they said in Vietnamese, simple enough Vietnamese for him to know what they were saying. This man is an Indian. An American, too, but he is an Indian. The lights were off in the theater, the projector was dead, but in the soft light of cigarettes hands that were not his people's hands grazed the curve of his spine. He was being touched again. Among the high narrow pines along the

Klamath he had once been looked for and found. He knew he was the one the Hupa had tapped. He knew, too, he was his father's son, son of a drunk broken shaman who barely knew the prayers anymore but knew how to pray through the words failing him. Another life was calling him to be lived, and he looked around him now at the life of a people he'd never believed he'd have to enter. The air was hot and sour and he ate some small hard wafers somebody'd handed him. They were stale, least they tasted stale, but maybe they were supposed to be that way, he couldn't tell, and as he ate he remembered how, last sweat, his father'd told him he would meet a woman in Vietnam. He'd love her, marry her, but she'd die before he could bring her home. He'd come home alone. His father had told him to prepare for that. For coming home alone.

Jenna said, "You mean she's your wife?"

"Leni's sister picked me out at the movie. That's the way it works here. It has to be done through the family."

"Then you can bring her back," Jenna told him.

"She doesn't have long," Petard said, not really listening to her. "But she's happy. I take her out for rides. She sits on the fender of my jeep."

"What's wrong with her?"

"A cancer," he said. "A rare kind of cancer."

"I'm sorry," said Jenna.

"Don't be." Petard covered his eyes with his hand. "She likes it here."

"You do, too, don't you?" Jenna asked him softly.

Petard didn't answer this, not right away at least. But he loosened up and started talking more easily. There was no grass in Vietnam, he told her, not grass the way he remembered it, white high dancing grass sweeping one way then the other, leaves from scrub oak blowing every which way in the wind when the wind was cold, the mountains bare and blue in the distance. Vietnam didn't have fog either, tule fog rising off the ground at night, but the country had enough steam to turn every turbine in every dam that'd ever be built. It wasn't California but his father was right. Petard said he remembered him on the mountain, standing mute up the side of Ukonom, not waving, the grass was waving goodbye, waving in the wind for them both, for him and the mountain where his mother was buried. His father hadn't said much that last day when they'd walked together up where the snow was melting and the orchids were just beginning to push through, just, you'll like it there, and he was right. There weren't lady's slippers in Vietnam, much less azalea and pines and ravines crammed so full of cedar each one smelled like a closet, but his father was right, he liked Vietnam. He thought now that was why he was so high up here, he liked it here. He liked the tin shacks along the Bien Hoa Highway and he liked the people in them, they were dirt-poor but they gambled with a ferocity he'd never seen. He liked the markets where you could buy garlic one bud at a time and smell ginger and arrowroot, a cleaner smell than the burning oil of American deep-fry, markets where everything, even birds, was sold by weight, balanced on battered brass scales, liked the bitter fruit they ate, tamarind and betel and carambole, liked their rice alcohol, liked it too much, but most of all he liked their Five Elements, they were a building people and he liked that. America had four elements, water and fire and earth and air, but Vietnam had five, water and fire and earth and metal and wood, because metal and wood were for making the things of the world and the Vietnamese understood the things of the world.

"I like it here, too," she told him when he was done. "I even have a house."

"In Saigon?"

"Cholon. But it's not really mine. I share it with some other journalists. They're never there, though, so I have it mostly to myself. Except for Defosse."

"Defosse?" Petard's eyes widened; he was startled and couldn't conceal it. He tore the wrapper off a piece of gum and put it in his mouth. "He's not American, is he?"

"No. French."

Petard traced his fingers along the line of an incipient crack in his teacup. "Better tell me what you know about him."

"You know him?"

"No. Not directly."

"Does he work for the Bureau of Reclamation?"

"He's an engineer. But not one of ours."

"Does he build dams?"

"He used to. But that was a long time ago."

"Not to hear him talk about it," said Jenna.

Jenna watched Petard smile at the woman who brought them soup. He pressed his hands together before taking the bowl from her. He leaned forward slightly while he ate, sipping soup from the bowl. Jenna took a long breath and began.

3

"I met Defosse," Jenna told Petard, "after taking the first photographs. Not the ones I showed you. Others. I didn't know what to do with them. I thought maybe the film was scored. So I went back and shot the dams three, four more times, using a different ASA film each time. But the cracks just got bigger. It was getting to me, I didn't know where to turn. So I went to this small augur's shop in Cholon. Defosse was waiting for me there, afterward, in the shadows."

Jenna said the shop she was looking for was an old shop

off Catinet with a pale blue awning and a window cut in two by a screen of dirty blankets. A few old travel posters taped to the window had faded to pastels. It was an augur's shop, one in a row of fortune-telling places, and she went in. Inside, two ceiling fans droned like a twin-engined plane. None of the usual stuff in here, though, no bottled snakes or pickled monkeys, no bowls of sand with small burnt brooms of bamboo shoved in them, no periodic tables of the alphabet either, just a sort of dentist chart dividing a schematic head into time zones. Laid out in a row on the counter were busts, Tiams mostly, kings the original Annamese'd kicked out when they stole the Delta country and drowned the great irrigators one at a time in their own ditches.

The augur's fingers were stained yellow with nicotine. His wrists were wire-thin. The metal strap of his big silver Seiko watch hung loose an inch off his skin. He stood behind the counter tending a tiny bamboo skillet with some red peppers cooking on it. He had a few in one hand and ate standing up. Somehow he knew right away she wasn't your usual American living off water tanked in from the Philippines. His rimless glasses slipped down his nose as he took her in. Jenna took off her floppy straw hat and let him look. She was thin and wore a white cotton dress with a scoop neck. Her hair was steel wool in a bun. Her eyes were light blue. And she had bangs like a girl out of the Delta.

"Révélation pour mademoiselle?" he asked her.

"Look at these," said Jenna, slipping the prints out of their manila envelope.

"1–2–3–4," he said after a moment's scrutiny. "These not 1–2–3–4."

"What are they, then?" she said, not knowing what he meant but wanting to hear him out.

"Future not first," said the augur. "Future second."

She took out her Leica but he shook his head before she could hand it to him. It wasn't the camera. It was her eye. He passed his light palmar hands over the prints like he was absolving them.

"You mean I did this?"

He gave her a dead untelling stare.

"I didn't mean to," she said. "I really didn't."

She knew then she'd taken a picture of the future, but didn't know what future or why. Turning around in the door, she saw the augur's wife sitting in a chair beside him. She'd taken his hand and put it in her lap. Out on the street was Defosse. He was leaning against a wall, wearing one of his soft white suits, his feet pointing at her. When he saw her he took the gum he was chewing out of his mouth and pressed it into a doorjamb with his thumb. He didn't have to say anything. She knew he'd been looking for her or someone like her. And he knew she knew.

"Then what?" asked Petard.

"He led me to a house a couple of doors down."

She followed him in there without exchanging a word. Inside, it was pretty stark. A long fluorescent bulb was suspended over a stool and an overstuffed chair. She looked at Defosse closely as she could in the swaying light. He was delicate. His neck was red against his white collar and his hair was stiff with too much oil. Once he sat down he didn't get up from his overstuffed chair. Sunken in it he didn't even look at her over its flanges, not straight on. He just talked, crossing and uncrossing his legs carefully to keep the creases sharp in his pants. He said he was the last of a family of concessionaires. After his father's death he had sold his family's rubber plantation, La Barbe de Saint Ratouille, and left for France to become an engineer. But he had not built dams for many years. Not since Dien Bien Phu.

"He told you he built dams?" asked Petard.

"Yes. But first he showed me pictures. That's why he'd followed me. He saw I'd taken pictures and that something wasn't right about them. You see, he had pictures, too."

"How many? What were they of?"

"Quite a few. He said they were of the battle of Dien Bien Phu. But they were strange. There was nothing of war in them. No soldiers, no weapons even. Just Defosse sitting in a chair with a little girl dressed in white attending on him."

"What's so strange about that?" asked Petard.

"Her face was wrapped in white, too," she said. "Thick white gauze."

There were other photos, she told Petard, and he'd let her flip through them, watching her with cold unvarying eyes.

"What are these of?" Jenna asked Defosse again when she was finished.

"Dien Bien Phu," said Defosse.

"That can't be," Jenna told Defosse. "This is a big house. You're sitting in an easy chair. The girl in the white bundle seems to be serving you."

She was serving him, Defosse started to say, just like she had at the siege. How a frail little girl figured in the last battle the French fought in Indochina, Jenna didn't know. That ended in May of 1956, seventeen years earlier, when the French dropped a garrison into a valley of poppy fields and watched a fortress turn into their last muddy stand in Indochina. Vietnam was a partitioned land now, but the way Defosse talked about it, the siege of Dien Bien Phu was still going on. Defosse talked about Dien Bien Phu like he was asleep, not far asleep, but snorkeling just below the surface. Opium, she thought, seeing the signs now, the slow-curing skin, the face with trampoline cheeks, the half-moons under his eyes. Defosse sat in a chair like he was lying on his side, his head resting on a small block of wood, twisting a bit of gum onto a needle, holding it over a flame to the bubbling point. She saw his eyes wavering at her behind a tiny lamp of smoke and watched him draw her in with concave calm. Across the street was a shop where a butcher was disjointing a goat. Defosse didn't see it, though. He didn't seem to have peripheral vision. His eyes kept dropping into the lining of a bowl where they went begging for equilibrium. He'd seen something at Dien Bien Phu and was seeing it still, detail by detail. He wanted to tell her what he'd done. He was a rubber planter. He'd cut down a tree. A tree? She was sure he'd done something more than gash a tree and drive an iron spout in. Jenna already knew that rubber planters didn't give a shit about trees. What had Defosse done at Dien Bien Phu?

Defosse remembered, remembered and talked for hours in the dark. Remembered the horizon trembling in the heat of the valley of Dien Bien Phu. The shelling had stopped. Over the wireless Defosse had heard Colonel Langlais's last message to Hanoi, saying he was about to surrender. He'd thought it was the end of the war. End of the miles of deserted rubber plantations. End of the matchbox forests burned from the air, the craters filled with purple water, the pear trees wilted by chlordane. End of him too, probably, because the Viet Minh were inside the compound now and they were tilting their fire his way. He wasn't scared. He was hungry and wondered if they'd feed him before they took him prisoner. What was left for him now besides some rice wrapped in palm leaves? His arm was in a splint, hanging by a camera strap. He couldn't bend his elbow. His mouth was dry from all the morphia, and at the end, when there was no water left, he'd taken to drinking the jacket water from shell casings. He adjusted the rag wound round his head in a turban and thought back to another world two months ago, when he'd held firm in his hands the taming power to divert a river. This was a war for engineers and in fifty-six days he'd built a dam. Surely that counted for something. Defosse felt the evenness of time and knew the morphine salts were taking effect, knew that, long as he lived, he'd never be able to draw breath again without them.

His orders were to get Dien Bien Phu out of the water. Travaux Cochinchine'd put him in charge of 3rd Company, 31st Engineering Battalion, Unit 90.8.6.1. It was a shitty assignment and the numbers showed how far down he was. The base was on the Nam Yum River, an unpredictable river with a history of bad spring flooding. The Nam Yum was asleep half the year but Defosse knew that, come April, the river'd roll out of its bed and hit the base with a hard bracing slap. He remembered how, back in Saigon, he used to rinse out his teaspoon under the tap ten minutes at a time, watching the water twist into a fan, an ear, a length of rope. He knew water went wherever it wanted to go. But when he told Colonel Langlais that a dam could not be built on the Nam Yum using conventional means, Langlais had laughed and hadn't even asked him what those unconventional means were. He said a few measly rubber trees would have to do for a dam, he couldn't spare sandbags. He gave him a few rolls of chicken wire and some empty wine bottles. He told him to do whatever he had to do for the dam to hold, and Defosse knew what he had to do. If only he hadn't known, but he had.

The first few weeks he didn't really think he'd have to build the dam. There weren't even a few sick rubber trees, just one old one alone on a bend in the river, so he did nothing. The first couple months of 1954 Dien Bien Phu wasn't Dien Bien Phu yet. It was just another ruin on the edge of France's colonial crumble. His family's plantation was a stretch of stumps now, clear-cut to pay off old debts. Used to be they tapped trees, let them dribble latex for twenty years. Now they pulled them over with bulldozers, stripped them into dowels, then incised the trunk, crushed the roots, ripped off the limbs, and stamped them into ruts where the rubber flowed out into pancakes they pressed into blocks. They tore the trees apart and didn't stop till there were two piles left, one pulp and one rubber. The corpses of his family's trees sickened Defosse. They had been magnificent creatures and they burned blue even at night because the blue they gave off was darker than black. He saw it but didn't stop it. The trees were his sole source of income and he'd lost touch with them. He knew how to take scrapings from cup and bark and how to watch for any drops falling to the ground, but mostly he knew how to set out neat mathematical rows of new trees, corridors planted two hundred to the acre, an immense formal garden of trees, a number for every tree, the terracing work that led him first to weeding and pruning, then to drain upkeep, then last to river work. This was all before he'd learned surveying from Travaux, learned that *the land is already marked*, that it loses its divisions when it gets bladed down to dough. The trees are posts, the forests fences, the rivers boundary lines, and they're all already there. He'd had to be taught this but his sister Hevea hadn't. He remembered the day they cut down the trees. He was twenty and had just acceded to the estate. She was eighteen. They'd gone fishing on the muddy river. She said she was ashamed of him. You don't wear the same clothes as me, Hevea told him, don't eat the same food, then why can't you see the trees are all different too, they're alive just like us. Snapping open her little blue plastic handbag, she'd handed him a zinc coin, just a couple of dong, but she said this was tree money and he'd have to take it, put it in his mouth and not swallow it, swallowing's too easy, Gerard, just live with your cold work, roll it around in there, live with the taste of corrosion between your teeth. Defosse the destroyer she'd called him, and maybe she was right. He never felt what they all called the tapping, not till later, not till it was too late to tap into anything anymore, not even his family tree, because, no matter how much money they all made off the rubber market, Defosse couldn't kick the feeling that all the Defosses were a dry and brittle line about to be obliterated by a fog that'd cover the plantation country like a blank white wall.

The great cutting was in 1937. By August 1939 Defosse was studying combat engineering at the Bernoulli Institute in Vincennes. That's when he'd decided he wanted to become a rebuilder, a reclaimer. He told himself when it was all over he'd never cut down another rubber tree again, and he hadn't, fact he'd started a reclaim plant for masticating old snips and cuttings of rubber into useful form again, hadn't even considered it, not till now. He was wary about cutting trees when there weren't many of them left but knew that immense power resided in killing the last of anything. After all, his great-grandfather Hercule'd planted the first rubber tree along the Bai d'Along in 1858. The Defosse line was one long tapering rubber conveyor belt from Hercule to him. His father hadn't even grown that much rubber. Aristide Defosse had simply been willing to mix almost anything into the gum just to see what would happen. He'd set up factories that cut it with fillers, accelerators, coloring agents, oils, asphalt from Trinidad's sticky lake, tar from the coke ovens of Ohio River steel towns, hardwood pitch from northern forests, pine tar from southern woods. The rubber heels he made were half clay, the tires he turned out were half soot, the kitchen tiles mostly sawdust. The factories were in Hanoi, where the rubber arrived in 250-pound oblong blocks, jacketed in woven straw matting. Defosse had long stopped believing in any future that had rubber in it. These days the Defosse estate went into foam-rubber toys that were rubber in name only. They had no tree milk in them. Would Defosse be the last Defosse, the one to pull the last rubber tree from the last plantation and leave the last of the soil exhausted?

The days passed at Dien Bien Phu. March into April. He drank tea and condensed milk spotted with tiny flies and his head buzzed from too much quinine. The edge of the base was going soft with water from the rains and the river was rising. Three strongpoints, Claudine, Françoise, Huguette, were already lost to muck. Langlais was furious. He wanted the camp kept dry. Defosse fingered the ball of unfigured rubber he carried around in his front pocket and kept an eye on the one rubber tree in camp. One day he took out his pocketknife, made a shallow cut in the bark, and tapped the gum. The rubber dried fast over the cut and sealed the incision clean. Clean and fast like it'd never been cut. It was a good tree, maybe the right tree. Defosse knew that a dam could be built from one tree if it was the right one. Other than this old tree there were no trees anywhere in sight. He knew how to make a dam using hard piles, cedar and hickory and oak. He even knew how to make one out of soft piles, usable pine, hemlock, spruce. But a dam out of one tree? He watched Langlais's skepticism turn to scorn. One tree? The rubber tree had a straight trunk and white bark with little sessile flowers in red and white. But Langlais was not cooperative. He turned down his requisition for a gunboat because, when he'd asked him why he needed it, Defosse'd said he needed to feel the sway of the river's will. Langlais had given him a hard ducal stare, then taken out a manila folder, slipped out a few sheets of paper, and made a note to himself with a stubby pencil. Probably requesting a replacement, Defosse thought, Legion and Travaux never did get along, but Langlais tried to make light of it in his swank way, saying, Why not stopcock the river, pinch her bottom with a little wooden children's dam, eh, Defosse?

"Not wood," he told him. "Rubber."

Defosse knew there was a place where the dam had to go, a zero point where the river swung into balance all on its own, with just enough weight on each pan of the balance to bring the waters into locking position. He tried to focus all his senses on the river the way he'd been taught but couldn't get a lock on it. The river shifted its weight from bank to bank, never rested passing mulberry and jujube, smelled like vinegar and moved like milk. The only map he had to go by was made of silk. Defosse burnt his face to pottery taking soil samples, brushing the ground with a camel-hair brush, gathering the crumbling leather soil into clumps, laying it onto glass plates touched with oil to make the marl legible to his eyes. Dram after dram had nothing to say to him but he kept at it. He fitted a Linhoff camera with a Red 3 filter and shot the soil with infrared film, exposed the soil at f.11 six minutes after sunrise and six before sundown. He did everything but whiten up the river with a little 2,4-D, but if he did, if he turned the gas on full and brought the river to a boil, there'd be no dam because there'd be no river, and there had to be a dam. So he spent truant days on end with his pants rolled up over his knees, kicking mud clouds into the river. Langlais threw a shitfit but there were limits to what he knew about rivers. He thought all you had to do was cut open the belly of the river, pull its intestines across the land, and call it a canal. He wanted to pin a *croix de guerre* on the current and be done with it. Didn't he know the old song about the bridge at Avignon where the caissons held for seven hundred years over the bayonet piles of the innocents? *Sur le pont d'Avignon, on y danse, on y danse.* The old rhymes were mnemonic devices for engineers. They called them totaling formulas now but the drift was the same. To make the river give blood, give blood to the river, but Defosse knew once the river bent his arm, rolled up his sleeve, and took the cement stab, no wad of pressed cotton'd stop the flow. Wheels have spokes, pots are clay, houses have windows and doors. And a dam, a dam has death at its floor . . .

It took him a while to splice the ceremony right. All those arranged accidents, Defosse knew about them, though he hadn't actually been to a kill. At Travaux people spoke about them in stage whispers, talked about what it took to get a dam up to burial strength. It wasn't the casting of the concrete but the *casting into* the concrete. God, they were canny about it. They knew how to cover the abutments with tricolor bunting on opening day, knew how to bring in VIPs to talk about what a nice public bath this deep black water'd make, how to hand out free terry-cloth robes and sandals, one size fits all, the same way the dam fits anyone shoved into it for a long fossil swim. Up here, though, all you see are the memorial plaques, the placenta faces bronzed in bas-relief, twisted little half faces lobing out of a bog of bronze, hair smashed wet against cheek and forehead, air entrained round their lips in tiny gasping bubbles, faces newly arrived at death with the pain barely fled out of them. Down below, down under the rows of families sitting on folding chairs with green slipcovers, shielded from the sun by a large tent flaring downward in seersucker stripes, the flags folded scalene on their laps, fine view of the spreading lake, though, were the bodies, pillars of society if only they knew, officially listed as lost but each epoxied into place using coordinates, three axes representing three dimensions, a and b and c. Like Pierre Cognet, dead at a level of 563m O.D. below the top water of the St. Pierre-Cognet reservoir, not one of your calendar saints but well bedded all the same, and if your tourists up top don't know, if they've forgotten or don't want to remember, if they want to pray to him, least they've come to the right place. With him in his reliquary the dam's not likely to budge. Remember, too, his name and use it, because no amount of aggregate poured from the gyres of cement trucks'll save the structure from slump if you get the name wrong. The name of a dam is a ululant cry, it has to be agony to hear, rammed down the ear like a tamping rod pushed into memory. Three sharp cries, because dams come in threes. These days Reclam's Yokut/Ah Pah/Tehama was considered classic textbook triangulation, laid out in a triangle not far from equilateral, the first setting being Yokut at 0.0 and the rest falling into place around the base like meridians, but back in '47 there was nothing that big to go by.

Back then Travaux sent Defosse to repair a dam at Tignes, a project on the headwaters of the Isère a few miles west of the Italian border. Tignes Dam sat on an old valley, a valley so old there were other valleys under it filled with debris. A few old walls inclined out of the ground. The stone courses were fault lines that might move any time and break the tablet of the dam. This was good flooding ground if only you knew how to read the names worked into the rock, but these engineers didn't, not anymore. All they were doing was running traverses from one known point to another and it wasn't working. The dam was sagging. Defosse told the engineers on site to go over to the village and listen to the stories the old men told. A little train-set village with white limestone houses, a church, a bar, and two telephone poles, Tignes went back to prehistory. The Tignes under Tignes lived on in those stories, all of them about an old buried river, the one about the bull impaling the river with its horns and easing it off to one side, the one about the unfillable gold cup of water, a cup with no bottom and no top, the one about the lost hillside cemetery where each grave had a moat round it instead of a wall. Find Aesop, Defosse told them, find him and make him talk till his throat's dry and don't take abridgment for an answer, then go back to your transits and levels, calculate the angle of incidence at which the bull's horns hit the water till you find the river's old course dipping through the valley, scrape away the copper of the soil till you uncover red and calcined ruins, five feet thick and hard as metal, remnants of a reservoir gilded at its edges, find the double-ring graves with the fosses intact and trace from them the top water level of the intended dam. The old stories are full of names and numbers. Get them right and over your bright opening days the sun will shine like coral and set like concrete.

He was getting them right now. Well into the siege, Langlais called him into his command moat, a trench covered by a tin roof. A neat pile of papers sat on his desk. Without much ceremony he said, "I've asked Travaux to replace you."

"They won't," said Defosse.

"You've done nothing but collect old pottery."

"The dam's almost done."

"Flakes and scraps," he said. "I don't see what's in them."

"A name," said Defosse. "I've found a name."

Scorn was the best cover for the work he had to do, and even though the colonel eventually commuted his dismissal to a reprimand, he gave up on him right then and there. Not that he didn't have to be careful. He had to make it look right, like a normal atrocity. They'd raped a few women on the dikes and left them for blood-drip but this was different. This was sacrifice. Defosse knew it had to be done on intercalary time, extra time added to the year to sync calendar time up with the sun's time. Ends of months were best, February being a leap year was best of all, but he knew that old rhyme, thirty days hath September, April, May, whatever, was an approximation. The months were arbitrary equations of state to engineers, who knew otherwise, knew how time was written in variables and not absolutes, how geologic time was a matter of magnitude, not signs, how hours and days and months and years were numbers on one ruler, one line among many, all length and no thickness, one dimension strung in a telephone line among all the possible dimensions. It was impossible to know if the time you chose was right but possible to make it final. That was the trick. There had to be finality to the way it was done. A line had to die out in the doing of it, preferably a daughter of a grandee in whom the hopes of a fond father reposed, and he'd have to be there, too, watching and shaking while he strangled her with a plastic hose, standing with the rest of them up to his knees in water and rice. If it went right, the dam'd be wedded to Old Man River, thin when he was thin, fat when he was fat, high when high and low when low. A dam couldn't have calculated life like a building or a bridge. A dam had to have eternal life built into it, and the only way you can get eternal life is to take it away from someone who has it, stamp her out, pull her soul through a die and draw it extruded into blue clay.

May 6, 1954. The time came but it was slow in coming. A decade of water seemed to run over the stones in spun rosary lines before there was any letup. The siege had drawn cold round Dien Bien Phu. The ground outside the compound was white with parachute shrouds of supply drops that'd missed their mark. The rains stopped for a bit in the morning and Defosse thought, This is it. Aerial recon showed approach trenches curling round the garrison, ready to strike any minute now. Orders went out and they were total cyanide. Bomb the local grave-yards, split the staves on the barrel crypts and raise the white dust of generations, set their spirits free and see what happens when all hell breaks loose. It was mad but ele-mental. What Defosse thought the dam would do he did not know, turn the trenches into canals, doubtful, make the river impassable, maybe, but the preparations were complete and he knew it could be done. They had lost this war and this dam was part of the loss, not France's loss but the beginning of another, larger loss he'd just found half buried in the future like a colossus in sand. Just before noon a Travaux plane, a Junkers JU 51 with the nose engine out and the other two not doing too well, touched down with the little girl. The pilot didn't even cut the engines for a rest, and before he swung the clunker round for takeoff, he gave Defosse the V sign. V wasn't victory. V was the drill bit. Travaux said go and Defosse knew what that meant. The little girl and a few villagers were bundled out the rear hatch, the girl hardly visible, her body covered with gauze to above the shoulders and her hair pinned up under a bonnet.

She came on a litter, on a thin mattress supported by two poles they carried like a sling. She was so small, her neck really no bigger than his wrist, so young and old, a little plaster of baby fat under her chin, but see that ravine wrinkling under her eyes. Around her was peace, the peace of innocence. Defosse wanted her peace for his dam, wanted it bad. The men around her brushed the flies from her eyes. He rubbed his eyes and wondered if he could go through with it. He shook his arm out of his sleeve and checked his watch. The time didn't matter but the gesture did. It said get on with it. As they carried her away from the airstrip she was looking at him and her eyes were saying, how far is it to your village, you don't work for one of those American agencies, do you? He didn't know why she thought he was an American till he remembered he had an eagle on his cap like a U.S. officer but this was an eagle on a dry riverbed, standard Travaux issue, and that'd happened before, because wherever Travaux sent him, there was that Bureau handing out pieces of that big rock-candy mountain they called Reclamation.

For years Defosse had been a Bureau watcher, stacking rocks in cairns while they built pyramids. The Americans did things step-by-step by the book, but theirs was a book of steps, each of unequal height, leading to an altar up top where they houseled themselves and said unspeakable things in a closely guarded Zend of name, number, and table. Their dams were words and their words were liquid. They were a Vatican, but what kind of Vatican built dams with small chapels hollowed into the base of them, lined galleries with unbaked bricks and purple plaster, laid granaries next to generators, dug keyways with petroglyphs riveted in, filled druse with documents, and left little bays in the towers where the river might live on till the waters subsided, as one day they would? Back in '48 when he was busy driving tunnels to shift the Loire round Donzère-Mondragon he'd written Denver, strictly a fan letter praising the cuneiform design of Yokut Dam, the one wedged up against the Klamath, but asking in a P.S. how the Anasazi in southern Colorado ever'd managed to cut a city into a cliff without drills to bite away at the rock, and after a while getting back a response incised on letterhead, just an underling scrawl but bad handwriting's nothing when you can make a river follow the point of your stylus, and when he made it out, it said, "They built the mesa first and put the city in later." This was an added dimension, but Reclam was always adding dimensions.

Heaven is high and earth is low but not if you're in reclamation and can get there by building earth on earth till the yielding sand settles autogenous on the ground and an arm of concrete reaches up so high and white that its hand is the hand you see pushing the sun across the sky.

"This is hard for me," said Defosse, the chair he held onto swaying with him now.

"Try to remember," said Jenna.

Try to remember, Defosse, remember the last minutes of her life. Her name was Ly Thoat and that was going to be the name of the dam. Unwrap the nameplate and show it to her, Defosse. She's literate, so don't let her eyes roll backward into winter when she sees her name cut in depressed roman characters, name and dates, 1944–1954, ten years of her own name plus the French name Defosse had to give her, Lina Valentin. Steady her, whisper to her that she has not been given a work beyond her bearing strength. Tell her her death will be light work. Let her drink a Coke while she watches the tiny striped fish feeding on the water side of the dam, the dam that is to be her dam. Stop looking back and forth between your watch face and hers. Don't hurry or delay because this is hard for you. The Chézy equation calls for death at critical depth where the discharge per unit width, q, is everywhere the same. Lay her across the first row of gambions, the bamboo bundles packed with stones floating the dam lightly on the light alluvial soil, and strap her down with plaited strips of bamboo, her back hung in a catenary curve, elbows and knees pulled tight together under the bale. Take out the shoes, the pile shoes, and slip them on her small feet. Then take her life, take it and give it to the pushing river, to the channels of the nine rivers and four lakes of Annam. Do not let her lag into death but slip her into very soft ground, cramped into the hollows, pinching open her eyes so that her death rushes out into the waters and seals the floor under the dam with its final fog. Take care to hear her last thoughts winding down helical, swept into the point of a cone, please, don't, no, oh . . . and at the very end cover her with a blanket so the last snuff comes in darkness and confusion, stop the uplift and push her spirit sheeting into the pile wall below, trace her end in a closed curve downward into the butt of the dam, tapering into the waiting silt. This is why you must say the words slowly, say them for her because she does not know how to say them anymore, say them because she is trembling and the words must be said without dilation or rotation, say them translate to her right, translate to her left, say them still but with a slight censor swing in your throat, say different words each time but say them in the right order because she is dying and hears you, say, Little girl, dig the channel deep and keep the spillways low, little girl, dredge the river's stones and pile them on the banks, little girl, fix the levels of high and low, and hold them, little girl, hold them good for a thousand, a thousand thousand years.

"Ly Thoat Dam." Jenna said it to hear it said, said it because Defosse hadn't.

"You've heard it before?"

"The way you say it," she told him, "I can't tell."

"I always call her Lina," said Defosse. "Never that other."

When Lina stopped breathing he cut the tree over her and gummed her eyes shut with tree milk. He'd have to build two more dams and till that happened this dam was DNA. Sure, the river looked tampered with, but that dilute black scuffing was all he or anyone was going to be able to see because whatever happened from now on was going to be outside time. There'd be no dome or tower or turret to mark this place. The others were walking back to the camp now, heads bent like statues with the heads knocked off, Defosse last in line, picking up the sashes tied round their foreheads that they were dropping behind them because it was all over now. The road back to the camp was empty and they were almost inside it when the shelling started.

Defosse knew right away this wasn't just random mortar fire. It was rain handed down from heaven. The rest ran for cover but Defosse stood still and waited for the rain to hit him. He didn't have to wait long for the hammer, but it wasn't one hammering down. The explosion hit him in jerks like he was a puppet, a little khaki doll of himself dressed in a white shirt and drill suit, hit him in marionette waves of shock and sound and fire. The waves came fast but slow too, slow enough so he could feel the timing of them. Did death tell time? Not for him, not now. He was still alive and dangling, alive on the windward side of death, alive against the shrapnel rain. He opened his eyes. He'd been thrown against a case of Chinese beer. His arm was stripped to a corncob. He'd seen other Legionnaires blown to bone but now he wasn't able to look at where his arm'd been and think, *my arm*. He tried to reach for his hat but gave up, thinking he still had an arm but'd lost manual control. It was so sad for him to see his new fedora sinking in the mud. He wanted to turn away from it but he couldn't move his head, only his eyes. Straining them he tried to look at the river but the river was like his hat, muddy and just beyond him. Old Man River ought to have gone into thrombosis by now, but look, there he was, all flow and no clot. Had the dam failed? Defosse didn't know and for the first time in weeks didn't care. Around him he saw the leaves wilting at the top of a tall tree, smelled the mimosa, felt the coolness of the river, waited for the surge of coming night. He didn't know how much time passed. He'd always lived and breathed numbers and now he was running out of numbers to breathe. Staked to the ground at the other end of the rubble, a dog barked. Defosse was conscious of his white jeep parked nearby, the steering column held in place by a sagging wire hanger.

The last he saw of Dien Bien Phu was a soldier on a bicycle. "Please, I can't walk," he'd told him in a weak voice. Defosse was so still the Viet Minh'd jumped in his seat, he was so startled to hear a dead man talk. But he brought a doctor and when they lifted him onto a stretcher Defosse slipped into a blackness as quiet as night. It wasn't unconsciousness. It was a burning blackness with a white crusted edge like powder, only he couldn't feel a thing. He was slipping away now. He was eating a bowl of noodle soup in the restaurant he ate lunch most days on a side street, the rue Taberd back in Saigon, sitting at the small round table next to the window where he always sat, staring at the china lions in the garden, when a spray truck passed by hissing out a heavy white mist of DDT. The cook pushed her daughter, a girl in a wheelchair with spina bifida, back into the back room and threw her apron over the soup pot. A lot of the strange white powder fell indolent to the ground but more blew back up in his face and he breathed it in. It didn't have the incense sting of DDT. He felt a metallic fastness forming around him, taste of opium, taste of a penny sucked dateless in his mouth. He didn't feel like moving ever again. He was in a bird cage with a blanket thrown over it and that was fine with him. Could he roll himself up in concrete and stay there? He wanted to, would have said yes if saying was something he could have done, but his memory wasn't a solid mass and he didn't know what concrete was anymore. What was concrete? Hard white stone was what he would have said but now he didn't know the answer. Concrete was not white, not hard, not stone. It was more like rubber . . .

He woke up in a field hospital where another doctor told him he was going to get a new arm, an American arm. He lay on a bed made out of gummy legion pine with a rush mat laid over it. There was no IV stuck in him, just a medicine dropper in a glass of fizzy water on a stand next to his bed. So there was compassion in this long narrow country that'd always reminded him of a cheekbone up north and a jawbone down south. But compassion was a drug, the drug was morphia, and it offered him everything except real refuge. On the other side of the opium curtain was the little girl Ly Thoat with her questions, the girl bundled in white. He never saw her save stealing into his camera in those prints he clutched in his one hand the day Jenna met him on the rue Catinet, hearing her voice through the hanging abacus beads, always asking those same questions, You left, you left, you had a good home and you left it, Defosse, why did you go and leave your refuge? She was right. Where was the refuge for him now? He had made two sacrifices that day in May. He'd sacrificed her knowingly and himself without knowing it. There must have been some other way to do it. He knew of a few dams named after their engineers and he'd never known why they'd held, not till now. Backing up behind Ly Thoat Dam he saw Lake Defosse. If he'd put trust in that dam, if he hadn't staked their two lives on it and instead put trust, and trust alone, could it have held?

"Could it?" Petard had asked Jenna.

"He didn't know. He never knew."

"Never knew what?"

"That it never happened," Jenna said. "That there was no sacrifice, no little girl."

"How are you so certain?" asked Petard.

"His story's unbelievable," said Jenna. "If he's right, the Bureau of Reclamation is full of sorcerers."

Petard rubbed his eyes and slid her packet of photos back across the table. "Then how do you explain these?"

"I can't."

"I can't either," he told her. "But I know what they mean."

Petard knew all right. He spoke with a cold, even finality about what was going to happen in Vietnam in the next six weeks. Two divisions of North Vietnamese regulars, aided by four brigades of Viet Cong, were helping an elite division of engineers from the United States Bureau of Reclamation build a dam across the Mekong Delta. The stated purpose of the dam was to moderate flood flow in the Delta. The real purpose was to divert the Mekong River and destroy the capacity of the Delta, the rice basket of Asia, to produce food. Petard was Chief Engineer, Division of Design, Bureau of Reclamation R&A, and he knew what diverting a river meant. The dams at Da Trinh Sanh were built to his exact specs.

"Engineering isn't what you think it is," Petard told her. "Building a dam is like building a pyramid. Only one man, the Chief Engineer, knows all the plans and he mostly carries them around in his head. It's safer that way. A dam is really quite a delicate thing. It has to last ten thousand years, but if you're off just a little, if you don't get the tolerances just right, it won't last six weeks."

"What about my pictures?" Jenna asked.

"Seems things are right on schedule," he said.

"So you know when the dams will break apart."

"No, not exactly. Not to the degree I'd like."

"Then you know where?"

"You've seen the photographs. The cracks will be right where they are. They are already waiting there."

"So you do know when."

"No, I already told you I don't know. Some magic is as slow as bureaucracy. What I know is the who. I know who designed the dams and who will destroy them. This knowledge is everything. It is what I will take back to my people after we leave Vietnam."

"Who designed them, then?"

"I did," he said.

"Then who will destroy them?"

Petard blanched. He sucked in his lips around his front teeth before he spoke.

"I will."

4

There was more, Jenna told me now, but it wasn't her story to tell; it was more my brother's than hers and I'd better ask him. After she finished her story she closed her eyes for a minute and leaned her head against the wheel of the pickup. She listened to the vibrating sounds the dam was making. Then she got out of the car. She went to the edge of the ravine. There was a picnic table next to the chain-link fence and she sat down facing the bridge across the canyon. The bridge hung across the canyon in a graceful catenary arch. The fog had mostly burned off, so now I could see the dam looming behind it.

"Death is a bridge," said Jenna, abstracted, more to herself than to me.

"A what?" I said, coming up next to her.

"A bridge. Death is a bridge. It's something Defosse told me once. I used to wonder what he meant by it. I thought he meant death was a bridge *to* something. You died, and your death was a bridge to some other life. But now I think he was saying something a lot simpler. That death *is* a bridge. That a bridge is made of death. That a bridge needs death."

"People jump off bridges," I said. "Not into them."

"Not according to Defosse. He said they have to jump. That they're drawn there."

She said in his last years Defosse had an apartment in the Pacific Heights section of San Francisco. Out his bay window, partly blocked by a hotel neon on Lombard Street, you could make out a sliver of the Golden Gate Bridge. He'd sit in that big chair of his, a calico cat in his lap, absently stroking the cat with his one hand. Next to the chair he'd rigged up an IV drip. Over and over again he'd stare fixedly out the window and tell her how the Golden Gate Bridge should've rocked by now, sideslipped in an earthquake, but for the ramming of lives into it, the suicides. Not all of them, he'd say, just the pure ones, the clear regretless ones, the ones who jumped out of their cars with the motors still running, climbed over the fence, a fence ten feet high but carefully striated with footholds. These were the ones who didn't pause, didn't hesitate, didn't look at the jelled black water before leaping, who clambered off into the cement ocean, stumbling down to darkness without a cry, without a fell doubt, without once wondering if this was the wrong darkness, lives given in a leap of faith that death would be final, that death on a bridge was a bridge to an end, not a bridge to a bridge. Souls go up or down at death, he told her, but a bridge was for tamping them down, dead straight down.

"What about dams?"

"He had all sorts of theories. There's this webbing of cable laid in the concrete fills of a dam. You know what it is; it looks like a spider's web."

"The deadman," I said.

"Right. It's called the deadman. Even the technical dictionaries use the name. Defosse said the name doesn't make much sense unless you took it literally. He'd sit there looking out the window at the bridge, breathing without moving, so still I'd wonder sometimes if he was alive. And then he'd come to and say, Jenna they're not jumping into the water, they're jumping into the bridge."

"He was a junkie, Jenna."

"Of course he was a junkie. And he got worse. You know it's not easy to get good opium in the U.S. Without the pure stuff he lost the pleasure he used to take in it. His last couple years he began to have trouble breathing. He said the air around him was bitter like lemon, a quarter lemon shoved in his mouth, no juice or pulp left in it, just dry rind with the zest scraped off. Sometimes he'd stop in the middle of a sentence and ask me to take the lemon out of his mouth. At the end he was hooked up to a respirator and didn't have the strength to turn his head. But he had his bed moved out into the living room so he could keep an eye on the Golden Gate Bridge. No matter how cold it got—by that point he had no fat at all on his body—he'd want the window thrown open. Defosse loved the sound of the foghorn. He said there were voices in it. Sad voices."

"This was 1978?"

"1979. He also liked his sheets wrapped tight around him. White and tight like a bundle. He called them his baptism dress."

"Like the little girl at Dien Bien Phu?"

"Like her. I think he died seeing her, but I have no idea if she really existed. Petard isn't sure either. But he has his own ideas, too. He won't talk about them around your brother because Jimbo will start ridiculing him, and you know what that's like. But I know he thinks dams are traps for spirits. He's pretty graphic about it. He says all valleys have spirits, specific spirits, and that when a dam floods a valley these spirits have nowhere to go. So these spirits hover round the intake towers and sometimes they get sucked in. They're driven down through tunnels and penstocks and wind up caught in the great spinning turbine. They want to get out but can't. Petard says spirits are prisoners of the laws of fluids. He says dams are built to these laws, says the Bureau of Reclamation knows them better than it knows anything else. I remember him telling me: *Spirits are fluids and they follow the rules. They don't have weight but they have mass and density. You can compress them, stuff them in jars, plug them in bottles. That's what a genie is, a trapped spirit, a prisoner of its own properties.*"

"And you believe this?"

"I'd hate to fall down an intake tower. I think about it every time I see a dam."

"But you're not some—spirit."

"But what he says makes sense. A dam is storage. They're strange dead places. You never see any moss on a dam."

My eyes followed the shadow of the heavy cable spanning the canyon. The chain-link fence next to us vibrated lightly. There was a green lawn on the dry side of the dam, an expanse of grass put there for no reason I could think of, save maybe to show the dry distant hills who was boss. Jenna saw me looking at the patch of green and started saying something I'd heard before from all of them, Petard and Travers and my brother. Irrigated societies don't work, she told me, not in the long run. Over time they exhaust the land, and that was happening here, though the dry day of reckoning was still a long time off. She leaned over to examine a softened embankment near where the pickup was parked. The bunchgrasses were gone off the top. Bugs can't live here, she went on to say, and the grass needs the bugs to take root. It was clear why. A sharp chemical scent lingered in the air. I didn't know what it was but Jenna lifted her nose in the air and said, very empirically, Dioxane. Jenna was practical about this. For her the land was a junkie same as any other miserable sweating junkie. This low land had been high for years and she accepted there was nothing she could do about it save radio in for more when the dioxin levels were low and the water grass was high. Some days the tule fog was green with phosphates but at least it was better than napalm, and after Vietnam, she knew what napalm did to the land.

"It's not like this," she said.

A crop duster flew over us in the other direction and tipped its wings at Jenna's pickup. Jenna waved without turning around. The plane looped round and let off a phosphate fog through a hose in the bottom of the fuselage. Some fell to the ground, and some blew up in our faces as we drove by on our way back to Turlock, where my brother was waiting for us. The sun was going down now and the tule fog was beginning to rise off the low ground. The rust of an old irrigation pump caught the sun. I looked across a savanna of rice. In a field beyond, on the other side of a canal, a bunch of workers kicked a soccer ball around, shouting in Spanish. The canal itself was laid out in pure American quadrangle. With a slight slope, its banks scraped of grass, it continued straight for maybe half a mile, then fell into a culvert under a highway, spitting out finally into some empty stubbled fields prepared for rice.

1

East Los Angeles. We were late getting back to Fontana because my brother wanted to see the Los Angeles River before he let me off. The L.A. River was just what I'd always imagined the river of the future to be, a long culvert made of concrete. My brother pulled off Whittier Boulevard and cut the engine. He waited a minute before he got out of the pickup and pressed his face up against the corrugated chain-link fence lining the river. He said it wasn't what he'd imagined. This river wasn't high tech at all. It was more like somebody's backyard. The concrete embankment was so dirty it looked unset. The river itself was dry and full of junk, rusted cars and broken lamps and treadless tires. It reminded him of the old road in Guttenberg, two miles leading to the state highway past a couple of boxcars on a spit of track that didn't go anywhere, past abandoned cars buried bullnose up and bathtubs filled with dirt. East Los Angeles was familiar Appalachian ground to him same as it was to me. Along the river, cars shot by on the San Bernadino Freeway, not really knowing West Virginia was in their midst.

"What do you think?" I asked.

My brother took a good look at the river, then smiled

like he knew something he wasn't going to tell me. "I wish I hadn't seen it."

Once in the pickup he started turning the radio dial back and forth, trying to get 1440 before he remembered that WAJR was back in Morgantown. Fontana was a straight drag west on the 10, and my brother drove the last few miles talking about Petard. It was one of those rare humid days in L.A. His breath fogged the windshield and from time to time he wiped the steam off with his elbow. Petard's pickup had one of those old two-piece windshields; while he talked, my half fogged over completely.

"I was thinking of going someplace," he told me. "Alaska maybe."

"What's in Alaska?" I asked.

"Petard has some friends up there," he said, rolling up his window as the palm trees passed by faster and faster. Then he turned to me and said, "He calls them friends but they're more like his relatives. I been along sometimes. Petard's idea of traveling is going from reservation to reservation. He just shows up somewhere and other Indians take him in. It's strange."

"What's so strange about that?"

"They all know who he is. You go someplace with him down some long road, winding into what you think is totally empty wilderness. There's no sign of anyone anywhere and Petard doesn't really know where he is either, he's just feeling his way through the mountains, then all of a sudden there's a village ready with a big welcoming committee. I swear they always know he's coming. The last mile or two you can hear the drums."

"What are they waiting for?"

"Him. Always him. He gets the VIP treatment even though they don't know who he is or why he's come. Last time we came up from Pecwan on the Klamath

River. There were no roads into Blue Creek, just cat tracks for loggers. It was a pretty awful place. The hills were raw and eroded. The trees were stripped off the sides of the mountains. When we got there the people were assembled. They were expecting him."

"What did he do?"

"Nothing. He told them some stories."

"What kind of stories?"

"Whatever came into his head. You've heard him. He has different ways of saying things, different each time."

"Does he talk about himself?"

"He doesn't have to. Word gets around. It's not like he's a hero or anything. It's not like he even thinks he does anything himself. With him it's the opposite of self-reliance. Petard *relies*. He relies on everything. People, water, the weather, the wind—you name it and he thinks it's on his side. I tell him he's full of shit but I know he's not. Not after what he did in Vietnam."

"He saved your life."

"He did a lot more than that." My brother ran his fingers through his hair. "He saved Vietnam."

2

It was after, my brother told me, not long after he was hit. After giving him the tattoo Petard had left him in a boat. He wasn't sure where he was or how far he'd been moved since the ambush. His head was bandaged and he was being conveyed down a canal. The boat was almost fifty feet long but didn't have a keel or ribs. Three wide planks ran the length of it. Posts and thwarts crossed the hull at intervals, fastened in place by wooden pegs and rattan lacing. He was propped up against a thwart facing the prow. When he opened his eyes he didn't know where he was. The air around him was moist and rich.

He remembered watching the land slide by and hearing voices speaking in Vietnamese. He managed to focus a few feet ahead of him. At the front of the boat was a small shaky wooden altar with blue candles stuck to it, dried in their own drippings. There was a bowl with yellow fruit, some wilted purple flowers, sliced bread wrapped in plastic, and a few dishes filled with sand, a stick or two of incense burning in each of them. For a second he thought he was dead and bundled up in a funeral boat, sailing off up the river of death. But no, this boat had a pilot and there he was, keeping an eye on the engine, making minor adjustments with his hand on a red knob, the engine turning smoothly with not too much vibration.

"The pilot turned around," my brother told me. "It wasn't Petard. He was NVA. A North Vietnamese regular in uniform. He turned around and smiled at me. I don't know why, but it didn't seem strange to see him smiling at me like that. I tried to remember what had happened to me, how I got there, but I couldn't. Most of it was gone."

He didn't remember much more, then or later, but he sure remembered his original orders. They'd been to secure a canal and they hadn't made any sense. The gunboats were all turning off the river. They were fanning off into the canal system. He didn't get it. They were all being led down a series of dead ends, *away from the dam*. Weren't they supposed to be guarding the dam? His own boat was going down a minor canal that didn't lead anywhere. It took three or four dips above and below an x-axis, then straightened out toward a dribbling end that didn't connect with any other canals. There was no maneuvering room, a foot maybe on each side, then dense twisted jungle. He remembered throttling down to a final slow troll, feeling his way along the canal beside the banks matted with bamboo. In that kind of tangle it wasn't even a fight. Stosser was hit first, a clean through-and-through to the heart that left him hanging in his cage. The next man had a head wound. Two more went down, one shot in the face, another in the neck. My brother moved on down the line, yelling over his shoulder for a medevac chopper to be called, stopping at the next man. A bullet had broken his femur and he was still alive. My brother pressed down on his thigh to stop the bleeding and tried to remember the treatment for shock. But before he could do anything the man's body shivered with another bullet and he was dead.

"Why didn't you fire back?" I asked.

"It didn't occur to me. My men were going down and that's all I cared about."

"You were on a gunboat."

"Some gunboat," he said. "It was a converted tug, all cab and motor, sort of thing you'd see on the Mon pushing a couple of barges upstream. A tug like that's a moving target. You can see the green starboard lights for miles."

My brother said he stumbled back to the wheelhouse and took the throttle. The engine was making stalling sounds but hadn't quit yet. His fingers slippery with blood, he gunned the engine way above idle and felt the boat lurch forward. The rubber bumper of the tug hit the banks and my brother jumped over and out. He knew their only chance was in the jungle. He was about to yell out, everybody out, everybody out *now*, when he stopped and saw where he was. The bow of the boat had come to rest against a mud flat that was short of the bank. He was in the open. Knee-deep in mud he waded toward an embankment. It was maybe fifteen feet ahead. He didn't have a prayer. One bullet ripped through him, then another. He made it to the embankment but not to the tree line, slumped over a stump the way Petard found him.

He didn't know it then, but Petard found him because

of that stump. When he fell he didn't know where he'd been hit. He tried to roll over but couldn't. His back was wedged against another stump. Those stumps were two in a row of thousands of stumps, pulled out by the roots and left to rot on the tops of embankments. It was one of Petard's ideas. All across the Mekong Delta the embankments were held in place by an elaborate root system of trees. The trees weren't really heavy-duty, they were mostly tung and sesame trees used for making oils, so they were easy to rip out with bulldozers and chains. Without the roots the embankments eroded rapidly and dropped into the canals. That same day Petard was checking the stump operation himself, flying over the rows of twisted trees, when he saw white smoke streaming behind the tugboat about a mile ahead. Bodies littered the clearing. He made two passes from the air and was about to break away when he thought he saw something moving. He tilted the nose down to get a better view. The embankment wasn't wide enough to put a helicopter there but the trees were gone and he managed to settle the Huey close to the ground, the high grass snapping every which way, wood splinters flying everywhere. Close enough; Petard waited till he felt Connor take the controls, then jumped the remaining four feet and waved his co-pilot away.

"Petard says I was hit in the stomach," my brother told me. "Says he stopped the bleeding by giving me a tattoo. I don't know what to believe. When I came to, my head was in a bandage and I was in that boat. My leg was trembling. I thought I'd been taken prisoner."

In the next few hours he saw more than he knew to explain, a hell of a lot more. It turned out he was taking a trip through Long Dam. It wasn't your usual fifty-minute tour through Hoover or Grand Coulee, because Long Dam wasn't one dam, wasn't ten dams, wasn't even a hundred dams. The boat bristled through the canal and my brother made out a dam every mile or two. He rubbed his eyes to see if he was seeing right. He didn't see how they could possibly have built so many dams in so short a time. He thought he knew a thing or two about the design of dams, but here they were, lines of them laid out in places where there was no water. The Panama Canal was like this before they'd opened the locks, wasn't it, a strange empty landscape of locks and dams? My brother saw the blazes, painted red and staked at intervals, marking the path the canal was going to take. He knew enough surveying to recognize that meridians had been marked out and azimuths taken. Just yesterday, drinking coffee out of a thermos, he'd been briefed over a stained set of river charts but he hadn't remembered hearing anything about this. Far as he knew, the Mekong River was going to have one dam on it, and that dam was going to be classic Bureau, a white arch of concrete embedded in the narrows six miles from the Cambodian border. He'd never stopped to ask what such a big dam was doing in such a low flat place. There was no valley back of the dam for a lake to rise in. All that water—no way there'd be enough room to store all that water. Where was it all going to go?

My brother wanted to answer the question but he couldn't keep his mind on it. A numbness was climbing up one of his legs. The pain was there, too, but somehow distant like it was sending its message to him in some secret strobe. He took in the river, the marsh chafing its banks, the careening flies, the banana palms. His tongue curled in his mouth as he watched the water in the nearby rice paddies clouding with green. He was drifting off, but not into sleep. For a moment he found himself remembering how he used to drive our mother into Morgantown to go shopping. He'd drive and she'd be quiet the whole time in the cab of the Plymouth on the way in, listening to the wind the way he listened to the radio, half hearing and half not, sitting on her hands because they were large, and shifting in her seat, her knees knobbed together and her dress pulled taut over them. To make herself look halfway decent Lydia had sewn a coarse lace edge over the frayed hem. But her skin was rubbed dry with soap and her nails were different lengths because she was always biting them. He knew why. The road into town ran along the neck of the river. Along the Mon they passed one dam, then another, then another.

"I knew I wasn't back in the Mon Valley," my brother said to me now. "It's just I'd never seen so many dams in one place. Every couple clicks we'd pass some kind of dam. Different dams every time, low dams, high dams, but none of them was made of concrete. Everything but."

"I thought you said there were concrete dams."

"There were. But only a few of them. They were centered around Da Trinh Sanh. They were the only modern dams in the Long Dam project. But you see, *they weren't designed to hold.*"

"Petard," I said shortly.

"Yes, Petard. Da Trinh Sanh was his baby. Travers thought of the truce, but it was Petard who chose the site, drafted the plans, set it aside."

He set it aside, my brother told me, for what was to come. Like Dresden, like Hiroshima, it had been held apart, a place in waiting. Until the end of the war Da Trinh Sanh was an unimportant little village located near the Cambodian border, a few miles above the point where the Mekong River broke into two tributaries and drove south into the Delta. This was the place where, starting in August of '72, shipments of stone had gone. Great hulking shipments of a strange kind of stone. The people who lived in the village did not know what conglomerate was. But they were afraid of the sacks piled along the pier. To Petard Davidson, Chief of Design, Bureau of Reclamation R&A, they sent a delegation to say that this was not right, not good. Only gods or the dead reside in buildings of stone. The French had not lived in wooden houses built up high on piles. They lived in stone houses faced with yellow plaster and look what happened to them at Dien Bien Phu, the stone cracked and their rule crumbled because, as it is written, *tensile is heaven's decree, in light and grain without end.* They told Petard he must learn his temple odes, the verses present in every pagoda tracing the lines of right worship. Petard was polite and thanked them for coming. The delegation left him sadly, thinking he did not know that what he was building must soon be destroyed.

"But Petard knew exactly what they were getting at," my brother continued. "It's incredible what he knew. He knew to build something they considered so horrible that they'd take it down themselves if it didn't fail on its own. So he built the dam higher than he had to and put a façade of boulders on it. He set the boulders in rows so they looked like a set of grinding teeth. He wanted to give the dam a face they'd recognize, an evil face."

"How did he know what to do?"

"He listened carefully to all their objections. Then he built the dam they were objecting to."

"So he played to their superstition."

"Call it superstition if you want. That's not how Petard sees it. You have to remember who he is. I mean, he married one of them. In a way, he's just like them. The Vietnamese are wary of anything made of stone. So are Digger Indians. It was in him to design a dam that everyone would want to destroy."

"So the Vietnamese destroyed it themselves," I said.

"It wasn't necessary," explained my brother. "Petard

planned it. He planned it all. It was brilliant. I never figured why some dams were cracked and others weren't, but that's because I didn't know my hydraulics. If you line up all the dams on a map and check the ones that were going to hold against the ones that weren't, you can see what he was doing. Petard wasn't diverting the Mekong River. He was setting up a new irrigation system for the Delta. The connecting dams taking the river toward Saigon were the ones that were going to fail. The dams moderating the flood flow to the Delta were going to hold. Petard knew what exactly he was doing. He knew the Vietnamese knew, too. They had their augurs crawling all over the dams all that autumn. They put it together just like he knew they would. They built the dams and they built them on time just like Travers said they would. And the dams failed, just as the Bureau had planned. *But not all the dams.* Remember after the war when everyone was expecting famine? Well, there was no famine. In 1975 Vietnam was exporting rice. The dams he built had taken and were holding. Petard's very proud of those dams. There hasn't been a flood in the Delta since 1972. Whenever the river rises, the water goes off into a chain of small holding lakes. The lakes are beautiful. The design is perfect."

"You've seen them?"

"No, but the world has." Out of his wallet he pulled a strip of stamps wrapped in cellophane. There were twelve stamps in red and green and blue. "These are the dams. These are the lakes. Just think of it. Every letter sent to America from Vietnam is a letter sent to Petard. Look at this one. It's called *Cam Kla Mat.* Klamath Dam."

"That showed them," I said.

"No it didn't. The Bureau knew what he was doing. Don't you understand? *They knew.* Petard made the best of it. Some of his dams held and now he's a big hero over there. But the other dams failed and the VC blew us out of the water at Da Trinh Sanh. It was all a setup. Failure was the reason we were there. Petard told me the whole time he was in Vietnam, he couldn't shake the feeling *he* was the agent of the Bureau's will in Vietnam. He was afraid he'd design the dams to fail and find that he was doing just what he was supposed to be doing. Petard doesn't quite believe it even now. He thinks he delivered the fatal blow. He just doesn't know."

"Know what?"

"That we were all pawns. That the Bureau took its best people and sacrificed them. That the dams were supposed to fail. Do you think an outfit like the Bureau would let an Indian like Petard near their dams unless they knew what he was likely to do? I'm not faulting what he did. He saw an opening and he took it. He told me that even if they'd wanted him to sabotage dams he would have done it anyway because that's what he was put on earth to do. I'm not so sure. I think he did what they wanted him to do. The reason he was perfect for the job is that there was complete agreement between Petard and the Bureau. Petard wanted to stop the Bureau of Reclamation from building dams. And the Bureau of Reclamation wanted him to stop them from building them."

"Jimbo," I told my brother. "That makes no sense."

"Think back," he said. "In 1973 there was no will in America to win that war. The Bureau had been in Vietnam since the mid-fifties. They didn't need to start a crash project that late in the war. They had all the fucking time in the world. The Bureau waited until the war was lost beyond any possible reversal. Then they brought in Travers and started building. I know Travers thinks Long Dam was some crazy revenge project, something like Hitler's V-2s, but he's wrong. It was deliberate. It was policy. *They wanted us to lose.*"

"Organizations don't destroy themselves," I told my brother.

"Sometimes they do. They destroy parts of themselves if they want to survive."

"There are no more dams being built in America."

"I know that."

"Then why were the dams at Da Trinh Sanh supposed to fail?"

"I don't know, little brother. That's the big question, isn't it? That's why we're all talking to you."

"You mean you don't know?"

"I'm just a guy with some theories. You're the smart one in the family. You figure it out."

"I'm not sure I can."

"I'm not saying you can," said my brother. "Engineers are sorcerers, for all I know. Look at Defosse. If any part of his story is true then Lydia was telling the truth when she said she—she and not the U.S. Army Corps of Engineers—was holding the river back from our house."

"So it's come to that?" I said. "Magic?"

"I'm not saying there's a lot you won't understand," he told me. "Just understand enough."

"How much is enough?"

"I don't know. That's for you to decide."

"But the stories I've heard. Do you know what they mean?"

"No. I already told you I don't."

"But what if I don't, either?"

"Then tell without knowing. The important thing is to tell."

3

My brother pulled up the truck behind a Buick in front of my house. It was getting dark. At the end of the block was a lit basketball court with some kids playing in it. Beyond were the outskirts, orange groves mostly, because my mother and I lived in a rural part of L.A. Lydia was standing in the door wearing her bathrobe. She said she'd eaten without us. My brother unloaded the truck and went in. Some cold chicken sat on a platter on the dining-room table, along with some empty Shasta cola cans. He took off his boots and put his feet up on the table. He was wearing socks, athletic socks with a couple of high-water marks printed on them. He sat there quietly while Lydia took the chicken back into the kitchen to heat it up. He tried reading a newspaper but the paper was yesterday's and he put it down.

It had been two days since we left Jenna at Turlock, two weeks since I met Petard at Eureka. It seemed to me that everything I'd said and thought for the past two weeks somehow suggested dams. For my brother it was different. He'd said what he wanted to say and now he was relieved it was over. If there was anything more to say he wasn't aware of it. When Lydia put the chicken on the table he ate without looking up. She stood in the corner watching him eat, smoking, shaking Kents one by one out of a gold mesh case. She drew her robe together at her throat. I knew what she was thinking. My brother was the kind of drinker who could drop it for a few days or weeks if he wanted to. Someday soon he was going to start up again, walking the way he always walked when he was drunk, holding his arms out to steady himself when he thought nobody was watching, stepping his way along a balance beam only he saw.

My brother lifted his head like he'd heard what she was thinking. But he hadn't. Instead he said he wanted to leave now and asked her to fill his thermos with coffee for the trip back north. Then he walked back through the house, snapping off lights and checking doors. For a while he stood looking out the kitchen window at an avocado tree in the backyard. The wind was picking up, and coming up next to him, I could hear an avocado drop from a branch above the kitchen, hitting the roof and rolling into a gutter.

"There's one more thing," he said.

I turned to look at him.

"Someone else wants to see you. I don't know when he's coming. I'm not in the right circles."

"You mean he's with the Bureau?"

"He's not *with* the Bureau. He *is* the Bureau."

"Not Navier-Stokes?"

"Navier-Stokes," my brother said.

I looked at him closely. "Why would Navier-Stokes come to see me?"

"He knows we're all talking to you. He probably wants the last word."

"Petard told me he's friendly with Jenna."

My brother twisted his shoe on the linoleum. "Jenna didn't lose a river."

"Petard lost a river and look at him."

"I'll never understand him," said my brother. "I know he thinks he's doing me some good, taking me on trips. But hearing what he did, shit, it just makes things worse."

I said, "Petard says you're afraid of going back."

My brother frowned. "What's there to go back to?"

"The Monongahela River Valley."

He wiped his face with the back of his hand. "I'm not going back any more than you are. We lost that river and that's why we're here. Half our valley moved to East L.A. to work in the mills. How many of those people are you going to get to go back with you? Face it, the Mon Valley is a lost cause."

"A cause is only lost when you let go of it."

"I don't see you running back to Pennsylvania."

He had a point, but a different one than he thought he was making. I didn't want to go back any more than he did. But going back wasn't the point. Staying was; both of us knew we should have stayed. Petard was raised on a river, he'd fought for it and lost but at least he'd put up a fight. He never gave up, never. He became an expert in a war of experts. He went to school and learned about resilience, strength, density. Later he took up soil mechanics and wrote the Davidson tests for the specific gravity of solids. When he went to Vietnam he taught himself Chinese hydrography and built dams using wooden piles, gambions, baskets. He continued to hate the Bureau of Reclamation but learned how to love the work he did. My brother had too much hate, that was his problem. He hated even knowing about dams. When he was in the Bureau he thought equations were a kind of secret language the higher-ups spoke. When he was in Vietnam he didn't learn Vietnamese, didn't even try. Even now, almost twenty years later, my brother remembered most of what he'd seen there but didn't really see the point of it. Guttenberg, Pennsylvania, didn't exist anymore and nothing he did was ever going to bring it back. Our town was underwater, along with a lot of other towns.

He walked out to the pickup with a thermos tucked under his arm and a ring of keys jingling on his belt. He opened the door and slid in from the passenger side. The junk on the floor clanked around as if the pickup was haunted but he didn't care, everything in his life was haunted and he was pretty much used to it. He'd put a few things in the back, mostly stuff Lydia had given him, a garden shovel with a curved back, some pails, a rolled-up tarp, a stiff pair of work gloves. In the yard a long green hose dribbled water from a spigot at the side of the house. He hopped out and went back to turn it off. My brother hated dripping faucets. No way he'd leave a gas-station bathroom till he'd shoved the spigots, and not just the one he'd used, hard off. Before he drove off Lydia handed him a parcel tied with string. He didn't open it. Later she told me it was a new set of green work clothes. "He won't wear them," I told her.

4

So my brother went back to Eureka and I stayed in Fontana, living with my mother. I spent many months putting down everything I'd seen and heard, trying to get it right. What was the Bureau of Reclamation? I went to the public library and checked out stacks of books. If you do the same thing, going through them as carefully as I did, you won't find anything like what Petard and Travers and Jenna told me. In all the books the Bureau of Reclamation is a faceless government agency in the Department of the Interior. A bureaucracy, not a bureau of magi. My eyes jumped around the pages, looking for something, anything. Most of it was straight technical talk about fluid mechanics. In hydraulic engineering there are certain constants for water, for measuring its pressure and density and viscosity, and dams are built to them. I came away with a head full of facts but nothing hard to go on. Only the emblem of the Bureau stamped on every document, a picture of a dam with sky above and fields below, circled by that strange motto I'd seen before, *Vox Reclamantis in Deserto*.

It means a voice reclaiming the wilderness. When I first heard it I thought it meant something like the voice of God. The way my brother talked, engineers were holy men, burdened with a God who spoke to them in equations and gave them visions of a new heaven and a new earth, a Holy Jerusalem of great public works. But now I thought the voice of God could just as easily be that voice

Petard heard once many years ago at the foot of Yokut Dam, a voice coming from a loudspeaker crackling out commands to a river, telling his people to leave their land and go into exile. For centuries engineers had the allotted power to build the biggest human things on earth. You would think that was power enough, but think about it. Imagine having the power to build a dam big as the Tower of Babel. Imagine improving on it. You get rid of those biblical labor problems when you recruit the people you flood out and teach them to speak one language, the language of engineering. You build your dams hundreds of miles from any city. You write equations making it possible for dams to be built to tolerances the other side of zero. In your hands engineering recedes from a science back into an art, a mystery, a legend. To a code stricter than Hammurabi's you build whole Gizas of dams, laid out to the height of pyramids. In time you begin to believe you can do anything, by any means; you start thinking engineering is magic, demanding cool precision of observance; you become like Defosse, who believed that all the ancient prohibitions against grave robbing, against disturbing the dead, were warnings to keep people away from dams.

Navier-Stokes did not contact me to say otherwise, at least not right away. But one week in October four months after my brother left, my mother was off visiting her sister in Santa Barbara and I decided to take a little trip of my own. I drove up US 395 in my beat old Chevy, the torn seat under me mended with tape and sticky in the heat. My plan was to follow the L.A. Aqueduct up into the Owens Valley, but I couldn't really see the canal from the road. A map spread out on my lap, I turned the Chevy off the highway toward a thin blue line near the mountains where the canal was supposed to be. The L.A. Aqueduct was a disappointing sight. It wasn't a castle with

ZERO

TOLERANCE

high walls and great towers like Yokut Dam. It was a low sunken moat. The water barely moved. I didn't even bother getting out of the car to look at it. I just sat in the front seat for an hour watching the water go by, rubbing my foot on the brake and turning up my collar when a cold wind came in. I didn't have any new thoughts. I knew engineering had a kind of power I couldn't exactly pin down, an exactness that wasn't just an illusion of some kind, but that was about all I knew. Driving home, I wondered if my brother had found work yet.

When I got back, Navier-Stokes was waiting for me. A long black limo idled in the street in front of my house. I had no idea how long it had been there. The window in the back seat was open a crack. When I brought the Chevy to an abrupt stop in the driveway the window closed and the door opened. A man, a very old man, got out of the limo and walked across the yard onto my doorstep.

"Needs water," he said.

Navier-Stokes was tall, so tall he hunched to talk. He wore a suit shiny from too much ironing. The pants were a little large for him. His white shirt was starched into mineral stiffness. His clothes were an old man's, but not his face. The crease was still sharp in his mouth. His jaw was slightly off-center and the pupils of his eyes were sharp as pinpoints. He was clean-shaven, he'd shaved off the mustache Petard said he used to have but still held his upper lip expressively like a third eyebrow.

"The Bureau sent you?" I asked him.

"The Bureau never *sends* anyone. I've come on my own."

Navier-Stokes talked without looking at me. His eyes clicked around my house in Fontana, taking a series of stills. He made a gesture, passing one hand delicately over another, he meant it to look soothing but I thought of a hand slipping into a rubber glove. A whiff of asphalt came in through the open door, so I asked him in and closed it. Outside, I could still hear the sigh of traffic locked in slow chancery.

"I know you are writing a book," he began. "Jenna told me."

"And you're here to stop me?"

"I am here to see you are—properly informed."

"You can't tell me what to write."

"Perhaps. In any case I don't want to. May I?"

Navier-Stokes took a chair, crossed his legs, and folded his palms face down on his lap. He unbuttoned his suit jacket and smoothed down his lapel. He didn't put his feet up. He pushed the ottoman away and slapped his folded newspaper down on it.

"I just want you to know."

"Know what?"

"The truth."

"Whose truth?"

"The simple truth. Reclamation has left America."

"Left? That can't be."

"Left, and left for good."

"Left for where?"

"I don't suppose you've heard of Salto Grande de Sete Quedas?"

"Don't suppose I have."

"You sound like your brother," said Navier-Stokes, shifting his weight, wincing with hip pain. "I know you don't trust me, but perhaps that doesn't matter. There will be no more new dams here."

His face was nearly expressionless as he said this, nearly because the tensions in his face were so evenly balanced they canceled out. His face was perfectly laminar; no sign of the unsteady flow of thought. I thought of the faces I knew best, Petard with stress lines for dimples, Travers with his loose oscillating jaw, my brother with his close viscid stare. Only Jenna had something of his canceling calm. And yet they all knew him and trusted him. I couldn't tell his exact age, just that when Navier-Stokes crossed his legs, his ankles were bald like an old man's. Jenna told me every summer this man stayed with her at Turlock, her houseguest, and the two of them'd drive up to Hetch Hetchy, where they'd take a midnight boat ride on the reservoir. Out on the edge of the deck Navier-Stokes would untie the ropes, toss them in the Chris-Craft, and jump in just as Jenna gunned the engine and corrugated the water with furrows and ridges. There were no lights near the reservoir, no other boats on it, no markers. An artificial lake was a lake stripped of its senses, and going for a boat ride on one was like going for a ride out on the void. The spotlight on the bow cast a white searching glare onto the black water. The more light you threw on the water, the blacker it got. Jenna closed her eyes, they weren't any good there, and felt her way to the dam. When she got there she cut the engine and the boat idled not far from the wall, the waves spanking the concrete with sharp little slaps, then threw the anthuriums over the side and watched them drift within nudging distance of the dam. Petard came along sometimes, clenching a wet cigar between his teeth. I'd even seen a picture of my brother slumped in the bucket seat aft of the engine, frowning fat and shirtless in Bermuda shorts; he, too, apparently tolerated Navier-Stokes, though, like most people raised in the Mon Valley, he didn't take to foreigners.

"Don't get me wrong," Navier-Stokes was saying to me now. "It's not that the Bureau of Reclamation has ceased to exist. Just that it's now in the process of becoming a minor agency, another Corps of Engineers. The Bureau will atrophy. Petard and your other friends will see to that."

"And you won't try to stop them?"

"Why should we? Petard was the best, the best we ever had. His designs were pure, very pure. And we owe more to Travers, to all the Traverses, than we could possibly repay."

"I don't get it. They defeated you."

"Not by design. Petard, Travers, Jenna were all accidents, but very powerful accidents. Without the enabling resistance they offered, most of our new dams would never have been built."

"You mean they helped you?"

"Not at all. They did everything they could to destroy us. They did not just sabotage public works, they did more and worse. They tampered with our dynasties. They learned our craft and learned it well, learned to live inside it well enough to turn it against us and stop us at Da Trinh Sanh. They did us a great service there."

"But they defeated you," I said again, stressing every word.

"No. They defined us. They taught us we could be stopped. You see, your Vietnam was your Vietnam, but it was our Vietnam, too. It ended our great days as it ended yours. Reclamation had always had its will with water, and for over three hundred years that water was American water. Our water, your water. Whose was whose? Over time the Bureau had come to identify its interests with American interests. That had happened before. Necos talked himself into believing he was an Egyptian and Frontinus into believing he was a Roman. They, too, had forgotten who they were. It happened more recently, at Leyden, in Holland, four hundred years ago, but never so completely."

"You mean the Bureau isn't American?"

"It isn't, but it became American. I saw this happen. We all did, but it was easier for me to see, not being one of you. The turning came in 1934, when Reclam didn't want to drain the Pontine marshes in central Italy. Not because it couldn't be done, or because Reclam didn't want to do it. Because they felt a revulsion for this man Mussolini, who had to do the job himself, with only a few of our advisors looking on. I ought to know. I was one of them."

"I'd have thought your engineers would have admired him."

"Some did. I did. But we were a few, a very few, who thought the Bureau had strayed too far from the path of Menes. Who thought the Bureau had become too American. Who thought it had come time."

"Come time to what?"

Navier-Stokes shifted his weight again. "Long Dam never stood a chance."

"You mean you knew it was going to fail?"

"The dam wasn't important. The Bureau had to fail. It could no longer carry on its ancient work as an American agency. It had to be purged of its—Americanness—and failure, large failure, was the best purgative. The Bureau had to lose the war and be blamed for it."

"But nobody knew what Reclam R&A did at Da Trinh Sanh. It didn't even make it into the papers. I know. I've checked."

"The right people knew," said Navier-Stokes. "Early as 1957, after the first accidents at Ah Pah Dam, I saw the only way we could leave America was in disgrace. Even the failure of the other two dams in the triangle—Ah Pah and Tehama—wasn't enough. Petard could force the Bureau to abandon its dams but not to abandon America. His despair drove him to Vietnam, and over time I'd learned to trust Petard's despair, to follow where it led him. Vietnam was then only a disgrace in the making, but it was very promising. I knew we had to pledge to pull

America out of a very desperate situation and then fail to deliver on that pledge. To give America her last best hope and then take all hope away, offering ourselves as a willing scapegoat. The role is sometimes misunderstood. The scapegoat is not the goat that is sacrificed but the goat that escapes and is blamed. Nixon and Kissinger were very desperate men, willing to believe us at the right time and willing to blame us at the right time. It was really very simple. The war was already lost, it was lost all along. Travers saw that and so did Petard. What we simply did was lose it unconditionally, and once we did, there was no turning back. Nixon took the Bureau down with him, and we let him. By 1975 the Bureau was effectively dismantled as an instrument of policy."

"So Petard, Jenna, Travers, my brother—they're safe?"

Navier-Stokes crinkled out a smile. "Safe? They're heroes in reclamation history. They performed a great and estimable service. They led us out of their country just in time. Little matter that they led an exodus by pushing, not pulling. If they hadn't pushed us out of America they might actually have destroyed us. Not us, meaning the American Bureau. Us, meaning the confederation of dam builders, the guild, the art, the mystery of reclamation itself. I don't think any of them know how close they came to severing the irrigation line extending back to the Fertile Crescent, to the land between the two rivers, the Tigris and the Euphrates."

"You mean it goes that far back?"

Navier-Stokes didn't answer but smiled a lengthening diasporic smile and reached for his hat off the coatrack near the door. He started digressing. Egypt was hydraulic in theory, Babylon hydraulic in practice. The Nile was the Mississippi; your Twain saw that for himself. The Euphrates was the ancient Colorado, a boiling river of great sediment content. A separate civilization developed on the

Euphrates, a hydraulic civilization in which all human institutions existed for purposes of flood control, water supply, irrigation. On the Nile they never got much further than controlling the annual flooding of farms. The land dried out too quickly and so did the crops. The Fertile Crescent was the first system of continual irrigation, the model for all things to come. The Colorado, too, was a desert river, and for a hundred years of reclamation the American West was Babylon. The first straight line wasn't Euclid's. It was drawn by some Babylonian engineer, name long lost, and his pen was a river. Everything Navier-Stokes had seen about the Bureau led him to one man, one presence at the hydraulic beginning of historical time. He was not a god any more than we are. Stealing fire was god's play, not even the sliver of a second elapsed between the willing of it and the doing of it, but stealing water was the work of untold dynasties of men. Prometheus stole fire and got nailed for it but he was a god. The Bureau was frail with men, men using men to break the backs of rivers. Concede the beginning of time to Prometheus: he started it all with his book of matches. But history, recorded history, began with moats scratched in sand, the canals laid by the men of the city of Ur. Navier-Stokes was adamant about this. The theft of fire was nothing compared to the theft of water by the Bureau under all its names and aliases of Reclamation.

"I think you understand what there is to understand," he told me now. "Well enough to do what you have to do."

"Set it down?"

"That's right."

"All of it?"

"All you want, however you want. Jenna is right. The way you choose will be the right way."

With that he gave the knot of his tie a quick tug, and

the blue tie with the white fleur-de-lis tightened into a baby's fist. He took a last look round my house in East L.A., a California matchbox with its shabby kitchen and sofa bed in the living room, took it all in sadly as if to say, this isn't equal to you. He left without saying good-bye. I dropped my chin and stared at the floor as he walked out of my house straight into some new America of reclamation.